THE STAR ROAD

Books by Gordon R. Dickson

THE STAR ROAD

THE TACTICS OF MISTAKE

DANGER—HUMAN

NONE BUT MAN

NECROMANCER

PLANET RUN (with Keith Laumer)

THE SPACE SWIMMERS

NAKED TO THE STARS

SPATIAL DELIVERY

ALIEN FROM ARCTURUS

MANKIND ON THE RUN

THE GENETIC GENERAL

DELUSION WORLD

TIME TO TELEPORT

THE ALIEN WAY

SECRET UNDER ANTARCTICA

SECRET UNDER THE CARIBBEAN

SECRET UNDER THE SEA

SPACE WINNERS

MISSION TO UNIVERSE

SPACEPAW

SOLDIER, ASK NOT

EARTHMAN'S BURDEN (with Poul Anderson)

MUTANTS

HOUR OF THE HORDE

THE STAR ROAD
Gordon R. Dickson

Doubleday & Company, Inc., Garden City, New York
1973

ISBN: 0-385-06811-5
Library of Congress Catalog Card Number 72–89304
Copyright © 1973 by Gordon R. Dickson
All Rights Reserved
Printed in the United States of America
First Edition

CONTENTS

WHATEVER GODS THERE BE   1

HILIFTER   19

BUILDING ON THE LINE   41

THE CHRISTMAS PRESENT   86

3-PART PUZZLE   97

ON MESSENGER MOUNTAIN   114

THE CATCH   173

JACKAL'S MEAL   188

THE MOUSETRAP   212

THE STAR ROAD

At 1420 hours of the eighth day on Mars, Major Robert L. (Doc) Greene was standing over a slide in a microscope in the tiny laboratory of Mars Ship Groundbreaker II. There was a hinged seat that could be pulled up and locked in position, to sit on; but Greene never used it. At the moment, he had been taking blood counts on the four of them that were left in the crew, when a high white and a low red blood cell count of one sample had caught his attention. He had proceeded to follow up the tentative diagnosis this suggested, as coldly as if the sample had been that of some complete stranger. But, suddenly, the scene in the field of the microscope had blurred. And for a moment he closed both eyes and rested his head lightly against the microscope. The metal eyepiece felt cool against his eyelid; and caused an after-image to blossom against the hooded retina—as of a volcanic redness welling outward against a blind-dark background. It was his own deep-held inner fury exploding against an intractible universe.

Caught up in this image and his own savage emotion, Greene did not hear Captain Edward Kronzy, who just then clumped into the lab, still wearing his suit, except for the helmet.

"Something wrong, Bob?" asked Kronzy. The youngest of the original six-officer crew, he was about average height—as were all the astronauts—and his reddish, cheerful complexion contrasted with the shock of stiff black hair and scowling, thirty-eight year old visage of Greene.

"Nothing," said Greene, harshly, straightening up and slipping the slide out of the microscope into a breast pocket. "What's the matter with you?"

"Nothing," said Kronzy, with a pale grin that only made more marked the dark circles under his eyes. "But Hal wants you outside to help jacking up."

"All right," said Greene. He put the other three slides back in their box; and led the way out of the lab toward the airlock. In the pocket, the glass slide pressed sharp-edged and unyielding against the skin of his chest, beneath. It had given Greene no choice but to diagnose a cancer of the blood—leukemia.

Ten minutes later, Greene and Kronzy joined the two other survivors of Project Mars Landing outside on the Martian surface.

These other two—Lt. Colonel Harold (Hal) Barth, and Captain James Wallach—were some eighty-five feet above the entrance of the airlock, on the floor of the crater in which they had landed. Greene and Kronzy came toiling up the rubbled slope of the pit where the ship lay; and emerged onto the crater floor just as Barth and Wallach finished hauling the jack into position at the pit's edge.

Around them, the crater floor on this eighth day resembled a junk yard. A winch had been set up about ten feet back from the pit five days before; and now oxygen tanks, plumbing fixtures, spare clothing, and a host of other items were spread out fanwise from the edge where the most easily ascendible slope of the pit met the crater floor—at the moment brilliantly outlined by the sun of the late Martian 'afternoon'. A little off to one side of the junk were two welded metal crosses propped erect by rocks.

The crosses represented 1st Lieutenant Saul Moulton and Captain Luthern J. White, who were somewhere under the rock rubble beneath the ship in the pit.

"Over here, Bob," Greene heard in the earphones of his helmet. He looked and saw Barth beckoning with a thick-gloved hand. "We're going to try setting her up as if in a posthole."

Greene led Kronzy over to the spot. When he got close, he could see through the faceplates of their helmets that the features of the other two men, particularly the thin, hand-some features of Barth, were shining with sweat. The eighteen-foot jack lay with its base end projecting over a hole ground out of solid rock.

"What's the plan?" said Greene.

Barth's lips puffed with a weary exhalation of breath be-fore he answered. The face of the Expedition's captain was finedrawn with exhaustion; but, Greene noted with secret sat-isfaction, with no hint of defeat in it yet. Greene relaxed slightly, sweeping his own grim glance around the crater, over the hole, the discarded equipment and the three other men.

A man, he thought, could do worse than to have made it this far.

"One man to anchor. The rest to lift," Barth was answering him.

"And I'm the anchor?" asked Greene.

"You're the anchor," answered Barth.

Greene went to the base end of the jack and picked up a length of metal pipe that was lying ready there. He shoved it into the hole and leaned his weight on it, against the base of the jack.

"Now!" he called, harshly.

The men at the other end heaved. It was not so much the jack's weight, under Mars' gravity, as the labor of working in the clumsy suits. The far end of the jack wavered, rose, slipped gratingly against Greene's length of pipe—swayed to one side, lifted again as the other three men moved hand under hand along below it—and approached the vertical.

The base of the jack slipped suddenly partway into the

hole, stuck, and threatened to collapse Greene's arms. His fingers were slippery in the gloves, he smelled the stink of his own perspiration inside the suit, and his feet skidded a little in the surface dust and rock.

"Will it go?" cried Barth gaspingly in Greene's earphones.

"Keep going!" snarled Greene, the universe dissolving into one of his white-hot rages—a passion in which only he and the jack existed; and it must yield. "Lift, damn you! Lift!"

The pipe vibrated and bent. The jack swayed—rose—and plunged suddenly into the socket hole, tearing the pipe from Greene's grasp. Greene, left pushing against nothing, fell forward, then rolled over on his back. Above him, twelve protruding feet of the jack quivered soundlessly.

Greene got to his feet. He was wringing wet. Barth's faceplate suddenly loomed before him.

"You all right?" Barth's voice asked in his earphones.

"All right?" said Greene. He stared; and burst suddenly into loud raucous laughter, that scaled upward toward uncontrollability. He choked it off. Barth was still staring at him. "No, I broke my neck from the fall," said Greene roughly. "What'd you think?"

Barth nodded and stepped back. He looked up at the jack. "That'll do," he said. "We'll get the winch cable from that to the ship's nose and jack her vertical with no sweat."

"Yeah," said Kronzy. He was standing looking down into the pit. "No sweat."

The other three turned and looked into the pit as well, down where the ship lay at a thirty degree angle against one of the pit's sides. It was a requiem moment for Moulton and White who lay buried there; and all the living men above felt it at the same time. Chance had made a choice among them —there was no more justice to it than that.

The ship had landed on what seemed a flat crater floor. Landed routinely, upright, and apparently solidly. Only, twenty hours later, as Moulton and White had been outside setting up the jack they had just assembled—the jack whose purpose was to correct the angle of the ship for takeoff—chance had taken its hand.

What caused it—Martian landslip, vibration over flawed rock, or the collapse of a bubble blown in the molten rock when the planet was young—would have to be for those who came after to figure out. All the four remaining men who were inside knew was that one moment all was well; and the next they were flung about like pellets in a rattle that a baby shakes. When they were able to get outside and check, they found the ship in a hundred foot deep pit, in which Moulton and White had vanished.

"Well," said Barth, "I guess we might as well knock off now, and eat. Then, Jimmy—" his faceplate turned toward Wallach, "you and Ed can come up here and get that cable attached while I go over the lists you all gave me of your equipment we can still strip from the ship; and I'll figure out if she's light enough to lift on the undamaged tubes. And Bob—you can get back to whatever you were doing."

"Yeah," said Greene. "Yeah, I'll do that."

After they had all eaten, Greene shut himself up once more in the tiny lab to try to come to a decision. From a military point of view, it was his duty to inform the commanding officer—Barth—of the diagnosis he had just made. But the peculiar relationship existing between himself and Barth—

There was a knock on the door.

"Come on in!" said Greene.

Barth opened the door and stuck his head in.

"You're not busy."

"Matter of opinion," he said. "What is it?"

Barth came all the way in, shut the door behind him, and leaned against the sink.

"You're looking pretty washed out, Bob," he said.

"We all are. Never mind me," said Greene. "What's on your mind?"

"A number of things," said Barth. "I don't have to tell you what it's like with the whole Space Program. You know as well as I do."

"Thanks," said Greene.

The sarcasm in his voice was almost absent-minded. Insofar as gratitude had a part in his makeup, he was grateful to Barth for recognizing what few other people had—how much the work of the Space Program had become a crusade to which his whole soul and body was committed.

"We just can't afford not to succeed," Barth was saying.

It was the difference between them, noted Greene. Barth admitted the possibility of not succeeding. Nineteen years the two men had been close friends—since high school. And nowadays, to many people, Barth *was* the Space Program. Good-looking, brilliant, brave—and possessing that elusive quality which makes for newsworthiness at public occasions and on the tv screens—Barth had been a shot in the arm to the Program these last six months.

And he had been needed. No doubt the Russian revelations of extensive undersea developments in the Black Sea Area had something to do with it. Probably the lessening of world tensions lately had contributed. But it had taken place—one of those unexplainable shifts in public interest which have been the despair of promotion men since the breed was invented.

The world had lost much of its interest in spatial exploration.

No matter that population pressures continued to mount. No matter that natural resources depletion was accelerating, in spite of all attempt at control. Suddenly—space exploration had become old hat; taken for granted.

And those who had been against it from the beginning began to gnaw, unchecked, at the roots of the Program. So that men like Barth, to whom the Space Program had become

a way of life, worried, seeing gradual strangulation as an alternative to progress. But men like Greene, to whom the
Program had become life itself, hated, seeing *no* alternative.

"Who isn't succeeding?" said Greene.

"We lost Luthern and Saul," said Barth, glancing downward almost instinctively toward where the two officers must
be buried. "We've got to get back."

"Sure. Sure," said Greene.

"I mean," said Barth, "we've got to get back, no matter
what the cost. We've got to show them we could get a ship up
here and get back again. You know, Bob—" he looked almost
appealingly at Greene—"the trouble with a lot of people who're
not in favor of the Project is they don't really believe in the
moon or Mars or anyplace like it. I mean—the way they'd
believe in Florida, or the South Pole. They're sort of half-
clinging to the notion it's just a sort of cut-out circle of silver
paper up in the air, there, after all. But if we go and come
back, they've *got to* believe!"

"Listen," said Greene. "Don't worry about people like that.
They'll all be dead in forty years, anyway.—Is this all you
wanted to talk to me about?"

"No. Yes—I guess," said Barth. He smiled tiredly at Greene.
"You pick me up, Bob. I guess it's just a matter of doing what
you have to."

"Do what you're going to do," said Greene with a shrug.
"Why make a production out of it?"

"Yes." Barth straightened up. "You're right. Well, I'll get
back to work. See you in a little while. We'll get together for
a pow-wow as soon as Ed and Jimmy get back in from
stringing that cable."

"Right," said Greene. He watched the slim back and square
shoulders of Barth go out the door and slumped against the
sink, himself, chewing savagely on a thumbnail. His instinct
had been right, he thought; it was not the time to tell Barth
about the diagnosis.

And not only that. Nineteen years had brought Greene to

the point where he could, in almost a practical sense, read the other man's mind. He had just done so; and right now he was willing to bet that he had a new reason for worry.

Barth had something eating on him. Chewing his fingernail, Greene set to work to puzzle out just what that could be.

A fist hammered on the lab door. "Bob?"

"What?" said Greene, starting up out of his brown study. Some little time had gone by. He recognized his caller now. Kronzy.

"Hal wants us in the control cabin, right away."

"Okay. Be right there."

Greene waited until Kronzy's boot sounds had gone away in the distance down the short corridor and up the ladder to the level overhead. Then he followed, more slowly.

He discovered the others already jammed in among the welter of instruments and controls that filled this central space of the ship.

"What's the occasion?" he asked, cramming himself in between the main control screen and an acceleration couch.

"Ways and means committee," said Barth, with a small smile. "I was waiting until we were all together before I said anything." He held up a sheet of paper. "I've just totalled up all the weight we can strip off the ship, using the lists of dispensable items each of you made up, and checked it against the thrust we can expect to get safely from the undamaged tubes. We're about fifteen hundred Earth pounds short. I made the decision to drop off the water tanks, the survival gear, and a few other items, which brings us down to being about five hundred pounds short."

He paused and laid down the paper on a hinge-up desk surface beside him.

"I'm asking for suggestions," he said.

Greene looked around the room with sudden fresh grimness. But he saw no comprehension yet, on the faces of the other two crew members.

"How about—" began Kronzy; then hesitated as the words broke off in the waiting silence of the others.

"Go on, Ed," said Barth.

"We're not short of fuel."

"That's right."

"Then why," said Kronzy, "can't we rig some sort of auxiliary burners—like the jato units you use to boost a plane off, you know?" He glanced at Greene and Wallach, then back at Barth. "We wouldn't have to care whether they burnt up or not—just as long as they lasted long enough to get us off."

"That's a good suggestion, Ed," said Barth, slowly. "The only hitch is, I looked into that possibility, myself. And it isn't possible. We'd need a machine shop. We'd need—it just isn't possible. It'd be easier to repair the damaged tubes."

"I suppose that isn't possible, either?" said Greene, sharply.

Barth looked over at him, then quickly looked away again.

"I wasn't serious," Barth said. "For that we'd need Cape Canaveral right here beside us.—And then, probably not."

He looked over at Wallach.

"Jimmy?" he said.

Wallach frowned.

"Hal," he said. "I don't know. I can think about it a bit. . . ."

"Maybe," said Barth, "that's what we all ought to do. Everybody go off by themselves and chew on the problem a bit." He turned around and seated himself at the desk surface. "I'm going to go over these figures again."

Slowly, they rose. Wallach went out, followed by Kronzy. Greene hesitated, looking at Barth, then he turned away and left the room.

Alone once more in the lab, Greene leaned against the sink again and thought. He did not, however, think of mass-to-weight ratios or clever ways of increasing the thrust of the rocket engines.

Instead, he thought of leukemia. And the fact that it was still a disease claiming its hundred per cent of fatalities. But also, he thought of Earth with its many-roomed hospitals; and the multitude of good men engaged in cancer research. Moreover, he thought of the old medical truism that while there is life, there is hope.

All this reminded him of Earth, itself. And his thoughts veered off to a memory of how pleasant it had been, on occasion, after working all the long night through, to step out through a door and find himself unexpectedly washed by the clean air of dawn. He thought of vacations he had never had, fishing he had never done, and the fact that he might have found a woman to love him if he had ever taken off enough time to look for her. He thought of good music—he had always loved good music. And he remembered that he had always intended someday to visit La Scala.

Then—hauling his mind back to duty with a jerk—he began to scowl and ponder the weak and strong points that he knew about in Barth's character. Not, this time, to anticipate what the man would say when they were all once more back in the control cabin. But for the purpose of circumventing and trapping Barth into a position where Barth would be fenced in by his own principles—the ultimate ju-jitsu of human character manipulation. Greene growled and muttered to himself, in the privacy of the lab marking important points with his forefinger in the artificial and flatly odorous air.

He was still at it, when Kronzy banged at his door again and told him everybody else was already back in the control cabin.

When he got to the control cabin again, the rest were in almost the identical positions they had taken previously.

"Well?" said Barth, when Greene had found himself a niche

of space. He looked about the room, at each in turn. "How about you, Jimmy?"

"The four acceleration couches we've still got in the ship—. With everything attached to them, they weigh better than two hundred apiece," said Wallach. "Get rid of two of them, and double up in the two left. That gets rid of four of our five hundred pounds. Taking off from Mars isn't as rough as taking off from Earth."

"I'm afraid it won't work," Kronzy commented.

"Why not?"

"Two to a couch, right?"

"Right."

"Well, look. They're made for one man. Just barely. You can cram two in by having both of them lying on their sides. That's all right for the two who're just passengers—but what about the man at the controls?" He nodded at Barth. "He's got to fly the ship. And how can he do that with half of what he needs to reach behind him, and the man next to him blocking off his reach at the other half?" Kronzy paused. "Besides, I'm telling you—half a couch isn't going to help hardly at all. You remember how the G's felt, taking off? And this time all that acceleration is going to be pressing against one set of ribs and a hipbone."

He stopped talking then.

"We'll have to think of something else. Any suggestions, Ed?" said Barth.

"Oh." Kronzy took a deep breath. "Toss out my position taking equipment. All the radio equipment, too. Shoot for Earth blind, deaf and dumb; and leave it up to them down there to find us and bring us home."

"How much weight would that save?" asked Wallach.

"A hundred and fifty pounds—about."

"A hundred and fifty! Where'd you figure the rest to come from?"

"I didn't know," said Kronzy, wearily. "It was all I could figure to toss, beyond what we've already planned to throw out. I was hoping you other guys could come up with the rest."

He looked at Barth.

"Well, it's a good possibility, Ed," said Barth. He turned his face to Greene. "How about you, Bob?"

"Get out and push!" said Greene. "My equipment's figured to go right down to the last gram. There isn't any more. You want my suggestion—we can all dehydrate ourselves about eight to ten pounds per man between now and takeoff. That's it."

"That's a good idea, too," said Barth. "Every pound counts." He looked haggard around the eyes, Greene noticed. It had the effect of making him seem older than he had half an hour before during their talk in the lab; but Greene knew this to be an illusion.

"Thank you," Barth went on. "I knew you'd all try hard. I'd been hoping you'd come up with some things I had overlooked myself. More important than any of us getting back, of course, is getting the ship back. Proving something like this will work, to the people who don't believe in it."

Greene coughed roughly; and roughly cleared his throat.

"—We can get rid of one acceleration couch as Ed suggests," Barth continued. "We can dehydrate ourselves as Bob suggested, too; just to be on the safe side. That's close to two hundred and fifty pounds reduction. Plus a hundred and fifty for the navigational and radio equipment. There's three hundred and ninety to four hundred. Add one man with his equipment and we're over the hump with a safe eighty to a hundred pound margin."

He had added the final item so quietly that for a minute it did not register on those around him.

—Then, abruptly, it did.

"A man?" said Kronzy.

There was a second moment of silence—but this was like the fractionary interval of no sound in which the crowd in the grandstand suddenly realizes that the stunt flyer in the small plane is not coming out of his spin.

"I think," said Barth, speaking suddenly and loudly in the stillness, "that, as I say, the important thing is getting the ship back down. We've got to convince those people that write letters to the newspapers that something like this is possible. So the job can go on."

They were still silent, looking at him.

"It's our duty, I believe," said Barth, "to the Space Project. And to the people back there; and to ourselves. I think it's something that has to be done."

He looked at each of them in turn.

"Now Hal—wait!" burst out Wallach, as Barth's eyes came on him. "That's going a little overboard, isn't it? I mean—we can figure out something!"

"Can we?" Barth shook his head. "Jimmy—. There just isn't any more. If they shoot you for not paying your bills, then it doesn't help to have a million dollars, if your debts add up to a million dollars and five cents. You know that. If the string doesn't reach, it doesn't reach. Everything we can get rid of on this ship won't be enough. Not if we want her to fly."

Wallach opened his mouth again; and then shut it. Kronzy looked down at his boots. Greene's glance went savagely across the room to Barth.

"Well," said Kronzy. He looked up. Kronzy, too, Greene thought, now looked older. "What do we do—draw straws?"

"No," Barth said. "I'm in command here. I'll pick the man."

"*Pick* the man!" burst out Wallach, staring. "You—"

"Shut up, Jimmy!" said Kronzy. He was looking hard at Barth. "Just what did you have in mind, Hal?" he said, slowly.

"That's all." Barth straightened up in his corner of the control room. "The rest is my responsibility. The rest of you get back to work tearing out the disposable stuff still in the ship—"

"I think," said Kronzy, quietly and stubbornly, "we ought to draw straws."

"You—" said Wallach. He had been staring at Barth ever since Kronzy had told him to shut up. *"You'd* be the one, Hal?"

"That's all," said Barth, again. "Gentlemen, this matter is not open for discussion."

"The hell," replied Kronzy, "you say. You may be paper CO of this bunch; but we are just not about to play Captain-go-down-with-his-ship. We all weigh between a hundred-sixty and a hundred and eighty pounds and that makes us equal in the sight of mathematics. Now, we're going to draw straws; and if you won't draw, Hal, we'll draw one for you; and if you won't abide by the draw, we'll strap you in the other acceleration couch and one of us can fly the ship out of here. Right, Jimmy? Bob?"

He glared around at the other two. Wallach opened his mouth, hesitated, then spoke.

"Yes," he said. "I guess that's right."

Kronzy stared at him suddenly. Wallach looked away.

"Just a minute," said Barth.

They looked at him. He was holding a small, black, automatic pistol.

"I'm sorry," Barth said. "But I am in command. And I intend to stay in command, even if I have to cripple every one of you, strip the ship and strap you into couches myself." He looked over at Greene. "Bob. *You'll* be sensible, won't you?"

Greene exploded suddenly into harsh laughter. He laughed so hard he had to blink tears out of his eyes before he could get himself under control.

"Sensible!" he said. "Sure, I'll be sensible. And look after myself at the same time—even if it does take some of the glory out of it." He grinned almost maliciously at Barth. "Much as I hate to rob anybody else of the spotlight—it just so happens one of us can stay behind here until rescued and live to tell his grandchildren about it."

They were all looking at him.

"Sure," said Greene. "There'll be more ships coming, won't there? In fact, they'll have no choice in the matter, if they got a man up here waiting to be rescued."

"How?" said Kronzy.

"Ever hear of suspended animation?" Greene turned to the younger man. "Deep freeze. Out there in permanent shadow we've got just about the best damn deep freeze that ever was invented. The man who stays behind just takes a little nap until saved. In fact, from his point of view, he'll barely close his eyes before they'll be waking him up; probably back on Earth."

"You mean this?" said Barth.

"Of course, I mean it!"

Barth looked at Kronzy.

"Well, Ed," he said. "I guess that takes care of your objections."

"Hold on a minute!" Greene said. "I hope you don't think still you're going to be the one to stay. This is my idea; and I've got first pick at it.—Besides, done up in suits the way we are outside there, I couldn't work it on anybody else. Whoever gets frozen has got to know what to do by himself; and I'm the only one who fits the bill." His eyes swept over all of them. "So that's the choice."

Barth frowned just slightly.

"Why didn't you mention this before, Bob?" he said.

"Didn't think of it—until you came up with your notion of leaving one man behind. And then it dawned on me. It's simple—for anyone who knows how."

Barth slowly put the little gun away in a pocket of his coveralls.

"I'm not sure still, I—" he began slowly.

"Why don't you drop it?" blazed Greene in sudden fury. "You think you're the only one who'd like to play hero? I've got news for you. I've given the Project everything I've got for a number of years now; but I'm the sort of man who gets forgotten easily. You can bet your boots I won't be forgotten when they have to come all the way from Earth to save me. It's my deal; and you're not going to cut me out of it. And what—" he thrust his chin at Barth—"are you going to do if I simply refuse to freeze anybody but myself? Shoot me?"

Barth shook his head slowly, his eyes shadowed with pain.

Rocket signal rifle held athwart behind him and legs spread, piratically, Greene stood where the men taking off in the rockets could see him in the single control screen that was left in the ship. Below, red light blossomed suddenly down in the pit. The surface trembled under Greene's feet and the noise of the engines reached him by conduction through the rocks and soles of his boots.

The rocket took off.

Greene waved after it. And then wondered why he had done so. Bravado? But there was no one around to witness bravado now. The other three were on their way to Earth— and they would make it. Greene walked over and shut off the equipment they had set up to record the takeoff. The surrounding area looked more like a junkyard than ever. He reached clumsy gloved fingers into an outside pocket of his suit and withdrew the glass slide. With one booted heel he ground it into the rock.

The first thing they would do with the others would be to give them thorough physical checks, after hauling them out of the south Atlantic. And when that happened, Barth's leukemia would immediately be discovered. In fact, it was a yet-to-be-solved mystery why it had not shown up during routine medical tests before this. After that—well, while there was life, there was hope.

At any rate, live or die, Barth, the natural identification

figure for those watching the Project, would hold the spotlight of public attention for another six months at least. And if he held it from a hospital bed, so much the better. Greene would pass and be forgotten between two bites of breakfast toast. But Barth—that was something else again.

The Project would be hard to starve to death with Barth dying slowly and uncomplaining before the eyes of taxpayers.

Greene dropped the silly signal rifle. The rocket flame was out of sight now. He felt with gloved hands at the heat control unit under the thick covering of his suit and clumsily crushed it. He felt it give and break. It was amazing, he thought, the readiness of the laity to expect miracles from the medical profession. Anyone with half a brain should have guessed that something which normally required the personnel and physical resources of a hospital, could not be managed alone, without equipment, and on the naked surface of Mars.

Barth would undoubtedly have guessed it—if he had not been blinded by Greene's wholly unfair implication that Barth was a glory-hunter. Of course, in the upper part of his mind, Barth must know it was not true; but he was too good a man not to doubt himself momentarily when accused. After that, he had been unable to wholly trust his own reasons for insisting on being the one to stay behind.

He'll forgive me, thought Greene. He'll forgive me, afterwards, when he figures it all out.

He shook off his sadness that had come with the thought. Barth had been his only friend. All his life, Greene's harsh, sardonic exterior had kept people at a distance. Only Barth had realized that under Greene's sarcasms and jibes he was as much a fool with stars in his eyes as the worst of them. Well, thank heaven he had kept his weakness decently hidden.

He started to lie down, then changed his mind. It was probably the most effective position for what time remained; but it went against his grain that the men who came after him should find him flat on his back in this junkyard.

Greene began hauling equipment together until he had a sort of low seat. But when he had it all constructed, this, too was unsatisfactory.

Finally he built it a little higher. The suit was very stiff, anyway. In the end, he needed only a little propping for his back and arms. He was turned in the direction in which the Earth would rise over the Martian horizon; and, although the upper half of him was still in sunlight, long shadows of utter blackness were pooling about his feet.

Definitely, the lower parts of his suit were cooling now. It occurred to him that possibly he would freeze by sections in this position. No matter, it was a relatively painless death. —Forgive me, he thought in Barth's direction, lost among the darkness of space and the light of the stars.—It would have been a quicker, easier end for you this way, I know. But you and I both were always blank checks to be filled out on demand and paid into the account of Man's future. It was only then that we could have had any claim to lives of our own.

As Greene had now, in these final seconds.

He pressed back against the equipment he had built up. It held him solidly. This little, harmless pleasure he gave his own grim soul. Up here in the airlessness of Mars' bare surface, nothing could topple him over now.

When the crew of the next ship came searching, they would find what was left of him still on his feet.

It was locked—from the outside.

Not only that, but the mechanical latch handle that would override the button lock on the tiny tourist cabin aboard the *Star of the North* was hidden by the very bed on which Cully When sat cross-legged, like some sinewy mountain man out of Cully's own pioneering ancestry. Cully grinned at the image in the mirror which went with the washstand now hidden by the bed beneath him. He would not have risked such an expression as that grin if there had been anyone around to see him. The grin, he knew, gave too much of him away to viewers. It was the hard, unconquerable humor of a man dealing for high stakes.

Here, in the privacy of this locked cabin, it was also a tribute to the skill of the steward who had imprisoned him. A dour and cautious individual with a long Scottish face, and no doubt the greater part of his back wages reinvested in the very spaceship line he worked for. Or had Cully done something to give himself away? No. Cully shook his head. If that had been the case, the steward would have done more than just lock the cabin. It occurred to Cully that his face, at last, might be becoming known.

"I'm sorry, sir," the steward had said, as he opened the cabin's sliding door and saw the unmade bed. "Off-watch steward's missed making it up." He clucked reprovingly. "I'll fix it for you, sir."

"No hurry," said Cully. "I just want to hang my clothes; and I can do that later."

"Oh, no, sir." The lean, dour face of the other—as primitive in a different way as Cully's own—looked shocked. "Regulations. Passengers' gear to be stowed and bunk made up before overdrive."

"Well, I can't just stand here in the corridor," said Cully. "I want to get rid of the stuff and get a drink." And indeed the corridor was so narrow, they were like two vehicles on a mountain road. One would have to back up to some wider spot to let the other past.

"Have the sheets in a moment, sir," said the steward. "Just a moment, sir. If you wouldn't mind sitting up on the bed, sir?"

"All right," said Cully. "But hurry. I want to step up for a drink in the lounge."

He hopped up on to the bed, which filled the little cabin in its down position; and drew his legs up tailor-fashion to clear them out of the corridor.

"Excuse me, sir," said the steward, closed the door, and went off. As soon as he heard the button lock latch, Cully had realized what the man was up to. But an unsuspecting man would have waited at least several minutes before hammering on the locked door and calling for someone to let him out. Cully had been forced to sit digesting the matter in silence.

At the thought of it now, however, he grinned again. That steward was a regular prize package. Cully must remember to think up something appropriate for him, afterwards. At the moment, there were more pressing things to think of.

Cully looked in the mirror again and was relieved at the sight of himself without the betraying grin. The face that looked back at him at the moment was lean and angular. A little peroxide solution on his thick, straight brows, had taken the sharp appearance off his high cheekbones and given his pale blue eyes a faintly innocent expression. When he really wanted to fail to impress sharply discerning eyes, he also made it a point to chew gum.

The present situation, he considered now, did not call for that extra touch. If the steward was already even vaguely suspicious of him, he could not wait around for an ideal opportunity. He would have to get busy now, while they were still working the spaceship out of the solar system to a safe distance where the overdrive could be engaged without risking a mass-proximity explosion.

And this, since he was imprisoned so neatly in his own shoebox of a cabin, promised to be a problem right from the start.

He looked around the cabin. Unlike the salon cabins on the level overhead, where it was possible to pull down the bed and still have a tiny space to stand upright in—either beside the bed, in the case of single-bed cabins, or between them, in the case of doubles—in the tourist cabins once the bed was down, the room was completely divided into two spaces—the space above the bed and the space below. In the space above, with him, were the light and temperature and ventilation controls, controls to provide him with soft music or the latest adventure tape, food and drink dispensers and a host of other minor comforts.

There were also a phone and a signal button, both connected with the steward's office. Thoughtfully he tried both. There was, of course, no answer.

At that moment a red light flashed on the wall opposite him; and a voice came out of the grille that usually provided the soft music.

"We are about to maneuver. This is the Captain's Section, speaking. We are about to maneuver. Will all lounge passengers return to their cabins? Will all passengers remain in their cabins, and fasten seat belts. We are about to maneuver. This is the Captain's Section—"

Cully stopped listening. The steward would have known

this announcement was coming. It meant that everybody but crew members would be in their cabins and crew members would be up top in control level at maneuver posts. And that meant nobody was likely to happen along to let Cully out. If Cully could get out of this cabin, however, those abandoned corridors could be a break for him.

However, as he looked about him now, Cully was rapidly revising downward his first cheerful assumption that he— who had gotten out of so many much more intentional prisons —would find this a relatively easy task. On the same principle that a pit with unclimbable walls and too deep to jump up from and catch an edge is one of the most perfect traps designable—the tourist room held Cully. He was on top of the bed; and he needed to be below it to operate the latch handle.

First question: How impenetrable was the bed itself? Cully dug down through the covers, pried up the mattress, peered through the springs, and saw a blank panel of metal. Well, he had not really expected much in that direction. He put the mattress and covers back and examined what he had to work with above-bed.

There were all the control switches and buttons on the wall, but nothing among them promised him any aid. The walls were the same metal paneling as the base of the bed. Cully began to turn out his pockets in the hope of finding something in them that would inspire him. And he did indeed turn out a number of interesting items, including a folded piece of notepaper which he looked at rather soberly before laying it aside, unfolded, with a boy scout type of knife that just happened to have a set of lock picks among its other tools. The note would only take up valuable time at the moment, and—the lock being out of reach in the door— the lock picks were no good either.

There was nothing in what he produced to inspire him, however. Whistling a little mournfully, he began to make the next best use of his pile of property. He unscrewed the nib and cap of his long, gold fountain pen, took out the ink cartridge and laid the tube remaining aside. He removed his belt, and the buckle from the belt. The buckle, it appeared, clipped on to the fountain pen tube in somewhat the manner of a pistol grip. He reached in his mouth, removed a bridge covering from the second premolar to the second molar, and combined this with a small metal throwaway dispenser of the sort designed to contain antacid tablets. The two together had a remarkable resemblance to the magazine and miniaturized trigger assembly of a small handgun; and when he attached them to the buckle-fountain-pen-tube combination the resemblance became so marked as to be practically inarguable.

Cully made a few adjustments in this and looked around himself again. For the second time, his eye came to rest on the folded note, and, frowning at himself in the mirror, he did pick it up and unfold it. Inside it read: "O wae the pow'r the Giftie gie us" Love, Lucy. Well, thought Cully, that was about what you could expect from a starry-eyed girl with Scottish ancestors, and romantic notions about present-day conditions on Alderbaran IV and the other new worlds.

". . . But if you have all that land on Asterope IV, why aren't you back there developing it?" she had asked him.

"The New Worlds are stifling to death," he had answered. But he saw then she did not believe him. To her, the New Worlds were still the romantic Frontier, as the Old Worlds Confederation newspapers capitalized it. She thought he had given up from lack of vision.

"You should try again . . ." she murmured. He gave up trying to make her understand. And then, when the cruise was over and their shipboard acquaintance—that was all it was, really—ended on the Miami dock, he had felt her slip something in his pocket so lightly only someone as self-trained as he would have noticed it. Later he had found it to be this note—which he had kept now for too long.

He started to throw it away, changed his mind for the sixtieth time and put it back in his pocket. He turned back to the

problem of getting out of the cabin. He looked it over, pulled
a sheet from the bed and used its length to measure a few
distances.

The bunk was pivoted near the point where the head of it
entered the recess in the wall that concealed it in Up position. Up, the bunk was designed to fit with its foot next to the
ceiling. Consequently, coming up, the foot would describe an
arc—
About a second and a half later he had discovered that
the arc of the foot, ascending, would leave just enough space
in the opposite top angle between wall and ceiling so that if
he could just manage to hang there, while releasing the safety
latch at the foot of the bed, he might be able to get the bed up
past him into the wall recess.

It was something which required the muscle and skill normally called for by so-called "chimney ascents" in mountain
climbing—where the climber wedges himself between two op-
posing walls of rock. A rather wide chimney—since the room
was a little more than four feet in width. But Cully had had
some little experience in that line.

He tried it. A few seconds later, pressed against walls and
ceiling, he reached down, managed to get the bed released,
and had the satisfaction of seeing it fold up by him. Half a
breath later he was free, out in the corridor of the Tourist
Section.

The corridor was deserted and silent. All doors were closed.
Cully closed his own thoughtfully behind him and went along
the corridor to the more open space in the center of the ship.
He looked up a steel ladder to the entrance of the Salon Section, where there would be another ladder to the Crew Section, and from there eventually to his objective—the Control
level and the Captain's Section. Had the way up those lad-
ders been open, it would have been simple. But level with the
top of the ladder he saw the way to the Salon section was

closed off by a metal cover capable of withstanding fifteen pounds per square inch of pressure.

It had been closed, of course, as the other covers would have been, at the beginning of the maneuver period.

Cully considered it thoughtfully, his fingers caressing the pistol grip of the little handgun he had just put together. He would have preferred, naturally, that the covers be open and the way available to him without the need for fuss or muss. But the steward had effectively ruled out that possibility by reacting as and when he had. Cully turned away from the staircase, and frowned, picturing the layout of the ship, as he had committed it to memory five days ago.

There was an emergency hatch leading through the ceiling of the end tourist cabin to the end salon cabin overhead, at both extremes of the corridor. He turned and went down to the end cabin nearest him, and laid his finger quietly on the outside latch-handle.

There was no sound from inside. He drew his put-together handgun from his belt; and, holding it in his left hand, calmly and without hesitation, opened the door and stepped inside.

He stopped abruptly. The bed in here was, of course, up in the wall, or he could never have entered. But the cabin's single occupant was asleep on the right-hand seat of the two seats that an upraised bed left exposed. The occupant was a small girl of about eight years old.

The slim golden barrel of the handgun had swung immediately to aim at the child's temple. For an automatic second, it hung poised there, Cully's finger half-pressing the trigger. But the little girl never stirred. In the silence, Cully heard the surge of his own blood in his ears and the faint crackle of the note in his shirt pocket. He lowered the gun and fumbled in the waistband of his pants, coming up with a child-sized anesthetic pellet. He slipped this into his gun above the regular load; aimed the gun, and fired. The child made a little uneasy movement all at once; and then lay still. Cully bent over her for a second, and heard the soft sound of her breathing. He

straightened up. The pellet worked not through the blood
stream, but immediately through a reaction of the nerves. In
fifteen minutes the effect would be worn off, and the girl's
sleep would be natural slumber again.

He turned away, stepped up on the opposite seat and laid
his free hand on the latch handle of the emergency hatch overhead. A murmur of voices from above made him hesitate. He
unscrewed the barrel of the handgun and put it in his ear
with the other hollow end resting against the ceiling which
was also the floor overhead. The voices came, faint and dis-
torted, but understandable to his listening.

". . . Hilifter," a female voice was saying.

"Oh, Patty!" another female voice answered. "He was just
trying to scare you. You believe everything."

"How about that ship that got hilifted just six months ago?
That ship going to one of the Pleiades, just like this one? The
Queen of Argyle—"

"*Princess of Argyle.*"

"Well, you know what I mean. Ships do get hilifted. Just
as long as there're governments on the pioneer worlds that'll
license them and no questions asked. And it could just as well
happen to this ship. But you don't worry about it a bit."

"No, I don't."

"When hilifters take over a ship, they kill off everyone who
can testify against them. None of the passengers or ship's
officers from the *Princess of Argyle* was ever heard of again."

"Says who?"

"Oh, everybody knows that!"

Cully took the barrel from his ear and screwed it back onto
his weapon. He glanced at the anesthetized child and thought
of trying the other cabin with an emergency hatch. But the
maneuver period would not last more than twenty minutes at
the most and five of that must be gone already. He put the
handgun between his teeth, jerked the latch to the overhead
hatch, and pulled it down and open.

He put both hands on the edge of the hatch opening; and with one spring went upward into the salon cabin overhead.

He erupted into the open space between a pair of facing seats, each of which held a girl in her twenties. The one on his left was a rather plump, short, blond girl who was sitting curled up on her particular seat with a towel across her knees, an open bottle of pink nail polish on the towel, and the brush-cap to the bottle poised in her hand. The other was a tall, dark-haired, very pretty lass with a lap-desk pulled down from the wall and a handscriber on the desk where she was apparently writing a letter. For a moment both stared at him, and his gun; and then the blonde gave a muffled shriek, pulled the towel over her head and lay still, while the brunette, staring at Cully, went slowly pale.

"Jim!" she said.

"Sorry," said Cully. "The real name's Cully When. Sorry about this, too, Lucy." He held the gun casually, but it was pointed in her general direction. "I didn't have any choice."

A little of the color came back. Her eyes were as still as fragments of green bottle glass.

"No choice about what?" she said.

"To come through this way," said Cully. "Believe me, if I'd known you were here, I'd have picked any other way. But there wasn't any other way; and I didn't know."

"I see," she said, and looked at the gun in his hand. "Do you have to point that at me?"

"I'm afraid," said Cully, gently, "I do."

She did not smile.

"I'd still like to know what you're doing here," she said.

"I'm just passing through," said Cully. He gestured with the gun to the emergency hatch to the Crew Section, overhead. "As I say, I'm sorry it has to be through your cabin. But I didn't even know you were serious about emigrating."

"People usually judge other people by themselves," she said expressionlessly. "As it happened, I believed you." She looked at the gun again. "How many of you are there on board?"

"I'm afraid I can't tell you that," said Cully.

"No. You couldn't, could you?" Her eyes held steady on him. "You know, there's an old poem about a man like you. He rides by a farm maiden and she falls in love with him, just like that. But he makes her guess what he is; and she guesses . . . oh, all sorts of honorable things, like soldier, or forester. But he tells her in the end he's just an outlaw, slinking through the wood."

Cully winced.

"Lucy—" he said. "Lucy—"

"Oh, that's all right," she said. "I should have known when you didn't call me or get in touch with me, after the boat docked." She glanced over at her friend, motionless under the towel. "You have the gun. What do you want us to do?"

"Just sit still," he said. "I'll go on up through here and be out of your way in a second. I'm afraid—" he reached over to the phone on the wall and pulled its cord loose. "You can buzz for the steward, still, after I'm gone," he said. "But he won't answer just a buzzer until after the maneuver period's over. And the stairway hatches are locked. Just sit tight and you'll be all right."

He tossed the phone aside and tucked the gun in the waistband.

"Excuse me," he said, stepping up on the seat beside her. She moved stiffly away from him. He unlatched the hatch overhead, pulled it down; and went up through it. When he glanced back down through it, he saw her face stiffly upturned to him.

He turned away and found himself in an equipment room. It was what he had expected from the ship's plans he had memorized before coming aboard. He went quickly out of the room and scouted the Section.

As he had expected, there was no one at all upon this level. Weight and space on interstellar liners being at the premium that they were, even a steward like the one who had locked him in his cabin did double duty. In overdrive, no one but the navigating officer had to do much of anything. But in ordinary operation, there were posts for all ships personnel, and all ships personnel were at them up in the Captain's Section at Control.

The stair hatch to this top and final section of the ship, he found to be closed as the rest. This, of course, was routine. He had not expected this to be unlocked, though a few years back ships like this might have been that careless. There were emergency hatches from this level as well, of course, up to the final section. But it was no part of Cully's plan to come up in the middle of a Control room or a Captain's Section filled with young, active, and almost certainly armed officers. The inside route was closed.

The outside route remained a possibility. Cully went down to the opposite end of the corridor and found the entry port closed, but sealed only by a standard lock. In an adjoining room there were outside suits. Cully spent a few minutes with his picks, breaking the lock of the seal; and then went in to put on the suit that came closest to fitting his six-foot-two frame.

A minute later he stepped out onto the outside skin of the ship.

As he watched the outer door of the entry port closing ponderously in the silence of airless space behind him, he felt the usual inner coldness that came over him at times like this. He had a mild but very definite phobia about open space with its myriads of unchanging stars. He knew what caused it—several psychiatrists had told him it was nothing to worry about, but he could not quite accept their unconcern. He knew he was a very lonely individual, underneath it all; and subconsciously he guessed he equated space with the final extinction in which he expected one day to disappear and be forgotten forever. He could not really believe it was possible for someone like him to make a dent in such a universe.

It was symptomatic, he thought now, plodding along with

the magnetic bootsoles of his suit clinging to the metal hull, that he had never had any success with women—like Lucy. A sort of bad luck seemed to put him always in the wrong position with anyone he stood a chance of loving. Inwardly, he was just as starry-eyed as Lucy, he admitted to himself, alone with the vastness of space and the stars, but he'd never had much success bringing it out into the open. Where she went all right, he seemed to go all wrong. Well, he thought, that was life. She went her way and he would go his. And it was probably a good thing.

He looked ahead up the side of the ship, and saw the slight bulge of the observation window of the navigator's section. It was just a few more steps now.

Modern ships were sound insulated, thankfully, or the crew inside would have heard his dragging footsteps on the hull. He reached the window and peered in. The room he looked into was empty.

Beside the window was a small, emergency port for cleaning and repairs of the window. Clumsily, and with a good deal of effort, he got the lock-bolt holding it down, unscrewed, and let himself in. The space between outer and inner ports here was just enough to contain a spacesuited man. He crouched in darkness after the outer port had closed behind him.

Incoming air screamed up to audibility. He cautiously cracked the interior door and looked into a room still empty of any crew members. He slipped inside and snapped the lock on the door before getting out of his suit.

As soon as he was out, he drew the handgun from his belt and cautiously opened the door he had previously locked. He looked out on a short corridor leading one way to the Control Room, and the other, if his memory of the memorized ship plans had not failed him, to the central room above the stairway hatch from below. Opening off this small circular space surrounding the hatch, would be another entrance directly to the Control Room, a door to the Captain's Quarters, and one to the Communications Room.

The corridor was deserted. He heard voices coming down it from the Control Room; and he slipped out the door that led instead to the space surrounding the stairway hatch. And checked abruptly.

The hatch was open. And it had not been open when he had checked it from the level below, ten minutes before.

For the first time he cocked an ear specifically to the kinds of voices coming from the Control Room. The acoustics of this part of the ship mangled all sense out of the words being said. But now that he listened, he had no trouble recognizing, among others, the voice of Lucy.

It occurred to him then with a kind of wonder at himself, that it would have been no feat for an active girl like herself to have followed him up through the open emergency hatch, and later mount the crew level stairs to the closed hatch there and pound on it until someone opened up.

He threw aside further caution and sprinted across to the doorway of the Captain's Quarters. The door was unlocked. He ducked inside and looked around him. It was empty. It occurred to him that Lucy and the rest of the ship's complement would probably still be expecting him to be below in the Crew's section. He closed the door and looked about him, at the room he was in.

The room was more lounge than anything else, being the place where the captain of a spaceship did his entertaining. But there was a large and businesslike desk in one corner of the room, and in the wall opposite, was a locked, glassed-in case holding an assortment of rifles and handguns.

He was across the room in a moment and in a few, savage, seconds, had the lock to the case picked open. He reached in and took down a short-barreled, flaring-muzzled riot gun. He checked the chamber. It was filled with a full thousand-clip of the deadly steel darts. Holding this in one hand and his handgun in the other, he went back out the door and toward the other entrance to the control room—the entrance from the central room around the stairway hatch.

". . . He wouldn't tell me if there were any others," Lucy was saying to a man in a captain's shoulder tabs, while eight other men, including the dour-faced steward who had locked Cully in his cabin, stood at their posts, but listening.

"There aren't any," said Cully, harshly. They all turned to him. He laid the handgun aside on a control table by the entrance to free his other hand, and lifted the heavy riot gun in both hands, covering them. "There's only me."

"What do you want?" said the man with the captain's tabs. His face was set, and a little pale. Cully ignored the question. He came into the room, circling to his right, so as to have a wall at his back.

"You're one man short," said Cully as he moved. "Where is he?"

"Off-shift steward's sleeping," said the steward who had locked Cully in his room.

"Move back," said Cully, picking up crew members from their stations at control boards around the room, and herding them before him back around the room's circular limit to the very entrance by which he had come in. "I don't believe you."

"Then I might as well tell you," said the captain, backing up now along with Lucy and the rest. "He's in Communications. We keep a steady contact with Solar Police right up until we go into overdrive. There are two of their ships pacing alongside us right now, lights off, a hundred miles each side of us."

"Tell me another," said Cully. "I don't believe that either." He was watching everybody in the room, but what he was most aware of were the eyes of Lucy, wide upon him. He spoke to her, harshly. "Why did you get into this?"

She was pale to the lips; and her eyes had a stunned look.

"I looked down and saw what you'd done to that child in

the cabin below—" her voice broke off into a whisper. "Oh, Cully—"

He laughed mournfully.

"Stop there," he ordered. He had driven them back into a corner near the entrance he had come in. "I've got to have all of you together. Now, one of you is going to tell me where that other man is—and I'm going to pick you off, one at a time until somebody does."

"You're a fool," said the captain. A little of his color had come back. "You're all alone. You don't have a chance of controlling this ship by yourself. You know what happens to Hilifters, don't you? It's not just a prison sentence. Give up now and we'll all put in a word for you. You might get off without mandatory execution."

"No thanks," said Cully. He gestured with the end of the riot gun. "We're going into overdrive. Start setting up the course as I give it to you."

"No," said the captain, looking hard at him.

"You're a brave man," said Cully. "But I'd like to point out something. I'm going to shoot you if you won't co-operate; and then I'm going to work down the line of your officers. Sooner or later somebody's going to preserve his life by doing what I tell him. So getting yourself killed isn't going to save the ship at all. It just means somebody with less courage than you lives. And you die."

There was a sharp, bitter intake of breath from the direction of Lucy. Cully kept his eyes on the captain.

"How about it?" Cully asked.

"No brush-pants of a colonial," said the captain, slowly and deliberately, "is going to stand in my Control Room and tell me where to take my ship."

"Did the captain and officers of the *Princess of Argyle* ever come back?" said Cully, somewhat cryptically.

"It's nothing to me whether they came or stayed."

"I take it all back," said Cully. "You're too valuable to

lose." The riot gun shifted to come to bear on the First Officer, a tall, thin, younger man whose hair was already receding at the temples. "But you aren't, friend. I'm not even going to tell you what I'm going to do. I'm just going to start counting; and when I decide to stop you've had it. One . . . two . . ."

"Don't! Don't shoot!" The First Officer jumped across the few steps that separated him from the Main Computer Panel. "What's your course? What do you want me to set up—"

The captain began to curse the First Officer. He spoke slowly and distinctly and in a manner that completely ignored the presence of Lucy in the Control Room. He went right on as Cully gave the First Officer the course and the First Officer set it up. He stopped only, as—abruptly—the lights went out, and the ship overdrove.

When the lights came on again—it was a matter of only a fraction of a second of real time—the captain was at last silent. He seemed to have sagged in the brief interval of darkness and his face looked older.

And then, slamming through the tense silence of the room came the sound of the Contact Alarm Bell.

"Turn it on," said Cully. The First Officer stepped over and pushed a button below the room's communication screen. It cleared suddenly to show a man in a white jacket.

"We're alongside, Cully," he said. "We'll take over now. How're you fixed for casualties?"

"At the moment—" began Cully. But he got no further than that. Behind him, three hard, spaced words in a man's voice cut him off.

"Drop it, Hilifter!"

Cully did not move. He cocked his eyebrows a little sadly and grinned his untamable grin for the first time at the ship's officers, and Lucy and the figure in the screen. Then the grin went away.

"Friend," he said to the man hidden behind him. "Your business is running a spaceship. Mine is taking them away

from people who run them. Right now you're figuring how
you make me give up or shoot me down and this ship dodges
back into overdrive, and you become a hero for saving it.
But it isn't going to work that way."

He waited for a moment to hear if the off-watch steward
behind him—or whoever the officer was—would answer. But
there was only silence.

"You're behind me," said Cully. "But I can turn pretty fast.
You may get me coming around, but unless you've got something like a small cannon, you're not going to stop me getting
you at this short range, whether you've got me or not. Now,
if you think I'm just talking, you better think again. For me,
this is one of the risks of the trade."

He turned. As he did so he went for the floor; and heard
the first shot go by his ear. As he hit the floor another shot hit
the deck beside him and ricocheted into his side. But by that
time he had the heavy riot gun aimed and he pressed the firing button. The stream of darts knocked the man backward
out of the entrance to the control room to lie, a still and
huddled shape, in the corridor outside.

Cully got to his feet, feeling the single dart in his side. The
room was beginning to waver around him, but he felt that he
could hold on for the necessary couple of minutes before the
people from the ship moving in alongside could breach the
lock and come aboard. His jacket was loose and would hide
the bleeding underneath. None of those facing him could
know he had been hit.

"All right, folks," he said, managing a grin. "It's all over
but the shouting—" And then Lucy broke suddenly from the
group and went running across the room toward the entrance
through which Cully had come a moment or so earlier.

"Lucy—" he barked at her. And then he saw her stop and
turn by the control table near the entrance, snatching up the
little handgun he had left there. "Lucy, do you want to get
shot?"

But she was bringing up the little handgun, held in the grip of both her hands and aiming it squarely at him. The tears were running down her face.

"It's better for you, Cully—" she was sobbing. "Better . . ."

He swung the riot gun to bear on her, but he saw she did not even see it.

"Lucy, I'll have to kill you!" he cried. But she no more heard him, apparently, than she saw the muzzle-on view of the riot gun in his hands. The wavering golden barrel in her grasp wobbled to bear on him.

"Oh, Cully!" she wept. "Cully—" And pulled the trigger.

"Oh, *hell!*" said Cully in despair. And let her shoot him down.

When he came back, things were very fuzzy there at first. He heard the voice of the man in the white jacket, arguing with the voice of Lucy.

"Hallucination—" muttered Cully. The voices broke off.

"Oh, he said something!" cried the voice of Lucy.

"Cully?" said the man's voice. Cully felt a two-finger grip on his wrist in the area where his pulse should be—if, that was, he had a pulse. "How're you feeling?"

"Ship's doctor?" muttered Cully, with great effort. "You got the *Star of the North?*"

"That's right. All under control. How do you feel?"

"Feel fine," mumbled Cully. The doctor laughed.

"Sure you do," said the doctor. "Nothing like being shot a couple of times and having a pellet and a dart removed to put a man in good shape."

"Not Lucy's fault—" muttered Cully. "Not understand." He made another great effort in the interests of explanation. "Stars'n eyes."

"Oh, what does he mean?" wept Lucy.

"He means," said the voice of the doctor harshly, "that you're just the sort of fine young idealist who makes the best sort of sucker for the sort of propaganda the Old World's Confederation dishes out."

"Oh, you'd say that!" flared Lucy's voice. "Of course, you'd say that!"

"Young lady," said the doctor, "how rich do you think our friend Cully, here, is?"

Cully heard her blow her nose, weakly.

"He's got millions, I suppose," she said, bitterly. "Hasn't he hilifted dozens of ships?"

"He's hilifted eight," said the doctor, dryly, "which, incidentally, puts him three ships ahead of any other contender for the title of hilifting champion around the populated stars. The mortality rate among single workers—and you can't get any more than a single 'lifter aboard Confederation ships nowadays—hits ninety per cent with the third ship captured. But I doubt Cully's been able to save many millions on a salary of six hundred a month, and a bonus of one tenth of one per cent of salvage value, at Colonial World rates."

There was a moment of profound silence.

"What do you mean?" said Lucy, in a voice that wavered a little.

"I'm trying," said the doctor, "for the sake of my patient—and perhaps for your own—to push aside what Cully calls those stars in your eyes and let a crack of surface daylight through."

"But why would he work for a salary—like that?" Disbelief was strong in her voice.

"Possibly," said the doctor, "just possibly because the picture of a bloodstained hilifter with a knife between his teeth, carousing in Colonial bars, shooting down Confederation officers for the fun of it, and dragging women passengers off by the hair, has very little to do with the real facts of a man like Cully."

"Smart girl," managed Cully. "S'little mixed up, s'all—" He managed to get his vision cleared a bit. The other two were standing facing each other, right beside his bed. The doctor had a slight flush above his cheekbones and looked angry.

Lucy, Cully noted anxiously, was looking decidedly pale.
"Mixed up—" Cully said again.

"Mixed up isn't the word for it," said the doctor angrily,
without looking down at him. "She and all ninety-nine out of a
hundred people on the Old Worlds." He went on to Lucy.
"You met Cully Earthside. Evidently you liked him there. He
didn't strike you as the scum of the stars, then.

"But all you have to do is hear him tagged with the name
'hilifter' and immediately your attitude changes."

Lucy swallowed.

"No," she said, in a small voice, "it didn't . . . change."

"Then who do you think's wrong—you or Cully?" The doctor snorted. "If I have to give you reasons, what's the use? If
you can't see things straight for yourself, who can help you?
That's what's wrong with all the people back on the Old
Worlds."

"I believe Cully," she said. "I just don't know why I
should."

"Who has lots of raw materials—the raw materials to support trade—but hasn't any trade?" asked the doctor.

She frowned at him.

"Why . . . the New Worlds haven't any trade on their
own," she said. "But they're too undeveloped yet, too young—"

"Young? There's three to five generations on most of them!"

"I mean they haven't got the industry, the commercial organization—" she faltered before the slightly satirical expression on the doctor's face. "All right, then, you tell me! If
they've got everything they need for trade, why don't they?
The Old Worlds did; why don't you?"

"In what?"

She stared at him.

"But the Confederation of the Old Worlds already has the
ships for interworld trade. And they're glad to ship Colonial
products. In fact they do," she said.

"So a load of miniaturized surgical power instruments made

on Asterope in the Pleiades, has to be shipped to Earth and then shipped clear back out to its destination on Electra, also in the Pleiades. Only by the time they get there they've doubled or tripled in price, and the difference is in the pockets of Earth shippers."

She was silent.

"It seems to me," said the doctor, "that girl who was with you mentioned something about your coming from Boston, back in the United States on Earth. Didn't they have a tea party there once? Followed by a revolution? And didn't it all have something to do with the fact that England at that time would not allow its colonies to own and operate their own ships for trade—so that it all had to be funneled through England in English ships to the advantage of English merchants?"

"But why can't you build your own ships?" she said. Cully felt it was time he got in on the conversation. He cleared his throat, weakly.

"Hey—" he managed to say. They both looked at him; but he himself was looking only at Lucy.

"You see," he said, rolling over and struggling up on one elbow, "the thing is—"

"Lie down," said the doctor.

"Go jump out the air lock," said Cully. "The thing is, honey, you can't build spaceships without a lot of expensive equipment and tools, and trained personnel. You need a spaceship-building industry. And you have to get the equipment, tools, and people from somewhere else to start with. You can't get 'em unless you can trade for 'em. And you can't trade freely without ships of your own, which the Confederation, by forcing us to ship through them, makes it impossible for us to have.

"So you see how it works out," said Cully. "It works out you've got to have shipping before you can build shipping. And if people on the outside refuse to let you have it by proper means, simply because they've got a good thing going and

don't want to give it up—then some of us just have to break
loose and go after it any way we can."

"Oh, Cully!"

Suddenly she was on her knees by the bed and her arms
were around him.

"Of course the Confederation news services have been trying to keep up the illusion we're sort of half jungle-jims, half
wild-west characters," said the doctor. "Once a person takes
a good look at the situation on the New Worlds, though, with
his eyes open—" He stopped. They were not listening.

"I might mention," he went on, a little more loudly, "while
Cully here may not be exactly rich, he does have a rather
impressive medal due him, and a commission as Brevet-
Admiral in the upcoming New Worlds Space Force. The
New Worlds Congress voted him both at their meeting just
last week on Asterope, as soon as they'd finished drafting their
Statement of Independence—"

But they were still not listening. It occurred to the doctor
then that he had better uses for his time—here on this vessel
where he had been Ship's Doctor ever since she first lifted
into space—than to stand around talking to deaf ears.

He went out, closing the door of the sick bay on the former
Princess of Argyle quietly behind him.

BUILDING ON THE LINE

I

Crack-voiced, off-key, in every way like a fingernail drawn across the blackboard of his soul, the song cauterwauled in John Clancy's helmet earphones:

> ". . . Building on the Line, Team. Building on the Line!
> "Building Transmit Stations all along the goddam Line!
> "Light-years out and all alone,
> "We have cannibalized the drone;
> "And there's no way to go home
> " 'Till we get the Station working on the goddam Line!"

Clancy closed his mind to the two thousandth, four hundred and—what? He had even got to the point where he had lost count of the times Arthur Plotchin had sung it. Was that a win, he wondered, suddenly—a point for Plotch, in finally driving him to lose count? Or was it a point for him, in that he had managed to shut out the singing, at least to the point of losing his involuntary count of the times Plotch had sung it?

A bright light hit him in the faceplate, momentarily blinding him; and the singing broke off.

"Heads up, Clance!" It was Plotch's voice, cracking like static now in the earphones. "Keep your mind on your work, dim-bulb! Time to fire the wire!"

Clancy deliberately did not answer, while he slowly counted off six seconds—*"One-Mississippi, two-Mississippi . . ."* It was one of the things he could be sure rubbed Plotch the wrong way; even as he knew Plotch was sure by this time that the endless repetition of the *Line Song* was like sandpaper to Clancy's raw nerves.

"What?" Clancy said, at the end of the sixth second.

"You heard me, you . . ." Plotch choked a little and went silent, in his turn.

Clancy grinned savagely inside his helmet. With the flash from Plotch's signal-light blinked out of his eyes, now, he could make out the other's silver-suited figure with the black rectangle of tinted glass that was its faceplate. Plotch stood holding his wire gun by the other of the last two terminal rods in the almost-completed Star-Point. He was some hundred yards off across the barren rock of this hell-born world, with its two hundred degrees below zero temperature, its atmosphere that was poisonous, and almost non-existent to boot, with its endless rock surface, its red clouds always roiling threateningly overhead and the not-quite-heard gibber of uneasy native spirits always nagging at a man just below the level of his hearing.

Plotch was trying to turn the deaf treatment back on Clancy. But that was a game Clancy played better than his dark-haired, round-headed teammate. Clancy waited; and, sure enough, after a few moments, Plotch broke first.

"Don't you want to get back to the ship, horse's-head," shouted Plotch, suddenly. "Don't you ever want to get home?"

Was Plotch starting to sound a little hysterical? Or was it Clancy himself, imagining the fact? Maybe it was neither. Maybe it was just the hobgoblins, as Line Team 349 had come to call the native life-form, putting the thought into Clancy's head.

For the hobgoblins were real enough. There was no doubt by this time that some form of immaterial life existed in the fugitive flickers of green light among the bare rocks of XN-4010, as this frozen chunk of a world had been officially named. Something was there in the green flickering, alive and inimical; and it had been trying to get at him and Plotch all through the five days they had been out on the job here, setting up Number Sixteen of the twenty-six Star-Points required for a Transmit Receive Line Relay Station. Luckily, one of the few good things about the survival suits they were wearing this trip was that they seemed to screen out at least part of whatever emanations the hobgoblins threw at them.

Clancy broke off in the middle of his thoughts to switch the living hate within him, for a moment, from Plotch to R. and E.—the Research and Experimental Service, which seemed to be just about taking over the Line Service, nowadays. Thanks to an evident lack of guts on the part of the Line Service Commandant.

The work on the Line Teams was bad enough. Fifteen men transmitted out to a drone receiver that had been lucky enough to hit a world suitable for a Relay or Terminal Station. Fifteen men, jammed into a transmit ship where every cubic inch of space and ounce of mass was precious because of their construction equipment, was balanced against the weak resolving powers of the drone. Jammed together, blind-transmitted on to a world like this, where you lived and worked in your suit for days on end. That was bad enough.

Add Plotch for a partner, and it became unbearable. But then add R. and E. and it went beyond unbearable. It was bad enough five years back, in the beginning, when a fifteen-man Team would be testing perhaps a dozen new items for R. and E. Now Clancy had a dozen new gadgets in his suit alone. He was a walking laboratory of specialized untried gimmicks, dreamed up on comfortable old Earth. Plotch had a dozen entirely different ones; and so did all the others. Though who could keep count.

Clancy bent ostentatiously to tug once more on the immovable terminal rod he had just spent three hard physical hours of labor in planting six feet deep in XN-4010's native rock.

He had in fact been down with the terminal for some minutes before Plotch called. But he had been pretending to be still working, for the sake of making Plotch struggle to get him to finish up. But now it was time to tie in. These terminals were the last two of the nineteen that made up a Star-Point, as the twenty-six Star-Points, spread out over a diameter of eighty miles, would, when finished, make a working Relay Station. Tying in these last two terminals would activate the Star-Point. They could go back to the transmit ship for ten blissful hours outside their suits before they were sent out on the next job. Head down, still tugging at the rod, Clancy grinned bitterly to himself.

There was usually a closeness between members of a Line Team that was like blood-brotherhood. But in this case, if the hobgoblins were trying to stir up trouble between Plotch and him, they were breaking their immaterial thumbs trying to punch a button that already stuck in *on* position. Clancy straightened up from the rod and spoke over his helmet phone to Plotch.

"Yeah," he said. "I'm done."

He drew his own wire gun and, resting it in the sighting touch of the terminal rod, aimed it at the rod Plotch had just set up. He saw Plotch's gun come up, glinting red light from the glowing clouds overhead, and aim in his direction. For a second the pinhole of light that was sighting beam from Plotch's gun flickered in his eyes. Then, looking at his post, he saw its illumination there, like a small white dot.

"Ready?" Plotch's voice sounded in his earphones.

"Ready!" answered Clancy. "On the count of three, fire together with me. *One . . . two . . . three!*"

He pressed the firing button of his wire gun as he spoke the final word. An incredibly thin streak of silver lightning leaped out from the end of his gun through the receptor on the side of the post before him and buried its far end in the receptor on the post beside Plotch. In almost the same second a similar streak of lightning-colored wire joined Plotch's post in reverse to his. The physical shock of the suddenly activated Star-Point field sent both men stumbling backward awkwardly in their protective suits; and a varicolored aurora of faint light sprang up about the star-shaped area of grounded Relay equipment, enclosed by the twenty rods joined by double lengths of fine wire.

Number Sixteen Star-Point of the Relay terminal on XN-4010 was in and working. Now they could get back to the ship.

But then, as if the Star-Point's completion had been a signal, the low-hung clouds just over them opened up in a sort of hailstorm. Objects came hurtling toward the surface below —objects of all shapes and sizes. They looked like large rocks or small boulders, most of them. But for one weird moment, incredibly, it seemed to Clancy that some of them had the shape of Mark-70 anti-personnel homing missiles; and one of these was headed right for Plotch.

"Plotch!" shouted Clancy. Plotch whirled and his dark faceplate jerked up to stare at the rain of strange objects arcing down at them. Then he made an effort to throw himself out of the path of whatever was coming at him.

But he was not quite fast enough. The missile, or whatever it was, struck him a glancing blow high on the shoulder, knocking him to the rock surface underfoot. Clancy himself huddled up on the ground having no place to hide. Something rang hard against his helmet, but the shock of the blow went into his shoulders, as the supporting metal collar of his suit—another of R. and E.'s test gadgets—for once paid its way by keeping the helmet from being driven down onto the top of his head, inside.

Around him there were heavy thuddings. One more, just beside him. Then silence.

He got up. There were no more rocks falling from the skies. All around him there was only the silent, shifting, colorful aurora of radiation from the connected terminal rods; and the motionless, spacesuited figure of Plotch was a hundred yards off.

Clancy scrambled to his feet and began to slog toward the still figure. It did not move as he got closer, in the stumbling run which was the best speed he could manage, wearing his suit.

II

When at last he stood over Plotch, he saw his teammate was completely unmoving. Plotch's suit had a bad dent at the top front of the right shoulder joint; and there was a small, dark, open crack in the suit at the center of the dent. There was only rock nearby; no sign of any missile. But Plotch lay still. With that crack in it, his suit had to have lost air and heat instantly. His faceplate was white now, plainly opaqued on the inside by a thick coat of ice crystals.

Clancy swore. The gibbering of the hobgoblins, just out beyond the frontiers of his consciousness, seemed to rise in volume triumphantly. He reached down instinctively and tried to straighten out Plotch's body, for the other man lay half-curled on his side. But the body would not straighten. It was as a figure of cast iron. There was no doubt about it. Within his suit, Plotch was now as rigid as the block of ice that, for all practical purposes, he now was.

Plotch was frozen. Dead.

Or was he?

Clancy abruptly remembered something about the experimental gadgets in Plotch's suit. Had not one of them been an emergency cryogenic unit of some sort? If that was so, maybe it was the unit that had frozen Plotch—working instantly to save him when the suit was pierced.

If that was so, maybe Plotch was salvagable after all. If it really was so. . . .

"Calling Duty Lineman at Transmit ship!" Clancy croaked automatically into his helmet phone, activating the long-distance intercom with his tongue. "Calling whoever's on duty, back on the *Xenophon!* Come in, Duty Lineman! Emergency! Repeat, Emergency! This is Clancy! Answer me, Duty Lineman. . . ."

Static—almost but not quite screening out the soundless gibbering of the hobgoblins—answered, roaring alone in Clancy's earphones. His head, a little dizzy since the rain of rocks, cleared somewhat and he remembered that he should not have expected an answer from this ship. There was interference on XN-4010 that broke communication between a suit transmitter and the mother ship. It cut off, at times, even communication between a flitter's more powerful communication unit and the *Xenophon.* He struggled to his feet and, bending down, took hold of Plotch's stiff body underneath the armpits of the suit. He began to drag it toward their flitter, just out of sight over a little rise of the rocky ground, a couple of hundred yards away.

The ground was rough, and Clancy sweated inside his suit. He sweated and swore at his frozen partner, the hobgoblins, the R. and E. Service for its experimenting—and Lief Janssen, the Line Service Commandant, for letting R. and E. do it. The gravity on XN-4010 was roughly .78 of Earth normal, but the rocky surface was so fissured and strewn with stones of all sizes from pebble to boulder that Plotch's unyielding figure kept getting stuck as it was pulled along. Eventually, Clancy was forced to pick it up clumsily in his arms and try to carry it that way. He made one attempt to put it over his shoulder in a grotesque variation of the fireman's lift; but the position of the arms, crook-elbowed at the sides prevented the

bend in the body from balancing on his shoulder. In the end
he was forced to carry what was possibly Plotch's corpse, like
an oversized and awkward baby in his arms.

So weighed down, he staggered along, tripping over rock,
detouring to avoid the wider cracks underfoot until he topped
the rise that hid the flitter from him. Just below him and less
than thirty feet off, it had been waiting—an end and solution
to the grisly and muscle-straining business of carrying the
frozen and suited figure of Plotch in his arms.

It was still there.

—But it was a wreck.

A boulder nearly two feet in circumference had struck
squarely in the midst of the aft repulsor units, and the tough
but lightweight hull of the flitter had cracked open like a
ceramic eggshell under the impact.

Clancy halted, swaying, where he stood, still holding
Plotch.

"I don't believe it," he muttered into the static-roar of his
helmet. "I just don't believe it. That flitter's *got* to fly!"

For a moment he felt nothing but numb shock. It rose and
threatened to overwhelm him. He fought his way up out of
it, however; not so much out of determination, as out of a
sudden rising panic at the thought of the nearly thirty miles
separating him from the transmit ship.

The flitter could not be wrecked. It could not be true that
he was stranded out here alone, with what was left of Plotch.
The flitter *had* to save them.

Then, suddenly, inspiration came to him. Hastily, he
dropped onto one knee and eased Plotch onto a flat area of
the rock under foot. Leaving Plotch there, balanced and rocking a little, grotesquely, behind him, Clancy plunged down
the rubbled slope to the smashed flitter, crawled over its torn
sides into what had been the main cabin and laid hands upon
the main control board. He plugged his suit into the board,
snatched up the intercom hand phone and punched the call
signal for *Xenophon*.

"Duty-Lineman!" he shouted into the phone. "Duty-Lineman! Come in, *Xenophon!* Come in!"

Suddenly, then, he realized that there were no operating lights glowing at him from the control panel before him. The phone in his hand was a useless weight, and his helmet earphones, which should have linked automatically with the flitter receivers of the intercom sounded only with the ceaseless static and the endless, soundless gibbering.

Slowly, almost tenderly, he unplugged his suit, laid the phone back down on the little shelf before the dark instrument panel and dropped down on the one of three seats before the control board that was not wrecked. For a little while he simply sat there, with the hobgoblins gibbering at him. His head swam. He found himself talking to Plotch.

"Plotch," he was saying, quite quietly into his helmet phone. "Plotch, there's nothing else for it. We're going to have to wait here until the ship figures there's something wrong and sends out another flitter to find out what happened to us."

He waited a few moments.

"You hear me, Plotch?"

Still there was only silence, static, voiceless gibbering in his earphones.

"We can stick it out of course, Plotch," Clancy muttered, staring at the dead control panel. "Inside of two days they ought to figure we're overdue. Then they'll wait a day, maybe, figuring it's nothing important. Finally they'll send one of the other teams out, even if it means taking them off one of the other jobs. Oh, they'll send somebody eventually, Plotch. They'll have to. Nobody gets abandoned on the Line, Plotch. You know that."

The five days of bone-grinding manual labor on the Star-Point took effect on him, suddenly. Clancy fell into a light doze, inside his suit, sitting in the wrecked control room of the flitter. In the doze he half-dreamed that the gibbering voices took on their real hobgoblin shape. They were strange, grotesque parodies of the human figure, with bulbous bodies, long skinny arms and legs and turnip-shaped heads with the point upward, possessing wide, grinning, lipless mouths, a couple of holes for a nose, and perfectly round, staring eyes with neither eyebrows nor eyelashes. They gibbered and grinned and danced around him, kicking up their heels and flinging their arms about in joy at the mess he was in. They stretched their faces like rubber masks into all sorts of ugly and leering shapes, while they chanted at him in their wordless gibberish that they had got Plotch—and now they were going to get him, too.

"*No!*" he said, suddenly aloud in his helmet—and the spoken word woke him.

III

He glanced around the ruined flitter. The hobgoblin shapes of his dream had disappeared, but their gibberish still yammered at him from somewhere unseen.

"No," he said to them, again. "If you could rain rocks like that all the time, you'd still be doing it. I don't think you can do that except now and then. Even if it was you who did it. All I've got to do is wait." He corrected himself. "All we've got to do is wait—Plotch and I. And a flitter will come to pick us up."

Plotch is dead! Plotch is dead! gibbered the hobgoblins triumphantly.

"Maybe," muttered Clancy. "Maybe not. Maybe the cryogenic unit caught him in time. Maybe it froze him in time to save him. You don't know. I don't know."

A thought struck him. He got wearily up from his seat, clambered out of the wrecked flitter and struggled up the slope to where Plotch's frozen body in its suit still sat balanced, although by now it had stopped rocking. Clancy stood staring down at it—at the thick coating of white on the inside of the faceplate, ruddied by the red light from the clouds overhead.

"You dead, Plotch?" he asked after a little while. But there was no answer.

"So, maybe you're alive, then, Plotch, after all," said Clancy out loud to himself in the helmet. "And if you're alive, then that cryogenic unit works. So you're safe. You won't even have to know about the time we spend waiting for them to send a flitter after us.–Or, maybe . . . ?"

A sudden, new cold doubt had struck Clancy. Something he half-remembered Plotch's saying about the unit.

"I can't remember, Plotch," he muttered fretfully. "Was it supposed to be good for as long as necessary, that cryogenic action? Or was it just supposed to keep you for a few hours, or a few days, until they could freeze you properly, back at the ship? I can't remember, Plotch. Help me out. You ought to remember. What was it? Permanent or temporary?"

Plotch did not answer.

"Because if it's temporary, Plotch," said Clancy, finally, "then even if you're alive now, maybe you won't still be alive by the time the rescue flitter gets here. That's not good, Plotch. It's a dirty trick; having a cryogenic unit that won't last for more than a few hours or a few days. . . ." For a moment he was on the verge of emotional reaction; but he got his feelings under control. Anger came to stiffen him.

"Well, how about it, Plotch?" he shouted after a moment into the silence and the gibbering. "How about it—can you last until the flitter gets here or not. Answer me!"

But Plotch still did not answer. And a cold, hollow feeling began to swell like a bubble under Clancy's breastbone. It was a realization of the dirtiest trick in the universe—and Plotch just lay there, saying nothing, letting him, Clancy, flounder about with it in him, like a hook in a fish.

"You dirty skull!" burst out Clancy. "You planned it like this! You deliberately got in the way of that rock or whatever it was! I saw you! You deliberately got yourself all frozen up the way you are now! Now you want me to let you just sit here; and maybe sit too long before the ship sends somebody to rescue us? Is that it? Well, you know what, Plotch?"

Clancy paused to give Plotch a chance to answer. But Plotch maintained his unchanging silence. He was finally learning how to outdo Clancy on the not-answering bit; that was it, thought Clancy lightheadedly. But Plotch's learning that was nothing now, compared to this other, dirtier trick he was pulling.

"Well, I'll tell you what, Plotch," said Clancy, more quietly, but venomously. "I'm not going to take you into the ship myself. How do you like that?"

Plotch obstinately said nothing. But the hobgoblin voices chanted their gibber in the back of Clancy's head.

All that way with a dead man! Plotch's dead! Plotch's dead! chanted the hobgoblin voices. But Clancy ignored them. He was busy calculating.

They had come out due east of the ship, Plotch and he. It was now afternoon where they were. All he had to do was to walk into where the clouds were reddest, because that was where the western sunlight was. The days were sixteen hours long right now in this latitude on XN-4010, and the nights were a brief four hours. He had a good six hours to walk now, before darkness came. Then he could rest for four hours before picking up Plotch again, keeping the brightest light at his back this time, and carry on. It would be six days at least before the ship would be likely to come to a certain conclusion that he and Plotch were in trouble—and at least another day, if not two, before another flitter and two-man team could be diverted from their regular job to investigate what had happened out here. Seven days at least—and thirty miles to the ship.

Thirty miles—why, that was only a little over four miles a day. He could do that any time, carrying Plotch. In fact, he ought to be able to do twice as much as that much in a day.

Three times as much. Ten or twelve miles in a sixteen-hour day ought to be nothing. It was less than a mile an hour. Clancy got Plotch up in his arms and started off, his feet in the boots of the suit jarring one after the other against the naked rock beneath them. He walked down, past the damaged flitter, no longer looking at it, and thumped away, carrying his unyielding load in the direction of the brightest red clouds.

Far ahead, as far as he could see to the horizon, the rock plain seemed fairly level. But this was an illusion. As he proceeded, he discovered that there were gentle rises and equally gentle hollows that blended into the general flatness of the area, but which caused him to spend at least a share of his time walking either downhill or uphill. His legs took this effort without complaint; but it was not long before his arms began to ache from holding Plotch's stiff body in front of him, although he leaned back as much as he could to counterbalance the weight.

Eventually he stopped and once more tried to find some other way of carrying his burden. Several times he tried to find a position in which Plotch could be balanced on one of his shoulders, but without success. Then, just before he was ready to give up completely, he had a stroke of genius, remembering the gimmick collar on his suit that kept the inside of his helmet top from touching the top of his head. Testing, he discovered that it was possible to carry Plotch grotesquely balanced on top of his head, with the top of Clancy's helmet resting against the frozen man's unyielding stomach and with a knee and an elbow resting on Clancy's right and left shoulders, respectively. The helmet pressed down upon the collar and the weight upon it was distributed to the rigid shoulders of Clancy's suit, with the assistance of Plotch's frozen knee and elbow—and for the first time Clancy had a balanced load to carry.

"Well, Plotch," said Clancy, pleased. "You aren't so bad to take after all."

The flush of success that spread through Clancy lightened
his spirits and all but drove away the unending gibbering of
the hobgoblins. For a moment his mind was almost clear;
and in that bit of clear-headedness it suddenly occurred to
him that he had not set his pedometer. Carefully rotating
about, holding Plotch balanced on his head and shoulders,
he looked back the way he had come.

The wrecked flitter was just barely visible in the distance,
its torn parts reflecting a few ruddy gleams of red light. Gazing at the smashed vehicle, Clancy did his best to estimate
the ground he had covered so far. After a few seconds, he
decided that he had come approximately a third of a mile.
That was very good going indeed, carrying Plotch the way
he had, to begin with. Carefully holding Plotch in place now
with his left hand, he reached down with his right and set
the pedometer, which was inset in the front leg of his suit
just above the knee, giving himself credit for that third of a
mile he had already covered. Only twenty-nine and some
two-thirds of a mile to go to reach the ship, he told himself
triumphantly.

"How do you like that, Plotch?" he asked his partner.

He started off with fresh energy. Perched on top of Clancy's
head, Plotch rode with a fine, easy balance, except when
Clancy came to one of the hollows and was forced to walk
downslope. Then it was necessary to hold hard to Plotch's
knee and elbow, to keep the frozen body from sliding forward off the helmet. For some reason, going upslope, the
knee and elbow dug Clancy's shoulders and helped hold
Plotch in place, almost by themselves. All in all, thought
Clancy, he was doing very well.

He continued to slog along, facing into the dwindling western light behind the fiery masses of the clouds. Like all Line
Team members, he was in Class Prime physical shape,
checked every two weeks in the field, and every two months
back on Earth to make sure he was maintaining his position

in that class. He was five feet eleven inches in height, somewhat large-boned and normally weighed around a hundred
and ninety. Here on XN-4010, his weight was reduced by
the lesser gravity to about a hundred and fifty pounds. Plotch,
who was five-nine, lighter boned and usually weighed around
a hundred and sixty on Earth, here weighed probably no
more than a hundred and thirty. On Earth, Clancy would
have expected himself to be able to put on a hundred and
thirty pound pack and equipment load on top of his suit
and make at least a mile an hour with it over terrain like this
—and for at least as many hours in a row as there were in the
ordinary working day. That was, provided he stopped routinely for a rest—something like a ten-minute break every
hour.

Here, he should do at least as well as that. Still, the calcu-
lation had reminded him that periodic rest was necessary. He
sat down, eased Plotch off his shoulders and looked at his
watch to measure off a rest period of ten minutes. He looked
almost genially at the figure of Plotch with its frosted faceplate, as he sat, elbows on knees, resting.

"How do you like that, Plotch, you bastard?" he asked
Plotch. "It's no trouble for me to carry you. No trouble at all.
Maybe you thought you'd get out of something by playing
dead on me. But you're not. I'm going to take you in; and
they're going to thaw you out and fix you up. How do you
like that, Plotch?"

Plotch maintained his silence. Clancy's thoughts wandered
off for a while and then came back to the present with a jerk.
He glanced down at his watch and stared at what he saw.
A good half hour had gone by—not just the ten minutes he
had planned on. Had he fallen asleep, or what?

The light filtering redly through clouds was now low on
the horizon ahead of him. He looked at the pedometer on his
leg and saw that he had only covered a little over a couple of
miles. Sudden fear woke in him. There would be no making

the ship in a few days if he went along at this pace—no hope
of it at all.

Suddenly his throat felt dry. He tongued his drinking tube
into position before his mouth and drank several swallows
before he realized what he was doing and pushed the tube
away again. The recycling equipment in these light-weight
survival suits could not be all that perfect. Certain amounts
of water were lost in the ejection of solid body wastes and in
various other ways which, though minuscule, were important.
That loss had to be made up from the emergency tank built
into the back shoulder plates of his suit; and with the flitter
wrecked, now some miles behind him, there would be no
chance of refilling that tank—which at best was only supposed to carry enough supplementary water for two or three
days. He would have to watch his liquid intake. Food he
could do without . . . but he suddenly remembered, he had
plenty of stimulants.

He tongued the stim dispenser lever in his helmet and
swallowed the small pill that rolled onto his outstretched
tongue, getting it down with only the saliva that was in his
mouth. Then he struggled to his feet. He had stiffened, even
in this short period of sitting; and he had to go down on one
knee again to get Plotch back up on his shoulders before
rising.

Once more burdened, he plodded ahead again toward the
horizon and the descending red light behind the unending
clouds. Now that he was once more on his feet and moving,
the voiceless gibber of the hobgoblins made itself noticeable
again. The stim pill was working through him now, sending
new energy throughout his body. Up on his shoulders, the
frozen body of Plotch felt literally light. But the increase of
energy he got from the pill had a bad side effect—for he
seemed to hear the hobgoblin voices louder, now.

IV

He had about another two and a quarter hours before the
sun started to set along the edge of the horizon; and the wide
rocky land began to mix long, eerie black shadows with its
furnace-glare of sunset light. He stopped at last for the night,
before the last of the light was gone, wanting to take time to
pick a spot where he could be comfortable. He found it, at
last, in a little hollow half-filled with stones, so small that they
could fairly be called gravel. But, when he laid Plotch down
and checked with the pedometer at his knee, he found that
the day's walk so far had brought him only a little over seven
miles—although the last two hours he had been making as
good speed as he could without working himself into breath-
lessness inside his suit—which could have been dangerous.

He lay down on the gravel. It felt almost soft, through the
protection of his suit. He stared up at the darkening cloud-
belly overhead. The hobgoblin voices began to increase in
volume until they roared in his head, and he began to imagine
he saw their faces and bodies as he had in his dream of
them, imagined now in the various, scarlet-marked forma-
tions of the blackening clouds. He tongued for a tranquilizer;
and as it took effect, the light and the forms faded together.
The roar sank to a whisper. He slept.

He woke abruptly—to find that the sun was already well
above the opposite horizon behind him. The roiling clouds
were furnace-bright with a morning redness too fierce to look
on, even through his tinted faceplate. He drank a little water,
took a stim pill to get himself started and got himself back on
his feet with Plotch on his shoulders. Turning his back on the
morning light he began a new day's march.

Even through the clouds, the light was strong enough to
throw shadows. He kept his own moving shadow pointing
straight ahead of him, to be sure he was headed due west.

Even with the best he could do about maintaining his bearings, the odds were all against his passing within sight of the ship, itself. On the other hand, once the pedometer showed he was within a three or four mile radius of the ship, he could try to reach them with a constant signal from his suit intercom. And even if the intercom had trouble, the regular scanar watch by the Duty-Lineman then should pick up his moving figure on its screen, if he passed anywhere within horizon distance of the ship.

He took his rest regularly every hour; and he was alert each time to see that he did not exceed the ten minutes he had allowed himself. Together with the exercise and the increasing daylight, he began to warm to his task—even to become expert at it, this business of plodding over an endless rocky desert with the frozen body of Plotch balanced on his shoulders. He grew clever to anticipate little dips, hollows or fissures. The hobgoblins were clamorous; but under the combined effect of the walking and the stim he almost welcomed them.

"Thought you'd helped Plotch to get away from me, didn't you?" he taunted their gibbering, voiceless voices. "Well, see what I'm doing? I'm hanging on to him, after all. How about that, you hobgoblins? Why don't you throw some more rocks at us?"

The voices jabbered without meaning. It struck him suddenly, as an almost humorous fact, that they were not entirely voiceless now. They had gained volume. He could actually—if he concentrated—hear them in his earphones; about as loud as a small crowd of buzzing gnats close to his ears.

"I'll tell you why you don't throw any more rocks at us," he told them, after a while. "It's the way I figured it out back at the flitter. You've got to work something like that up; and that takes several days. And you've got to work it up for a particular spot—and I'm moving all the time now. You can't hit a moving target."

His own last words sent him off into a humorous cackle, which he stopped abruptly when he realized it was hurting his dry throat to laugh. He plodded along, trying to remember whether it was time for him to allow himself a drink. Finally, he worked out that it was time—in fact, it was past time. He allowed himself three sips of the recycled water. If he was correct, his shoulder tanks should still be about half full.

But as he went on through the day and as his shadow shortened before him until the most glaring cloud light was directly overhead, he began to feel the effort of his labors, after all. He took advantage of the sunlight being overhead to rest for a little longer than usual, until XN-4010's star should once more have moved ahead of him.

It was still too high in the cloud-filled sky for him to use it as a directional guide, when he forced himself to his feet once more. But he walked with his faceplate looking ahead and down, noting the short shadows thrown backward by the rocks he passed and making sure that he walked parallel to those shadows.

Meanwhile, the hobgoblin voices got louder. By mid-afternoon they were very nearly deafening. He was tempted to take a tranquilizer, which he knew would tune them down. But he was afraid that a tranquilizer would have just enough of a sedative effect to make the now almost intolerable job of carrying Plotch over the uneven ground too much for him.

By the time the sun was far enough down the western sky to be visible as a bright spot behind the clouds ahead of him, he was staggering with fatigue. He stopped for one of his breaks and fell instantly asleep—waking over an hour later. It took two stim pills this time, washed down with several extra swallows of the precious water to get him on his feet and moving. But once he was upright he cackled at the hobgoblin voices which had once more thronged around him.

"Just call me Iron Man Clancy!" he jeered at them hoarsely, through a raw throat and staggered on toward the horizon.

At the end of the day, his pedometer showed that he had covered nearly sixteen miles. He exulted over this; and, exulting, fell into sleep the way a man might fall into a thousand-foot-deep mine shaft. When he woke, the next day was well started. The sun was a full quarter of the way up the eastern horizon.

Cursing himself and Plotch both, he stimulated himself and struggled to his feet and set out once more. That day he began to walk into nightmares. The hobgoblin voices became quite clear—even if they still gibbered without sense—in his earphones. Moreover, now as he staggered along, it seemed to him that from time to time he caught glimpses of turnip heads and skinny limbs peering at him from time to time, or flickering out of sight when he glanced quickly in the direction of some boulder larger than the others.

Also, this third day of walking, he found he had lost all logical track of the time and the periods of his rest halts. Several times he fell asleep during a halt in spite of himself; and, by the time the red furnace-glow of the sun was low behind the clouds on the horizon before him, he was simply walking until he could walk no more, then resting until he could walk again . . . and so on . . .

At the end of the day the pedometer showed that, to the nearly sixteen miles covered the previous two days, he had added only seven. There was a good eight miles to go yet before he would be—theoretically at least—in the neighborhood of the spaceship.

Eight miles seemed little after covering more than twenty. But also, it seemed to him, as he sank down for the night and unloaded Plotch from his shoulders, that the eight miles might as well be eight hundred. Literally, he felt as if he could not take another step. Without bothering to find a comfortable position, he stretched out on the bare rock beneath him; and sleep took him with the suddenness of a rabbit taken by the silent swoop of a great horned owl.

—When he woke on the fourth day, he had Plotch on his

shoulders and was already walking. It seemed to him that he had been walking for some time, and the moving shadow of himself projected before him, which he followed, was already short.

Around him, the desert of bare rock had altered. Its loose boulders, its little rises and hollows, its fissures—all of these had somehow melted together and changed so that they made up the walls and rooftops of a strange weird city of low buildings, straggling in every direction to the horizon. The flat rock he walked on flowed upward off to his left to become a wall, tilted away to his right to become a roof; and among all these buildings, the city was aswarm with the hobgoblins.

v

Gray-bodied, turnip-headed and skinny-limbed, they swarmed the streets of their city; and all those within view of Clancy were concerned with him and Plotch. They were concerned *for* him, they implied, in their leering, jeering way. Their gibber still would not resolve itself into words; but somehow he understood that they were trying to tell him that the way he was going he would never make the spaceship. For one thing, he had gotten turned around and was headed in the wrong direction. His only hope of making it to the ship was to sit down and rest.—Or, at least, to leave Plotch behind, turn around and head back the way he had come. They were trying to help him, they suggested, even as they sniggered, and postured and danced about him. But somehow, a certain sort of animal cunning would not let him believe them.

"No!" he stumbled on through their insubstantial mass of gesticulating bodies. "Got to get Plotch to the ship. If I leave him, he'll get away from me." Clancy giggled suddenly, and was shocked for a second at hearing the high-pitched sound within the close confines of his own helmet. "I want him back Earthside."

No! No! The hobgoblins gibbered and made faces and jostled about him. *Plotch is through living. Clancy will be through unless he leaves Plotch behind.*

"You don't fool me," Clancy muttered, reeling and stumbling ahead with the dead weight of Plotch on his shoulders. "You don't fool me!"

After a while, he fell.

He twisted as he went down, so that the stiff body of Plotch landed on top of him. Lying flat on his back on the ground with the hobgoblin's bodies and faces forming a dome over them, Clancy giggled once again at Plotch.

"Hope I didn't chip you any, old boy." He grinned at Plotch.

He lay there for a while, thinking about everything and nothing. The labor of getting back to his feet and getting Plotch once more up on his head and shoulders loomed before him like the labor of climbing up the vertical side of a mile-high mountain. It was just not to be done. It was humanly impossible. But, after a while, he found himself trying it.

He got to his knees, and after a great deal of slow effort, managed to get Plotch balanced once more stiffly on his helmet and his shoulders. But when he came to rise from his knees to his feet, bearing Plotch's weight, he found his legs would not respond.

You see, said a large hobgoblin smirking and pulling his rubbery face into different grotesque shapes directly in front of Clancy's faceplate, *Clancy has to leave Plotch if Clancy is going to get to the spaceship.*

"To hell with you!"

Somehow, with some terrific effort and a strength that he did not know was still in him, Clancy found himself back on his feet once more, carrying Plotch. He tottered forward, wading through the hobgoblins that clustered around him. There was nothing substantial about their bodies to clog and hold back the movement of his legs, but their attempts to stop him wearied his mind. After forty or fifty steps he stumbled and fell again, this time losing his grip on Plotch, who tumbled to the rock, but lay there, apparently unbroken. Clancy crawled to the unmoving figure through the clutching mist of gray hobgoblin bodies.

"You all right, Plotch?" Clancy muttered.

He patted Plotch's stiff, suited body from helmet to boots. As far as touch could tell, there was no damage done. Then he saw that above the frost the faceplate was starred with cracks. Gently he probed it with the gloved fingers of his right hand. But, while cracked, the faceplate seemed to be still holding together.

"All right, Plotch," he muttered. He made one more effort to get Plotch on his shoulders, and himself on his feet; but his body would no longer obey him. Still kneeling, half-crouching over the figure of Plotch, he fell asleep. At first the sleep was like all the other sleeps, then gradually a difference began to creep in.

He found himself dreaming.

He was dreaming of his appointment ceremony as a Lineman back in the main tower of Line Service Headquarters, back on Earth. He and all the other cadets were dressed in the stiff, old-fashioned green dress uniforms, which, in his case, he had not put on again since. The uniforms had a high stand-up collar; and the collar edge of the cadet in front of him had already worn a red line on the back of the cadet's neck. The man kept tilting his head forward a little to get the tender, abraded skin away from the collar edge, while the voice of the Commandant droned on:

". . . *You are dedicating yourself today,*" the Commandant was saying, harshly, "*to the Line, to that whole project of effort by which our human race is reaching out to occupy and inhabit the further stars. Therefore you are dedicating your-selves to the service of your race; and that service is found within the Line from everyone in our headquarters staff out*

to the most far-flung, two-man teams on new Terminal or
Relay Worlds. All of us together make up the Team which
extends and maintains the Line; and we are bound together
by the fact that we are teammates. . . ."

The Commandant, Lief Janssen, was still senior officer of
the Line Service. He was a tall, stiff military-looking man
with gray hair and gray mustache, trim and almost grimly
neat in his green uniform with its rows of Station Clusters.
He made an imposing figure up on the rostrum; and at the
time of the appointment ceremony Clancy had admired the
Commandant greatly. It was the past five years that had
changed Clancy's mind. Janssen was plainly pretty much a
man of straw—at least where R. and E. was concerned. It
was strange that such an effective-looking man should prove
so weak; and that a small bookkeeperish-looking character
like Charles Li, the Head of R. and E., should turn out to
be such a successful battler. Theoretically, the two Services
were independent and equal, but lately R. and E. had been
doing anything it wanted to the Line Team.

Up on the platform, in Clancy's dream, the Commandant
continued to drone on. . . .

". . . For, just as the human race is the Line, so the Line
is the Line Team, in its single ship sent out to hook up a new
Relay or Terminal Station. And the Team in essence is its
two and three-man units, sent out to work on planetary sur-
faces heretofore untrodden by human foot. The race is the
Line Service. The Service is the Line Team, and the Line
Team is each and every one of your fellow Linemen. . . ."

The speech was interminable. Clancy searched for something in his mind to occupy himself with; and for no particular
reason he remembered an old film made of the hunting of
elephants in Africa, before such hunting was outlawed completely. The hunters rode in a wheeled car after the elephant
herd, which, after some show of defiance had turned to run
away. Standing up in the back of the wheeled car, one of the

hunters shot—and one of the large bull elephants staggered and broke his stride.

Clearly the animal had been hit. Soon he slowed. A couple of the other bulls, evidently concerned, slowed also. The hit elephant was staggering; and they closed in on either side of him, pushing against him with their great gray flanks to hold him upright.

For a while this seemed to work. But the effects of the shot were telling—or perhaps the hunter had fired again, Clancy could not remember. The wounded elephant slowed at last to a walk, then to a standstill. He went down on his front knees.

The other two bulls would not abandon him. They tried to lift him with their trunks and tusks; but he was too heavy for them. Up close, the hunter in the wheeled cart fired another shot in close. There was a puff of dust from behind the elephant's ear where the bullet hit. The wounded bull shivered and rolled over on its side and lay there very still.

It was plain he was finally dead. Only then did the other two bulls abandon him. Screaming with upcurled trunks at the wheeled cart, they faced the hunter for a moment, stamping, then turned and ran with the rest of the herd. The hunter and the others in the wheeled cart let them go . . .

In his dream, it seemed to Clancy that the elephant was suddenly buried. He lay in a cemetery with a headstone above his grave. Going close, Clancy saw that the name on the headstone was *Art*. There was something else written there; but when he tried to go closer to see—for it was just twilight in the graveyard and not easy to read the headstones —a dog lying on the grave, whom he had not noticed, growled and bared its fangs at him, so that he was forced to back off. . . .

Slowly, from his dreams of graduating ceremonies, elephants and graveyards, Clancy drifted back up into consciousness. It seemed that he must have been sleeping for some time; and his mouth was wet, which meant that somehow he must have been drinking water—whether from his suit reserves, or from some other source. But he did not feel now as if he had his suit around him.

VI

He opened his eyes and saw, at first, nothing but white, the white walls and ceiling of a small room aboard a spaceship. Then he became conscious of a girl standing beside the bed.

She was dressed in white, also, so at first he thought that she was a nurse—and then he noticed that she wore no nurse's cap, only a small, strange-looking gold button in the lapel of her white jacket.

"Who're you?" asked Clancy, wonderingly. "Where is this?"

"It's all right, you can get up now," the girl answered. "You're on our ship. We're Research and Experimentation Service, and we just happened to land less than half a mile from where you were. So we picked you up and brought you in. Luckily for you. You were headed exactly in the wrong direction."

"And Plotch?" Clancy demanded.

"We brought in your teammate, too," she answered.

Clancy sat up on what he now saw was a bunk, and sat on the edge of it for a moment. He was wearing the working coveralls he normally wore underneath the suit; but they seemed to have been freshly cleaned and pressed—which was good. He would not have liked to face this very good-looking girl in his coveralls, as they must have been after six days of his wearing the suit.

"R. and E.?" he echoed. For a second her words seemed to make sense. Then the great impossibility of what she was saying, struck him.

"But you can't have landed a ship on XN-4010!" he said to the girl, getting to his feet. "We're still just putting out the

Star-Point terminals. The only way another ship could get here would be to home in on the drone that our Line ship homed in on; and that's been inactive since our second day here, when we started cannibalizing it for Station parts!"

"Oh, no. This ship," she answered, "uses a new experimental process, designed to bypass the wasteful process of sending out a thousand drones in hopes that one may home in on a planet that may be used as a Terminal or Relay point for a ship shifted from Earth. But here comes someone who can explain it much better than I can."

A short, round-faced man with black hair and a short, black mustache had come briskly into the room. After a second, Clancy recognized him from seeing him on news broadcasts, back on Earth. He was Charles Li, Head of the Research and Experimentation Service; and he wore a long white coat, or smock, buttoned in front, with a small gold button like the girl's in his lapel.

It was strange, thought Clancy woozily, how an impressive figure like Janssen could turn out to be so incapable of protecting his own Service, while someone like this fuzzy-looking little man could prove to be so effective. You certainly could not judge by appearances. . . .

"I heard what you said, young man," snapped Li, now, "and I'd warn you against judging by appearances. The method that brought this special ship here is a gadget of my own invention. Of course, it's a million-to-one chance that we should land right beside you, out here; but that's what scientific research and experimentation deal with today, isn't it? Million-to-one chances?"

Clancy had to admit silently that it was. Certainly most of the R. and E. gadgets in their survival suits seemed to represent million-to-one shots at coming up with something useful. But Li was already taking Clancy by the arm and leading him out into and down a white-painted corridor of the ship.

"But there's something you need to do for us," he said in steely, commanding tones, his grip hard on Clancy's arm. "It's imperative your transmit ship be told of our arrival, as soon as possible. But the very nature of the device which brought us here—top secret, I'm afraid, so I can't explain it to you now—places us under certain restrictions. None of us aboard here can be spared to make the trip to your ship; and the nature of our equipment makes it impossible for us to send a message over ordinary inter-ship channels."

He led Clancy into a room which Clancy recognized as an airlock. His suit was waiting for him there.

"We're sorry to put you to this trouble, particularly just after recovering from a good deal of exhaustion and exposure," said the black-mustached man briskly. "But we have to ask you to put your suit on once again and finish your walk to your spaceship, to tell them that we're here."

"Why not?" said Clancy. He began to get into his spacesuit, while the other two watched; the girl, he thought, with a certain amount of admiration in her eyes.

"Yes, it's too bad one of us can't be spared to go with you," said the mustached man. "But we have no outside suits aboard the ship, and then if nothing else one would be needed for protection from the hobgoblins."

"Protection—?" echoed Clancy. He paused, in the midst of sealing the trunk of his suit. For the first time it struck him that he could not hear the voiceless gibber of the hobgoblins here.

The mustached man must have divined his thought, for he answered it.

"Yes," he said. "The special hull materials of this ship shield us from hobgoblin attempts to control us. A refinement of the shielding material in your suits. That same sort of protection we now have will be necessary for future Line Teams and whoever chooses this planet. I will have to recommend it once we get back to Earth."

"Yeah," said Clancy, putting on his helmet, but with the

faceplate still open. "I could have used some of that shielding myself, before this."

"You've done a marvelous job, Lineman," said Charles Li, "in resisting hobgoblin attack so far. They haven't been able to affect you at all, no matter how exhausted you've become. That will be going in my report, too. Well—good luck! And remember, head back the way you came."

Li reached out to shake hands. But, just at that moment, Clancy remembered something.

"Plotch!" he said. "I've got to take Plotch on in with me! He'll need medical attention."

"I'm afraid it's too late for medical attention." Li shook his head sharply. "Your teammate is dead."

"No, he isn't!" insisted Clancy. "You don't understand. There was a cryogenic unit in his suit."

"Yes, I know all about that," Li interrupted, "but you're mistaken. The cryogenic unit was actually in one of the other suits. Your teammate is indeed dead. Come along, I'll show him to you."

He turned and led the way once more into the corridor, the girl and Clancy following. They went down the corridor a little way and into another room with a single bunk in it. On this bunk lay Plotch, in his suit, but with the faceplate open and unfrosted; and with his hands folded on his chest. His face had the stiff, powdered and rouged look of a body that has been embalmed.

"You see?" said Li, after a moment. "I sympathize with you. But your friend is quite dead; and carrying him, you might not have the strength to make it to your ship. You can leave him safely to us to be taken care of." Clancy stared at Plotch, he did not believe Li. He thought he detected a slight rise and fall of Plotch's chest, under his coveralls, which were now as clean and pressed as Clancy's own.

But cleverly, Clancy saw the futility of arguing with the powerful Head of the R. and E. Service. Clancy nodded his

head and went back out into the corridor; he began to fasten
up his faceplate.

"Don't bother to show me out," he said, grinning. "I can
handle the airlock by myself."

"Good luck, then," said the mustached man. He and the
girl shook hands with him and then went off down the corridor, around a bend of it, and disappeared. Clancy turned
and walked heavily to the airlock entrance, walked into it,
waited a second, then turned and tiptoed back into the corridor and back up to the room in which Plotch lay.

Even thawed out in his suit, Plotch was a heavy load to
get up from the bunk, but Clancy closed his faceplate and got
him up in his arms in the same awkward, front-carrying
position in which he had first tried to carry the other away
from the smashed flitter. Carrying Plotch, he tiptoed back out
into the corridor into the airlock and cycled the lock open.
Once outside, with the airlock's outer door closed behind him,
he started tiptoeing off toward a sunlight-blazoned patch of
clouds, which was only an hour or two above horizon. He
was almost sure it was nearly sunset and that he was still
headed in his original direction.

As he went, the weight of Plotch forced him down off his
toes, to walk flat-footedly. Slowly, Plotch seemed to gain
heaviness, and tremendous weariness began to flood back into
Clancy. He was dreadfully thirsty. But when he gave in at last
to temptation and sucked on the water tube in his helmet,
only a little raspy gasp of moisture-laden air came through
his mouth. Somehow, although he could not remember doing
it, he must have emptied his reserve water supply. But he
could have sworn that there had been some liquid still in
reserve.

However, there was no help for him now. As if in com-
pensation, he made the discovery that Plotch had frozen stiff
once more in the same old position. Almost without thought,
he maneuvered the frozen body back up on his helmet and

shoulders in the same position in which he had carried it so far and tottered on toward the red, glaring patch of sunlight-illumined cloud before him.

His head swam. With every step, the efforts of moving seemed to grow greater. But now he had no strength left, even for the process of reason. He did not know exactly why he was carrying Plotch, with such great effort, toward the sunset; and it was too great an effort to reason it out. All he had strength for was to plod onward, one foot after another, one foot after another. . . .

Several times it seemed to him that he passed out, or went to sleep on his feet. But when he woke up he was still walking. . . .

Finally, he had lost all contact with his body and its strange desire to carry a frozen Plotch into the sunset. He stood as if apart from it in his mind and watched with a detached and uncurious amazement as that body staggered on, tilting precariously now and then under its burden, but never quite going down, while the landscape danced about it, one moment being rocky plain—the next a fantastic, low-walled city thronged with hobgoblins—the next a dusty African plain where elephants fled before hunters in a wheeled cart. . . .

He was still walking when the sun went down. And after that he remembered nothing . . . when he finally came to again, it was to a fuzzy, unreal state. He was lying on some flat surface and a body was bending over him; but the features in the face of the body danced so that he could not identify whoever it was. But, in spite of the unreality of it all, the smells were hard and familiar—the interior stink of a Line transmit ship, the smell of his own bunk aboard it, a mingled odor of men and grease.

VII

"He'll be all right," a familiar voice said above him. It came from the figure with the mixed-up features, but it was the voice of Jeph Wasca, his Team Captain.

"Plotch?" Clancy managed to croak.

"What?" The blurry figure with the dancing features bent down close to Clancy's face.

"Plotch. . . ." Clancy felt the strength draining out of him. After a few seconds, the figure straightened up, the dancing face withdrawing.

"I can't understand you. Tell me later, then," said Jeph's voice, brusquely. "I haven't got time to talk to you now, Clance. You go to sleep. When you wake up, you'll be back Earthside."

The indefinite figure withdrew, and all the fuzzy lights, colors, sounds and smells surrounding Clancy whirled themselves into a funnel that drew him down into dark unconsciousness.

When he woke this third time, he was indeed—as Jeph had promised—Earthside. He could tell it, if no way else, by the added pull of gravity, holding him down harder upon the bed in which he lay. The room he opened his eyes upon was plainly a hospital room, and there was a bottle of glucose solution with a tube leading to a needle inserted in his wrist.

He felt as if he had spent half a year locked up in a packing case with a pack of angry bobcats. Where he was not sore, he ached; and he did not feel as if he had strength enough to move the little finger of one hand. He lay for a while, placidly and contentedly watching the featureless white ceiling above him, and then a nurse came in. She put a thermometer sensor-strip into his mouth briefly, and then took it out again to examine it. Once his lips were free, he spoke to her.

"You're a real nurse?" he asked.

She laughed. She had freckles on her short nose, and they crowded together when she laughed out loud.

"They don't let imitations work in this ward," she said. "How're you feeling?"

"Terrible," he said. "But just as long as I don't try to move, I feel fine."

"That's good," she said. "You just go on not trying to move. That's doctor's orders for you anyway. Do you think you're up to having some visitors later on this afternoon?"

"Visitors?" he asked.

"Your Line Team Captain," she said. "Maybe some other people."

"Sure," Clancy said. She went out; and Clancy fell asleep.

He was awakened by someone speaking gently in his ear and a light touch on his shoulder. He opened his eyes and looked up into the face of Jeph standing at his bedside with another man—a tall man standing a little behind him.

"How are you feeling, Clance?" Jeph asked.

"Fine," answered Clancy sleepily. His fingers groped automatically for the bed-control lever at the bedside and closed upon it. He set the little motors whirring to raise him up into half-sitting position. "The nurse said you might be in to see me."

"I've been waiting to see you," said Jeph. "Got somebody here to see you." The man behind Jeph moved forward; but Clancy's eyes were all on Jeph.

"Plotch?" Clancy asked.

"He's going to be all right," Jeph answered. "They've got him defrosted and on his way back to normal—thanks to you."

"Don't thank me!" exploded Clancy. "Jeph, I can't take that guy any more! If I have to take any more of him, I'll kill him!"

"Relax," said Jeph. "I've known that for some time. I made up my mind some months back that one of you had to leave the Team."

"One of us—" Clancy went rigid, under the covers of the bed.

"Plotch's being transferred."

Clancy relaxed.

"Thanks," he muttered.

"Don't thank me," said Jeph. "You earned it. You saved all our necks out there on XN-4010—and more. That's why the Commandant's here to talk to you."

Clancy's gaze shot past Jeph for the first time; and the tall man stepped right up to the bedside. It was Janssen all right, with his gray, bristling little military mustache, just as Clancy remembered him. Janssen smiled stiffly down at Clancy.

Clancy's nerves, abraded by his sessions with the hobgoblins, took sudden alarm.

"What about?" he demanded warily.

"Let's get you briefed first," said Janssen sharply. He pulled up a chair and sat down, kicking another chair over to Jeph, who also sat down.

"Sorry to put you through your paces like this," Janssen said, not sounding sorry at all, "just the minute you get your eyes open. But when the time's ripe, the time's ripe. We've got someone else due to meet us here; and he may want to ask you some questions. I'm going to be asking you some questions for his benefit, in any case; and what I want you to do is just speak up. Give us both straight answers, just the way they come to you. You've got that?"

Clancy nodded again, warily.

"All right. Now, to get you briefed on the situation," said Janssen. "First, it seems you ran into something new out there on XN-4010. That planet's got an actual sentient life form, which exists as something like clouds of free electrons. Beyond that, we don't know much about them, except for three things; none of which we'd have known if you hadn't managed to carry Plotch on foot all the way back to the ship. One—"

Janssen held up a knobby forefinger to mark the point.

"—They can move material objects up to a certain size, with a great deal of effort—as in that shower of rocks you remember," he said. "But evidently it's not easy for them. Also, they can affect human thinking processes—up to a point. Again, though, it's not easy for them. For one thing, any kind of material envelope, like the body of a ship, or a flitter, or a suit like you were wearing, shields them out to a certain extent, depending on its thickness. For another, it seems they only become really effective if the human is the way you were, near the end of your walk—in a highly exhausted condition; the kind of condition where lack of sleep or extreme effort might have brought you to the point of hallucinations, anyway. Third—and most important—they were trying to kill off all the men of your Team. It seems they were able to understand that with the drone dismantled, the ship unmanned and the terminal not yet fully built and operative, there'd be no way for another ship out to XN-4010. In fact, the chances of our hitting the planet on a blind-transmit once more, let alone getting another drone safely landed on it, were microscopic. For some reason they didn't want us to know about their existence; and that suggests that maybe they wanted to make preparations of some kind—either for defense or offense against the human race."

He paused.

"Lucky for us," he said brusquely to Clancy, *"you* frustrated them."

"Just by bringing Plotch in?" Clancy demanded. There was something disproportionate in all this. He did not trust Janssen at all.

"That's right, Clance," said Jeph. "There's something you don't know. If you'd decided to sit down out there and wait for rescue, you'd have dried up to dust inside your suit before any rescue came."

Clancy stared at the Team Captain.

"All but one flitter and two-man crew," said Jeph slowly,

"were out on jobs—and the closest one out was farther away from the ship than you and Plotch were. Clance, every one of those flitters was smashed by rock showers, and its crew killed or stranded."

VIII

Clancy swallowed for the moment forgetting the Line Commandant.

"Who . . ." he could not finish the question. He only stared at Jeph with bright eyes. Jeph answered slowly, but without any attempt at emotion.

"Fletch," the Team Leader said, "Jim, Wally, Pockets, Ush and Pappy."

Clancy lay still for a moment, gazing at the wall of the room opposite. Then he looked back at Jeph.

"What kind of replacements are we getting?" he asked. He looked at Janssen challengingly.

"The best," answered the Commandant. "And I'll keep that promise. Again, because of you and your bringing Plotch in on foot."

"I still don't see what that did—" Clancy broke off, suddenly thoughtful.

"Now you start to see it, don't you?" said Jeph. "There were three of us and one flitter left in the spaceship. Twelve men and six flitters—including you and Plotch, all the other flitters and men we had—were out on work location. All of them overdue, and none of them back. What was I going to do? I could not risk sending out the two men I had left for fear the same thing would happen to them—they might not come back. On the other hand, without the Star-points all finished, there was no way we could transmit the ship back Earthside. The only thing was for the three of us to stay put and keep the ship powered. We couldn't transmit or receive, but with luck we could act as a beacon for another blind drone transmit from Earth—once Earth figured we were in trouble."

Jeph paused. Clancy slowly nodded.

"Then you came staggering in, with your load of frozen Plotch," said Jeph. "We shoved Plotch into the freeze-chamber and tried to find out from you what had happened. You weren't up to talking consciously; but I pumped you full of parasympathetic narcos, and you babbled in your sleep. You babbled it all. Once I knew what I was up against, I was able to risk my last flitter and my last two men to go out on quick rescue missions to each of the work-points. After that we went out with the men who were left for only a couple of hours on the job at a time, until the last Star-point was finished and we could transmit ourselves back here."

Clancy nodded again. He was thinking of Jim, Wally, and all the rest who had not come back, looking out the window of his room at the green hospital grounds outside with unfocused eyes. Someone else had just come into the room; but Clancy was too full of feeling to bother to look to see who it was. He was aware of Jeph and the Commandant turning briefly to glance toward the newcomer, then they were back looking at him.

"All right," Janssen said grimly, with one eye still on who-ever had just come in. "Let's have your attention Lineman. There's a question some people may be wanting to ask you. That's how you were able to see through what the hobgoblins were trying to do to you, in making you leave Plotchin and go off in the wrong direction; once they'd gotten you to hal-lucinating about a new experimental type ship that didn't need the Line to shift from Earth out to XN-4010?"

Clancy scowled down at the white bedspread.

"Hell," he grumbled, "I didn't see through it! I mean I didn't start adding up reasons until later. Like the rescue ship land-ing right beside me; and the people on her using our Team's own word for the 'hobgoblins'; when they hadn't heard me calling them that myself."

"But you didn't leave Plotchin the way they wanted you to. And you didn't take their word for it that you were headed wrong for your ship," said Janssen.

"Of course not!" Clancy growled. "But it was just because I felt there was something wrong about it all; and I wasn't going to leave Plotch behind, as long as there was a chance they were lying about his being dead."

"All right. Wait a minute." It was the newcomer to the room speaking. He stepped close to the bedside. "Wasn't I given to understand you hated this teammate of yours—this, uh, Plotchin?"

Clancy looked up and goggled. He was gazing at a short man with a round face, black hair and a little black mustache. The man of his hallucination, only this time he was real: Charles Li, the head of Research and Experimentation Service.

Li's voice was not as deep as it had been in Clancy's hallucination—in fact there was almost a querulous note in it. But he sounded decisive enough.

"Why—I still hate him!" snapped Clancy. "I hate his guts! But that didn't mean I was going to leave him out there!"

He stared at Li. Li stared back down at him.

"I guess you haven't heard the latest interpretation of that, Charlie," Janssen said stiffly to Li, and the head of R. and E. turned about to face the Commandant. "Our Service psychologists came up with a paper on it just a couple of hours ago—I'll see you get a copy of it by the end of the day."

Li frowned suddenly at Janssen.

"Never mind," Li said, "just give me the gist of it."

"It's simple enough," said Janssen. "The immaterial life forms on XN-4010 got control of Clancy's conscious mind. But the only way they could make him hallucinate was by telling him what he *ought* to see and then letting him drag the parts to build the hallucination out of his own mind and memory. So while they had control of him pretty well, consciously, they never did get down into the part of him where his unconscious reflexes live. And did you know that team loyalty lives down among the instincts in some men, Charlie?"

"Team loyalty, an instinct?" Li frowned again. "I don't know if I can see that."

"Take my word for it, then," said Janssen, "but it's easy enough to check." He looked down at the shorter man. "Not only humans, a lot of the social animals have the same reflex. Porpoises hold another porpoise up on top of the water after he's been knocked unconscious, so that he won't drown—that's because the porpoise breathing mechanism is conscious, not unconscious like ours. Land animals too."

"Elephants . . ." muttered Clancy, suddenly remembering. But none of the other men were paying any attention to him.

"Under an instinct like that," Janssen was going on, raspingly, to the R. and E. Service Head, "the loyalty of every team member is to the team. And every other man on it. And the loyalty of the team's to him, in return. As long as there's a spark of life left in him, his teammates will do anything they can, at any cost to themselves, to care for him, to rescue him, or bring him home safely—"

"Lief, not one of your spiels, please—" began the shorter man, but Janssen overrode him by sheer power of voice.

"*But,*" went on the Commandant, "the minute he's dead, their obligation's lifted. Because they all know that now he has to be replaced by a new man on the Team, someone to whom the loyalty they used to owe the dead man will have to be transferred. What tripped up those hobgoblins on XN-4010 was the fact that Clancy here couldn't be sure Plotchin was dead. It didn't matter how much be hated Plotchin; or how overwhelming the evidence was that Plotchin was dead, or that trying to save Plotchin might only mean throwing his own life away, too. As long as the slightest chance was there that Plotchin could be rescued, Clancy was obligated by his Team instinct to do his best for his teammate. That's why Clancy brought the man in, in spite of how he felt about him, personally, and in spite of all those aliens could do, and in spite of the near physical impossibility, even under the lower gravity there, of carting a frozen dead man, weighing nearly as much as he did, for miles."

Janssen stopped talking. All the while he had been speaking, Li's face had been growing sourer and sourer, like a man who has discovered a worm in the apple into which he has just bitten.

"Can I talk now?" demanded Li. The querulous note in his voice was mounting to a pugnacious whine.

"Go ahead," said Janssen.

"All right." The smaller man drew a deep breath. "What's this all about? You got me over here to see this man, telling me you had something to show me. Evidently you wanted to prove to me he's a hero. All right, I agree. He's a hero. Now, what about it?"

Janssen turned to Jeph.

"Shut the door, there," he ordered. Jeph complied. Janssen's eyes raked from the Line Team Captain to Clancy. "And if either of you breathe a word of what you hear in this room from now on, I'll personally see that you get posted out on a job two hundred light-years from Earth, and forgotten there."

IX

Clancy's stomach floated suddenly inside him, as if an elevator he was in had just dropped away under the soles of his feet. His premonitions of trouble on seeing Janssen had been only too correct. Here, the man who had evidently lost five years of battles with the head of R. and E. was about to take one more swing at the other Service Head, using Clancy as a club. Two guesses, thought Clancy, as to what the outcome would be—and what would happen to Clancy himself as a result.

He had escaped the hobgoblins on XN-4010, only to be trapped and used by the super-hobgoblin of all—his own tough-talking, but ineffective Line Service Commandant. There he was now—Janssen—tying into Li as if he'd been the winner all these last five years, instead of the other way around.

"I'm glad to hear you admit that, Charlie," Janssen was snapping, "because Clancy here *is* a hero. A real, live hero. A man who damn near killed himself doing a superhuman job in the face of inimical alien action to save his teammate. Only he nearly didn't make it, because he was already chewed down past the exhaustion point when he started. Not just from fighting his job and the aliens—but from being worn thin by a round damn dozen of your Service's useless ivory-tower experiments, built into his working suit!"

Li stared at him.

"What're you talking about?" bristled Li. "It was the collar-innovation on his own suit that kept him from being brained when that rock hit his helmet. If it hadn't been for the experi-mental cryogenic unit in Plotchin's suit, Plotchin wouldn't be alive now!"

"Sure. Two!" snarled Janssen. "Two gadgets paid off, but of—what? A total of twenty-three, for both men's suits? What did the other twenty-one gadgets do for either of them? I'll tell you. Nothing! Nothing, except to wear them out to the point where they were ready to cut each other's throat like half the rest of my men on the Line Teams nowadays!"

Li's face was palely furious behind the black mustache.

"Sorry. I don't see that!" he snapped. "Your man's still only a hero because the cryogenic unit gave him a revivable team-mate to bring back. And credit for the cryogenic unit being in Plotchin's suit belongs to us!"

"You think so?" grated Janssen. Li's voice had gone high in tone with the argument. Janssen's was going down into a bass growl. Both men looked ready to start swinging at each other at any minute. Janssen's gray mustache bristled at Li. "Stop and think again for a moment. What if your cryogenic unit hadn't worked? What if Plotchin had actually been dead? Clancy wouldn't have had any way of knowing it, for sure. *And so he'd have brought Plotchin in, anyway!* You think you can take his hero status away from him just because your unit worked? He did what he did out of a sense of duty to his teammate—and whether there was a live man or a dead one on top of him at the time doesn't matter."

"So?" snarled Li.

"So!" barked Janssen. "I've been lying back and waiting for something to hang you with, Charlie, for four years. Now I've got it. I'm starting to punch buttons the minute I leave this hospital. We're both of us responsible to Earth Central, and Earth Central's responsible to the taxpayers. I'm going to set the wheels going to bring my hero up in front of a full-dress Central Investigating Committee—to determine whether the excessive number of experiments your Service has been forcing upon my Line Teams might not have caused the Relay Station installation on XN-4010 to fail in the face of attack by inimical aliens, who then might have gone undiscovered and eventually posed a threat to the whole Line, if not to the whole human race."

Clancy had a sudden, irrational impulse to pull the bed-covers up over his head and pretend they had all gone away.

"Are you crazy?" snarled Li. "You tried fighting me, five years ago, when we first got Central permission to test experimental equipment under working conditions, on your Line Teams. And Central went right along with me all the way."

"That was then, Charlie!" Janssen grated. "That was *then,* when you had all the little glittery, magic-seeming wonder-world-tomorrow type of gadgets to demonstrate on the TV screens and grab the headlines. All I had was honest argument. But now it's the other way around. All you've got is more of the same—but I've got the real glitter. I've got a hero. Not a fake hero, flanged up for the purpose. But a true hero—an honest hero. You can't shoot him down no matter what angle you try from. And I've got villains—real villains, in those alien hobgoblins, or whatever they are. I'm going to win this inquiry the same way you won the last one. Not in the Committee Room, but out in the News Services. I can get you and your experiment wiped clean out of my Service, Charlie! And I'll play hell with your next year's appropriations, to boot!"

Janssen shut up, his mustache stiff with anger. Clancy held his breath, resisting the impulse to shut his eyes. The Line Service Commandant had taken his swing; and now—how, Clancy did not know, but there would undoubtedly turn out to be a way—Li would lower the boom.

"All right," said Li, bitterly. "Damn you, Lief! You know I can't afford any threat to next year's appropriations now that the drone by-pass system is ready to go into field testing! Name your price!"

Clancy blinked. He opened his eyes very wide and stared at Li.

"But you wipe me out, and you'll regret it, Lief!" continued the R. and E. Head, bursting out before Clancy could get his brains unscrambled. "Admit it or not, but a lot of our ivory-tower gadgets, as you call them, have ended up as standard equipment, saving the lives of men on your Teams!"

"Don't deny it!" snapped Janssen. "I don't deny it and never did. And I don't want to wipe you out. I just want to get back the right to put some limit on the number of wild-eyed ideas my men have to test for your lab jockeys! That's all!"

"All right," said Li. He, too was relaxing, though his face was still sour. "You've got it."

"And we'll draw up an intra-Service agreement," said Janssen.

"All right." Li's glance swung balefully to fasten for a second on Clancy. "I suppose you know you'll be holding up progress?"

"That won't matter so much," said Janssen, "as long as I'm upholding my Linemen."

"Excuse me," Li answered stiffly, looking back at him, "I don't see that. As far as I'm concerned, progress comes before the individual."

"It does, does it?" said Janssen. "Well, let me tell you something. You get yourself a fresh crop of laboratory boys out of the colleges, every year, all you want, to work in your nice, neat, air-conditioned labs. But I get only so many men for work on the Line—because it takes a special type and there's only so many of that type born each generation!"

Clancy stared guiltily at Janssen. Clancy's conscience was undergoing an uncomfortable feeling—as if he had just been punched in the pit of his stomach.

"I know," Li was answering, with a sour glance at Clancy. "Heroes."

"Heroes, hell!" exploded Janssen. "Race horses! That's what my boys are—race horses! And you wanted to turn them into pack mules for your own purposes. Not damn likely! Not any more damn likely than I was to roll over on my back and let you get away with using a full-dress Central Investigation Committee to get permission to stick your nose into my Line Service! Open your eyes for once, Charlie! Use your imagination on something living! Can you imagine what it's like to do what these men do, jammed at best into the few clear cubic feet of a tiny transit ship you could cover with a large tent? And at worst—living in their suits out on the job for days on end, working harder than any manual laborer's worked on Earth in fifty years, always under strange conditions and unknown dangers like those hobgoblins on XN-4010?"

Janssen had to stop for a second to draw breath.

"Can you imagine doing that?" he went on. "Just to put in a Line Station for a million fat tourists to use; just about the time you're maybe getting killed or crippled putting in another Station out on some world the tourists have never heard of yet?"

"No, I can't," he said, dryly. "And I don't believe any normal, sensible man can. If the work's that bad, what makes any of your men want to do it?"

"Listen." Clancy propped himself up on one elbow. His conscience and the recognition of how wrong he had been about Janssen was finally bringing him into the fight. It was late. But better late than never.

"Listen—" he said again to Li. "You get a feeling you can't describe at the end of a job—when a working Station finally goes into the line. You feel good. You know you've done something, out there. Nobody else did it, but *you*—and nobody can take it away from you, that you've done it!"

"I see." The short man's mustache lifted a little. He turned to the door, opened it, and looked back at Janssen. "They're romantics, your Linemen. That's it in a nutshell. Isn't it?"

"That's right, Charlie," said the Commandant coldly. "You named it."

"Yes," said Li, "and no doubt the rest of the race has to have them for things like building the Line. But, if you'll excuse me, personally I can't see romantics. Or romanticism, either."

He went out shutting the door.

"No," said Janssen, grimly, looking at the closed door. "You wouldn't. Your kind never does. But we manage to get things done in spite of you, one way or another."

He glared suddenly at Clancy, who was staring at him with a powerful intensity.

"What're you gawking at, Lineman?" he barked.

Nothing," said Clancy.

"What is Christmas?" asked Harvey.

"It's the time when they give you presents," Allan Dumay told him. Allan was squatted on his mudshoes, a grubby figure of a little six-year-old boy, in the waning light over the inlet, talking to the Cidorian. "Tonight's Christmas Eve. My daddy cut a thorn tree and my mother's inside now, trimming it."

"Trimming?" echoed the Cidorian. He floated awash in the cool water of the inlet. Someone—perhaps it was Allan's father—had named him Harvey a long time ago. Now nobody called him by any other name.

"That's putting things on the tree," said Allan. "To make it beautiful. Do you know what beautiful is, Harvey?"

"No," said Harvey. "I have never seen beautiful." But he was wrong—even as, for a different reason, those humans were wrong who called Cidor an ugly swamp-planet because there was nothing green or familiar on the low mudflats that rose from its planet-wide fresh-water sea—only the stunted, dangerous thorn tree and the trailing weed. There was beauty on Cidor, but it was a different beauty. It was a black-and-silver world where the thorn trees stood up like fine ink sketches against the cloud-torn sky; and this was beautiful. The great and solemn fishes that moved about the uncharted pathways of its seas were beautiful with the beauty of large, far-traveled ships. And even Harvey, though he did not know it himself, was most beautiful of all with his swelling iridescent jellyfish body and the yard-long mantle of silver filaments spreading out through it and down through the water. Only his voice was croaky and unbeautiful, for a constricted air-sac is not built for the manufacture of human words.

"You can look at my tree when it's ready," said Allan. "That way you can tell."

"Thank you," said Harvey.

"You wait and see. There'll be colored lights. And bright balls and stars; and presents all wrapped up."

"I would like to see it," said Harvey.

Up the slope of the dyked land that was the edge of the Dumay farm, reclaimed from the sea, the kitchen door of the house opened and a pale, warm finger of light reached out long over the black earth to touch the boy and the Cidorian. A woman stood silhouetted against the light.

"Time to come in, Allan," called his mother's voice.

"I'm coming," he called back.

"Right away! Right now!"

Slowly, he got to his feet.

"If she's got the tree ready, I'll come tell you," he said, to Harvey.

"I will wait," said Harvey.

Allan turned and went slowly up the slope to the house, swinging his small body in the automatic rhythm of the mud-shoes. The open doorway waited for him and took him in—into the light and human comfort of the house.

"Take your shoes off," said his mother, "so you don't track mud in."

"Is the tree all ready?" asked Allan, fumbling with the fastenings of his calf-high boots.

"I want you to eat first," said his mother. "Dinner's all ready." She steered him to the table. "Now, don't gulp. There's plenty of time."

"Is Daddy going to be home in time for us to open the presents?"

"You don't open your presents until morning. Daddy'll be

back by then. He just had to go upriver to the supply house. He'll start back as soon as it's light; he'll be here before you wake up."

"That's right," said Allan, solemnly, above his plate; "he shouldn't go out on the water at night because that's when the water-bulls come up under your boat and you can't see them in the dark."

"Hush," said his mother, patting him on the shoulder. "There's no water-bulls around here."

"There's water-bulls everywhere. Harvey says so."

"Hush now, and eat your dinner. Your daddy's not going out on the water at night."

Allan hurried with his dinner.

"My plate's clean!" he called at last. "Can I go now?"

"All right," she said. "Put your plate and silverware into the dishwasher."

He gathered up his eating utensils and crammed them into the dishwasher; then ran into the next room. He stopped suddenly, staring at the thorn tree. He could not move—it was as if a huge, cold wave had suddenly risen up to smash into him and wash all the happy warmth out of him. Then he was aware of the sound of his mother's footsteps coming up behind him; and suddenly her arms were around him.

"Oh, honey!" she said, holding him close, "you didn't expect it to be like last year, did you, on the ship that brought us here? They had a real Christmas tree, supplied by the space lines, and real ornaments. We had to just make do with what we had."

Suddenly he was sobbing violently. He turned around and clung to her. "—not a—Christmas tree—" he managed to choke out.

"But, sweetheart, it is!" He felt her hand, soothing the rumpled hair of his head. "It isn't how it looks that makes it a Christmas tree. It's how we think about it, and what it means to us. What makes Christmas is the loving and the giving—

not how the Christmas tree looks, or how the presents are wrapped. Don't you know that?"

"But—I—" He was lost in a fresh spate of sobs.

"What, sweetheart?"

"I—promised—Harvey—"

"Hush," she said. "Here—" The violence of his grief was abating. She produced a clean white tissue from the pocket of her apron. "Blow your nose. That's right. Now, what did you promise Harvey?"

"To—" He hiccupped. "To show him a Christmas tree."

"Oh," she said, softly. She rocked him a little in her arms. "Well, you know honey," she said, "Harvey's a Cidorian; and he's never seen a Christmas tree at all before. So this one would seem just as wonderful to him as that tree on the spaceship did to you last Christmas."

He blinked and sniffed and looked at her doubtfully.

"Yes, it would," she assured him gently. "Honey—Cidorians aren't like people. I know Harvey can talk and even make pretty good sense sometimes—but he isn't really like a human person. When you get older, you'll understand that better. His world is out there in the water and everything on land like we have it is a little hard for him to understand."

"Didn't he *ever* know about Christmas?"

"No, he never did."

"Or see a Christmas tree, or get presents?"

"No, dear." She gave him a final hug. "So why don't you go out and get him and let him take a look at the tree. I'll bet he'll think it's beautiful."

"Well . . . all right!" Allan turned and ran suddenly to the kitchen, where he began to climb into his boots.

"Don't forget your jacket," said his mother. "The breeze comes up after the sun goes down."

He struggled into his jacket, snapped on his mudshoes and ran down to the inlet. Harvey was there waiting for him. Allan let the Cidorian climb onto the arm of his jacket and carried the great light bubble of him back into the house.

"See there," he said, after he had taken off his boots with one hand and carried Harvey into the living room. "That's a Christmas tree, Harvey."

Harvey did not answer immediately. He shimmered, balanced in the crook of Allan's elbow, his long filaments spread like silver hair over and around the jacket of the boy.

"It's not a real Christmas tree, Harvey," said Allan. "But that doesn't matter. We have to make do with what we have because what makes Christmas is the loving and the giving. Do you know that?"

"I did not know," said Harvey.

"Well, that's what it is."

"It is beautiful," said Harvey. "A Christmas tree beautiful."

"There, you see," said Allan's mother, who had been standing to one side and watching. "I told you Harvey would think it was beautiful, Allan."

"Well, it'd be more beautiful if we had some real shiny ornaments to put on it, instead of little bits of foil and beads and things. But we don't care about that, Harvey."

"We do not care," said Harvey.

"I think, Allan," said his mother, "you better take Harvey back now. He's not built to be out of the water too long, and there's just time to wrap your presents before bed."

"All right," said Allan. He started for the kitchen, then stopped. "Did you want to say good night to Harvey, Mommy?"

"Good night, Harvey," she said.

"Good night," answered Harvey, in his croaking voice.

Allan dressed and took the Cidorian back to the inlet. When he returned, his mother already had the wrapping papers in all their colors, and the ribbons and boxes laid out on his bed in the bedroom. Also laid out was the pocket whetstone he was giving his father for Christmas and a little inch-and-a-half-high figure he had molded out of native clay, kiln-baked and painted to send home to Allan's grandmother and grandfather, who were his mother's parents. It cost fifty units to ship an ounce of weight back to Earth, and the little figure was just under an ounce—but the grandparents would pay the freight on it from their end. Seeing everything ready, Allan went over to the top drawer of his closet.

"Close your eyes," he said. His mother closed them, tight.

He got out the pair of work gloves he was giving his mother and smuggled them into one of the boxes.

They wrapped the presents together. After they were finished and had put the presents under the thorn tree, with its meager assortment of homemade ornaments, Allan lingered over the wrappings. After a moment, he went to the box that held his toys and got out the container of toy spacemen. They were molded of the same clay as his present to his grandparents. His father had made and fired them, his mother had painted them. They were all in good shape except the astrogator, and his right hand—the one that held the pencil—was broken off. He carried the astrogator over to his mother.

"Let's wrap this, please," he said.

"Why, who's that for?" she asked, looking down at him. He rubbed the broken stump of the astrogator's arm, shyly.

"It's a Christmas present . . . for Harvey."

She gazed at him.

"Your astrogator?" she said. "How'll you run your spaceship without him?"

"Oh, I'll manage," he said.

"But, honey," she said. "Harvey's not like a little boy. What could he do with the astrogator? He can't very well play with it."

"No," said Allan. "But he could keep it. Couldn't he?"

She smiled, suddenly.

"Yes," she said. "He could keep it. Do you want to wrap it and put it under the tree for him?"

He shook his head, seriously.

"No," he said. "I don't think Harvey can open packages very well. I'll get dressed and take it down to the inlet and give it to him now."

"Not tonight, Allan," his mother said. "It's too late. You should be in bed already. You can take it to him tomorrow."

"Then he won't have it when he wakes up in the morning!"

"All right, then," she said. "I'll take it. But you've got to pop right into bed, now."

"I will." Allan turned to his closet and began to dig out his pajamas. When he was securely established in the warm, blanketing field of the bed, she kissed him and turned out everything but the night light.

"Sleep tight," she said, and taking the broken-armed astrogator, went out of the bedroom, closing the door all but a crack behind her.

She set the dishwasher and turned it on. Then, taking the astrogator again, she put on her own jacket and mudshoes and went down to the shores of the inlet.

"Harvey?" she called.

But Harvey was not in sight. She stood for a moment, looking out over the darkened night country of low-lying earth and water, dimly revealed under the cloud-obscured face of Cidor's nearest moon. A loneliness crept into her from the alien land and she caught herself wishing her husband was home. She shivered a little under her jacket and stooped down to leave the astrogator by the water's edge. She had turned away and was half-way up the slope to the house when she heard Harvey's voice calling her.

She turned about. The Cidorian was at the water's edge—halfway out onto the land, holding wrapped up in his filaments the small shape of the astrogator. She went back down to him, and he slipped gratefully back into the water. He could move on land, but found the labor exhausting.

"You have lost this," he said, lifting up the astrogator.

"No, Harvey," she answered. "It's a Christmas present. From Allan. For you."

He floated where he was without answering, for a long moment. Finally:

"I do not understand," he said.

"I know you don't," she sighed, and smiled a little at the same time. "Christmas just happens to be a time when we all give gifts to each other. It goes a long way back . . ." Standing there in the dark, she found herself trying to explain; and wondered, listening to the sound of her own voice, that she should feel so much comfort in talking to only Harvey. When she was finished with the story of Christmas and what the reasons were that had moved Allan, she fell silent. And the Cidorian rocked equally silent before her on the dark water, not answering.

"Do you understand?" she asked at last.

"No," said Harvey. "But it is a beautiful."

"Yes," she said, "it's a beautiful, all right." She shivered suddenly, coming back to this chill damp world from the warm country of her childhood. "Harvey," she said suddenly. "What's it like out on the river—and the sea? Is it dangerous?"

"Dangerous?" he echoed.

"I mean with the water-bulls and all. Would one really attack a man in a boat?"

"One will. One will not," said Harvey.

"Now I don't understand you, Harvey."

"At night," said Harvey, "they come up from deep in the water. They are different. One will swim away. One will come up on the land to get you. One will lie still and wait."

She shuddered.

"Why?" she said.

"They are hungry. They are angry," said Harvey. "They are water-bulls. You do not like them?" She shuddered.

"I'm petrified." She hesitated. "Don't they ever bother you?"

"No. I am . . ." Harvey searched for the word. "Electric."

"Oh." She folded her arms about her, hugging the warmth in to her body. "It's cold," she said. "I'm going in."

In the water, Harvey stirred.

"I would like to give a present," he said. "I will make a present."

Her breath caught a little in her throat.

"Thank you, Harvey," she said, gently and solemnly. "We will be very happy to have you make us a present."

"You are welcome," said Harvey.

Strangely warmed and cheered, she turned and went back up the slope and into the peaceful warmth of the house. Harvey, floating still on the water, watched her go. When at last the door had shut behind her, and all light was out, he turned and moved toward the entrance to the inlet.

It appeared he floated, but actually he was swimming very swiftly. His hundreds of hair-like filaments drove him through the dark water at amazing speed, but without a ripple. Almost, it seemed as if the water was no heavy substance to him but a matter as light as gas through which he traveled on the faintest impulse of a thought. He emerged from the mouth of the inlet and turned upriver, moving with the same ease and swiftness past the little flats and islands. He traveled upriver until he came to a place between two islands where the water was black and deep and the thorn bushes threw their sharp shadows across it in the silver path of the moonlight.

Here he halted. And there rose slowly before him, breaking the smooth surface of the water, a huge and frog-like head, surmounted by two stubby cartilaginous projections above the tiny eyes. The head was as big as an oil drum, but it had come up in perfect silence. It spoke to him in vibrations through the water that Harvey understood.

"Is there a sickness among the shocking people that drives them out of their senses, to make you come here?"

"I have come for beautiful Christmas," said Harvey, "to make you into a present."

It was an hour past dawn the following morning that Chester Dumay, Allan's father, came down the river. The Colony's soil expert was traveling with him and their two boats were tied together, proceeding on a single motor. As they came around the bend between the two islands, they had been talking about an acid condition in the soil of Chester's fields, where they bordered the river. But the soil expert—his name was Père Hama, a lean little dark man—checked himself suddenly in mid-sentence.

"Just a minute—" he said, gazing off and away past Chester Dumay's shoulder. "Look at that."

Chester looked, and saw something large and dark floating half-away, caught against the snag of a half-drowned tree that rose up from the muddy bottom of the river some thirty feet out from the far shore. He turned the boat-wheel and drove across toward it.

"What the devil—"

They came up close and Chester cut the motor to let the boats drift in upon the object. The current took them down and the nearer hull bumped against a great black expanse of swollen hide, laced with fragile silver threads and gray-scarred all over by what would appear to have been a fiery whip. It rolled idly in the water.

"A water-bull!" said Hama.

"Is that what it is?" queried Chester, fascinated. "I never saw one."

"I did—at Third Landing. This one's a monster. And *dead!*" There was a note of puzzlement in the soil expert's voice.

Chester poked gingerly at the great carcass and it turned a little. Something like a gray bubble rose to show itself for a second dimly through several feet of murky water, then rolled under out of sight again.

"A Cidorian," said Chester. He whistled. "All crushed. But who'd have thought one of them could take on one of these!" He stared at the water-bull body.

Hama shuddered a little, in spite of the fact that the sun was bright.

"And win—that's the thing," the soil expert said. "Nobody ever suspected—" He broke off suddenly. "What's the matter with you?"

"Oh, we've got one in our inlet that my son plays with a

lot—call him Harvey," said Chester. "I was just wondering . . ."

"I wouldn't let my kid near something that could kill a water-bull," said Hama.

"Oh, Harvey's all right," said Chester. "Still . . ." Frowning, he picked up the boathook and shoved off from the carcass, turning about to start up the motor again. The hum of its vibration picked up in their ears as they headed downriver once more. "All the same, I think there's no point in mentioning this to the wife and boy—no point in spoiling their Christmas. And later on, when I get a chance to get rid of Harvey quietly . . ."

"Sure," said Hama. "I won't say a word. No point in it."

They purred away down the river.

Behind them, the water-bull carcass, disturbed, slid free of the waterlogged tree and began to drift downriver. The current swung it and rolled, slowly, over and over until the crushed central body of the dead Cidorian rose into the clean air. And the yellow rays of the clear sunlight gleamed from the glazed pottery countenance of a small toy astrogator, all wrapped about with silver threads, and gilded it.

3-PART PUZZLE

The Mologhese ship twinkled across the light years separating the human-conquered planets of the Bahrin system from Mologh. Aboard her, the Mologh Envoy sat deep in study. For he was a thinker as well as a warrior, the Envoy, and his duties had gone far beyond obtaining the capsule propped on the Mologhese version of a desk before him—a sealed message capsule containing the diplomatic response of the human authorities to the proposal he had brought from Mologh. His object of study at the moment, however, was not the capsule, but a translation of something human he had painfully resolved into Mologhese terms. His furry brow wrinkled and his bulldog-shaped jaw clamped as he worked his way through it. He had been over it a number of times, but he still could not conceive of a reason for a reaction he had observed among human young to its message. It was, he had been reliably informed, one of a group of such stories for the human young. —What he was looking at in translation was approximately this:—

THE THREE (Name) (Domestic animals) (Name)

Once upon a time there was a (horrendous, carnivorous, mythical creature) who lived under a bridge and one day he became very hungry. He was sitting there thinking of good things to eat when he heard the sounds of someone crossing the bridge over his head. (Sharp hoof-sound)—(sharp hoof-sound) went the sounds on the bridge overhead.

"Who's there?" cried the (horrendous, carnivorous, mythical creature).

"It's only I, the smallest (Name) (Domestic animal) (Name)" came back the answer.

"Well, I am the (horrendous, carnivorous, mythical creature) who lives under the bridge," replied the (horrendous, carnivorous, mythical creature) "and I'm coming up to eat you all up."

"Oh, don't do that, please!" cried the smallest (Name) (Domestic animal) (Name). "I wouldn't even make you a good meal. My (relative), the (middle-sized? next-oldest?) (Name) (Domestic animal) (Name) will be along in a minute. Let me go. He's much bigger than I. You'll get a much better meal out of him. Let me go and eat him instead."

"Very well," said the (horrendous, carnivorous, mythical creature); and (hoof-sound)—(hoof-sound) the (Name) (Domestic animal) (Name) hurried across the bridge to safety.

After a while the (horrendous, carnivorous, mythical creature) heard (heavier hoof-sound)—(heavier hoof-sound) on the bridge overhead.

"Who's there?" he cried.

"It is I, the (middle-sized?) (Name) (Domestic animal) (Name)," replied a (deeper?) voice.

"Then I am coming up to eat you up," said the (horrendous, carnivorous, mythical creature). "Your smaller (relative?) the smallest (Name) (Domestic animal) (Name) told me you were coming and I let him go by so I could have a bigger meal by eating you. So here I come."

"Oh, you are, are you?" said the (middle-sized) (Name) (Domestic animal) (Name). "Well, suit yourself; but our oldest (relative?), the big (Name) (Domestic animal) (Name) will be along in just a moment. If you want to wait for him, you'll really have a meal to remember."

"Is that so?" said the (horrendous, carnivorous, mythical creature), who was very (greedy? Avaricious? Gluttonous?).

"All right, go ahead." And the (middle-sized) (Name) (Domestic animal) (Name) went (heavier hoof-sound)—(heavier hoof-sound) across the bridge to safety.

It was not long before the (horrendous, carnivorous, mythical creature) heard (thunderous hoof-sound)—(thunderous hoof-sound) shaking the bridge overhead.

"Who's there?" cried the (horrendous, carnivorous, mythical creature).

"It is I!" rumbled an (earth-shaking?) deep (bass?) voice. "The biggest (Name) (Domestic animal) (Name). Who calls?"

"I do!" cried the (horrendous, carnivorous, mythical creature). "And I'm coming up to eat you all up!" And he sprang up on the bridge. But the big (Name) (Domestic animal) (Name) merely took one look at him, and lowered (his?) head and came charging forward, with his (horns?) down. And he butted that (horrendous, carnivorous, mythical creature) over the hills and so far away he could never find his way back to bother anyone ever again.

The Mologhese Envoy put the translation aside and blinked his red-brown eyes wearily. It was ridiculous, he thought, to let such a small conundrum bother him this way. The story was perfectly simple and obvious; it related how an organization of three individuals delayed conflict with a dangerous enemy until their strongest member arrived to deal with the situation. Perfectly usual and good Conqueror indoctrination literature for Conqueror young.

But still, there was something—a difference about it he could not quite put his finger on. The human children he had observed having it told to them at that school he had visited had greeted the ending with an entirely disproportionate glee. Why? Even to a student of tactics like himself the lesson was a simple and rather boring one. It was as if a set of young students were suddenly to become jubilant on being informed that two plus two equaled four. Was there some hidden value in the lesson that he failed to discover? Or merely some freakish twist to the human character that caused the emotional response to be disproportionate?

If there was, the Envoy would be everlastingly destroyed if he could not lay the finger of his perception on what it was. Perhaps, thought the Envoy, leaning back in the piece of furniture in which he sat, this problem was merely part and parcel of that larger and more wide-spread anomaly he had remarked during the several weeks, local time, he had been the guest of the human HQ on Bahrin II. . . .

The humans had emerged on to the galactic scene rather suddenly, but not too suddenly to escape notice by potentially interested parties. They had fanned out from their home system; doing it at first the hard way by taking over and attempting to pioneer uninhabited planets of nearby systems. Eventually they had bumped into the nearest Conqueror civilization—which was that of the Bahrin, a ursinoid type established over four small but respectable systems and having three Submissive types in bondage, one of which was a degraded Conqueror strain.

Like most primitive races, the humans did not at first seem to realize what they were up against. They attempted at first to establish friendly relations with the Bahrin without attempting any proof of their own. Conqueror instincts. The Bahrin, of course, recognized Conqueror elements potential in the form of the human civilization; and for that reason struck all the harder, to take advantage of their own age and experience. They managed to destroy nearly all the major planetary installations of the humans, and over twenty per cent of the population at first strike. However, the humans rebounded with surprising ferocity and speed, to drop guerrilla land troops on the Bahrin planets while they gathered power for a strikeback. The strikeback was an overwhelming success, the Bahrin power being enfeebled by the unexpected fierceness of the human guerrillas and the fact that these seemed to have the unusual ability to enlist the sympathy of the Submissives under the Bahrin rule. The Bahrin were utterly broken; and the humans had for some little time been occupying the Bahrin worlds.

Meanwhile, the ponderous mills of the Galactic social order had been grinding up the information all this had provided. It was known that human exploration ships had stumbled across their first contact with one of the Shielded Worlds; and immediately made eager overtures of friendship to the people upon it. It was reported that when the Shielded peoples went on about their apparently meaningless business under that transparent protective element which no known Conqueror had ever been able to breach; (and the human overtures were ignored, as all Conqueror attempts at contact had always been), that a storm of emotion swept over the humans—a storm involving the whole spectrum of emotions. It was as if the rejection had had the equivalent of a calculated insult from an equivalent, Conqueror, race.

In that particular neighborhood of the galaxy the Mologhese currently held the balance of power among the Conqueror races. They sent an Envoy with a proposal to the human authorities.

—And that, thought the Envoy, aboard the returning spaceship as he put aside the problem of the translation to examine the larger question, was the beginning of an educative process on both sides.

His job had been to point out politely but firmly that there were many races in the galaxy; but that they had all evolved on the same type of world, and they all fell into one of three temperamental categories. They were by nature Conquerors, Submissives, or Invulnerables. The Invulnerables were, of course, the people of the Shielded Worlds; who went their own pacific, non-technologic ways. And if these could not be dominated behind the protections of their strange abilities, they did not seem interested in dominating themselves, or interfering with the Conquerors. So the situation worked out to equalities and they could be safely ignored.

The Submissive races, of course, were there for any Conqueror race's taking. That disposed of them. But there were certain elements entering into inter-Conqueror relationships, that were important for the humans to know.

No Conqueror race could, naturally, be denied its birthright, which was to take as much as it could from Submissives and its fellow-Conquerors. On the other hand, there were advantages to be gained by semi-peaceful existence even within the laws of a society of Conqueror races. Obvious advantages dealing with trade, travel, and a reciprocal recognition of rights and customs. To be entitled to these, the one prime requirement upon any Conqueror race was that it should not rock the boat. It might take on one or more of its neighbors, or make an attempt to move up a notch in the pecking order in this neck of the galactic woods; but it must not become a bother to the local community of Conquerors as a whole by such things as general piracy, et cetera.

"In short," had replied the Envoy's opposite number—a tall, rather thin and elderly human with a sad smile, "a gentleman's agreement?"

"Please?" said the Envoy. The Opposite Number explained.

"Essentially, yes," said the Envoy, feeling pleased. He was pleased enough, in fact, to take time out for a little dissertation on this as an example of the striking cultural similarities between Conqueror races that often produced parallel terms in completely different languages, and out of completely different backgrounds.

". . . In fact," he wound up, "let me say that personally, I find you people very much akin. That is one of the things that makes me so certain that you will eventually be very pleased that you have agreed to this proposal I brought. Essentially, all it asks is that you subscribe to the principles of a Conqueror intersociety—which is, after all, your own kind of society—and recognize its limitations as well as its privileges by pledging to maintain the principles which are the hard facts of its existence."

"Well," said his Opposite Number, whose name was Harrigan or Hargan, or some such, "that is something to be decided on in executive committee. Meanwhile, suppose I show you around here; and you can tell me more about the galaxy."

There followed several weeks in which the Envoy found himself being convoyed around the planet which had originally been the seat of the former Bahrin ruling group. It was quite obviously a tactic to observe him over a period of time and under various conditions; and he did not try to resist it. He had his own observations to make, and this gave him an excellent opportunity to do so.

For one thing, he noted down as his opinion that they were an exceedingly touchy people where slights were concerned. Here they had just finished their war with the Bahrin in the last decade and were facing entrance into an interstellar society of races as violent as themselves; and yet the first questions on the tips of the tongues of nearly all those he met were concerned with the Shielded Worlds. Even Harrigan, or whatever his name was, confessed to an interest in the people on the Invulnerable planets.

"How long have they been like that?" Harrigan asked.

The Envoy could not shrug. His pause before answering fulfilled the same function.

"There is no way of telling," he said. "Things on Shielded Worlds are as the people there make them. Take away the signs of a technical civilization from a planet—turn it all into parkland—and how do you tell how long the people there have been as they are? All we ever knew is that they are older than any of *our* histories."

"Older?" said Harrigan. "There must be some legend, at least, about how they came to be?"

"No," said the Envoy. "Oh, once in a great while some worthless planet without a population will suddenly develop a shield and become fertile, forested and populated—but this is pretty clearly a case of colonization. The Invulnerables seem to be able to move from point to point in space by some nonphysical means. That's all."

"All?" said Harrigan.

"All," said the Envoy. "Except for an old Submissive superstition that the Shielded Peoples are a mixed race sprung from an interbreeding between a Conqueror and a Submissive type—something we know, of course, to be a genetic impossibility."

"I see," said Harrigan.

Harrigan took the Envoy around to most of the major cities of the planet. They did not visit any military installations (the Envoy had not expected that they would) but they viewed a lot of new construction taking the place of Bahrin building that had been obliterated by the angry scars of the war. It was going up with surprising swiftness—or perhaps not so surprising, noted the Envoy thoughtfully, since the humans seemed to have been able to enlist the enthusiastic co-operation of the Submissives they had taken over. The humans appeared to have a knack for making conquered peoples willing to work with them. Even the Bahrin, what there were left of them, were behaving most unlike a recently crushed race of Conquerors, in the extent of their co-operation. Certainly the humans seemed to be allowing their former enemies a great deal of freedom, and even responsibility in the new era. The Envoy sought for an opportunity, and eventually found the chance to talk to one of the Bahrin alone. This particular Bahrin was an assistant architect on a school that was being erected on the outskirts of one city. (The humans seemed slightly crazy on the subject of schools; and only slightly less crazy on the subjects of hospitals, libraries, museums, and recreation areas. Large numbers of these were going up all over the planet.) This particular Bahrin, however, was a male who had been through the recent war. He was middle-aged and had lost an arm in the previous conflict. The Envoy found him free to talk, not particularly bitter, but considerably impressed emotionally by his new overlords.

". . . May your courage be with you," he told the Envoy. "You will have to face them sooner or later; and they are demons."

"What kind of demons?" said the Envoy, skeptically.

"A new kind," said the Bahrin. He rested his heavy, furry, bear-like forearm upon the desk in front of him and stared out a window at a changing landscape. "Demons full of fear and strange notions. Who understands them? Half their history is made up of efforts to understand themselves—and they still don't." He glanced significantly at the Envoy. "Did you know the Submissives are already starting to call them the Mixed People?"

The Envoy wrinkled his furry brow.

"What's that supposed to mean?" he said.

"The Submissives think the humans are really Submissives who have learned how to fight."

The Envoy snorted.

"That's ridiculous."

"Of course," said the Bahrin; and sighed heavily. "But what isn't, these days?" He turned back to his work. "Anyway, don't ask me about them. The more I see of them, the less I understand."

They parted on that note—and the Envoy's private conviction that the loss of the Bahrin's arm had driven him slightly insane.

Nonetheless, during the following days as he was escorted around from spot to spot, the essence of that anomaly over which he was later to puzzle during his trip home, emerged. For one thing, there were the schools. The humans, evidently, in addition to being education crazy themselves, believed in wholesale education for their cattle as well. One of the schools he was taken to was an education center for young Bahrin pupils; and—evidently due to a shortage of Bahrin instructors following the war—a good share of the teachers were human.

". . . I just *love* my class!" one female human teacher told the Envoy, as they stood together watching young Bahrin at play during their relaxation period.

"Please?" said the Envoy, astounded.

"They're so quick and eager to learn," said the teacher. One of the young Bahrin at play dashed up to her, was overcome with shyness at seeing the Envoy, and hung back. She reached out and patted him on the head. A peculiar shiver ran down the Envoy's back; but the young Bahrin nestled up to her.

"They *respond* so," said the teacher. "Don't you think so?"

"They were a quite worthy race at one time," replied the Envoy, with mingled diplomatic confusion and caution.

"Oh, yes!" said the teacher enthusiastically; and proceeded to overwhelm him with facts he already knew about the history of the Bahrin, until the Envoy found himself rescued by Harrigan. The Envoy went off wondering a little to himself whether the humans had indeed conquered the Bahrin or whether, perhaps, it had not been the other way around.

Food for that same wonderment seemed to be supplied by just about everything else that Harrigan let him see. The humans, having just about wiped the Bahrin out of existence, seemed absolutely determined to repair the damage they had done, but improve upon the former situation by way of interest. Why? What kept the Bahrin from seething with plans for revolt at this very minute? The young ones of course—like that pupil with the teacher—might not know any better; but the older ones . . . ? The Envoy thought of the one-armed Bahrin architect he had talked to, and felt further doubt. If they were all like that one—but then what kind of magic had the humans worked to produce such an intellectual and emotional victory? The Envoy went back to his quarters and took a nap to quiet the febrillations of his thinking process.

When he woke up, he set about getting hold of what history he could on the war just past. Accounts both human and

Bahrin were available; and, plowing through them, reading them for statistics rather than reports, he was reluctantly forced to the conclusion that the one-armed Bahrin had been right. The humans were demons.—Or at least, they had fought like demons against the Bahrin. A memory of the shiver that had run down his back as he watched the female human teacher patting the young Bahrin on head, troubled the Envoy again. Would this same female be perfectly capable of mowing down adult Bahrin by the automatic hand-weapon clipful? Apparently her exact counterparts had. If so, which was the normal characteristic of the human nature —the head-patting, or the trigger-pulling?

It was almost a relief when the human authorities gave him a sealed answer to the proposal he had brought, and sent him on his way home a few days later. He carried that last question of his away with him.

The only conclusion I can come to," said the Envoy to the chief authority among the Mologhese, a week and a half later as they both sat in the Chief's office, "is that there is some kind of racial insanity that sets in in times of peace. In other words, they're Conquerors in the true sense only when engaged in Conquest."

The Chief frowned at the proposal answer, still sealed on the desk before him. He had asked for the Envoy's report before opening it; and now he wondered if this traditional procedure had been the wisest move under the circumstances. He rather suspected the Envoy's wits of having gone somewhat astray during his mission.

"You don't expect me to believe something like that," said the Chief. "No culture that was insane half the time could survive. And if they tried to maintain sanity by continual Conquest, they would bleed to death in two generations."

The Envoy said nothing. His Chief's arguments were logically unassailable.

"The sensible way to look at it," said the Chief, "is to rec-

ognize them as simply another Conqueror strain with somewhat more marked individual peculiarities than most. This
is—let us say—their form of recreation, of amusement, between conquests. Perhaps they enjoy playing with the danger
of cultivating strength in their conquered races."

"Of course, there is that," admitted the Envoy. "You may
be right."

"I think," said the Chief, "that it's the only sensible all-
around explanation."

"On the other hand—" the Envoy hesitated, remembering.
"There was the business of that female human patting the
small Bahrin on the head."

"What about it?"

The Envoy looked at his Chief.

"Have *you* ever been patted on the head?" he asked. The
Chief stiffened.

"Of course not!" He relaxed slowly, staring at the Envoy.
"Why? What makes you ask that?"

"Well, I never have either, of course—especially by anyone
of another race. But that little Bahrin liked it. And seeing it
gave me—" the Envoy stopped to shiver again.

"Gave you what?" said the Chief.

"A . . . a sort of horrible, affectionate feeling—" The Envoy stopped speaking in helplessness.

"You've been overworking," said the Chief, coldly. "Is
there anything more to report?"

"No," said the Envoy. "No. But aside from all this, there's
no doubt they'd be a tough nut to crack, those humans. My
recommendation is that we wait for optimum conditions before we choose to move against them."

"Your recommendation will go into the record, of course,"
said the Chief. He picked up the human message capsule.
"And now I think it's time I listened to this. They didn't play
it for you?"

The Envoy shook his head.

The Chief picked up the capsule (it was one the Envoy

had taken along for the humans to use in replying), broke its seal and put it into the speaker unit of his desk. The speaker unit began to murmur a message tight-beamed toward the Chief's ear alone. The Envoy sat, nursing the faint hope that the Chief would see fit to let him hear, later. The Envoy was very curious as to the contents of that message. He watched his Chief closely, and saw the other's face slowly gather in a frown that deepened as the message purred on.

Abruptly it stopped. The Chief looked up; and his eyes met the Envoy's.

"It just may be," said the Chief slowly, "that I owe you an apology."

"An apology?" said the Envoy.

"Listen to this—" The Chief adjusted a volume control and pressed a button. A human voice speaking translated Mologhese filled the room.

"The Committee of Control for the human race wishes to express its appreciation for—"

"No, no—" said the Chief. "Not this diplomatic slush. Farther on—" He did things with his controls, the voice speeded up to a gabble, a whine, then slowed toward understandability again. "Ah, listen to this."

". . . Association," said the voice, "but without endorsement of what the Mologhese Authority is pleased to term the Conqueror temperament. While our two races have a great deal in common, the human race has as its ultimate aims not the exercises of war and oppression, plundering, general destruction and the establishment of a tyranny in a community of tyrants; but rather the establishment of an environment of peace for all races. The human race believes in the ultimate establishment of universal freedom, justice, and the inviolable rights of the individual whoever he may be. We believe that our destiny lies neither within the pattern of conquest nor submission, but with the enlightened maturity of independence characterized by what are known as the Shielded Worlds; and, while not ceasing to defend our people and our borders from all attacks foreign and domestic, we intend to emulate these older, protected peoples in hope that they may eventually find us worthy of association. In this hope—"

The Chief clicked off the set and looked grimly at the Envoy. The Envoy stared back at him in shock.

"Insane," said the Envoy. "I was right—quite insane." He sank back in his seat. "At any rate, you too were correct. They're too irrational, too unrealistic to survive. We needn't worry about them."

"On the contrary," said his Chief. "And I'm to blame for not spotting it sooner. There were indications of this in some of the preliminary reports we had on them. They are very dangerous."

The Envoy shook his head.

"I don't see—" he began.

"But I do!" said the Chief. "And I don't hold down this position among our people for nothing. Think for a moment, Envoy! Don't you see it? These people are *causal!*"

"Causal?"

"Exactly," replied the Chief. "They don't act or react to practical or realistic stimuli. They react to emotional or philosophic conclusions of their own."

"I don't see what's so dangerous about that?" said the Envoy, wrinkling his forehead.

"It wouldn't be dangerous if they were a different sort of race," said the Chief. "But these people seem to be able to rationalize their emotional and philosophic conclusions in terms of hard logic and harder science.—You don't believe me? Do you remember that story for the human young you told me about, about the three hoofed and horned creatures crossing a bridge?"

"Of course," said the Envoy.

"All right. It puzzled you that the human young should react so strongly to what was merely a lesson in elementary tactics. But—it wasn't the lesson they were reacting to. It was the emotional message overlaying the lesson. The notion of some sort of abstract right and wrong, so that when the some-how *wrong* mythical creature under the bridge gets what the humans might describe as his just deserts at the horns of the triumphing biggest *right* creature—the humans are tremendously stimulated."

"But I still don't see the danger—"

"The danger," said the Chief, "lies in the fact that while such a story has its existence apparently—to humans—only for its moral and emotional values, the tactical lesson which we so obviously recognize is not lost, either. To us, this story shows a way of conquering. To the humans it shows not only a way but a reason, a justification. A race whose motives are founded upon such justifications is tremendously dangerous to us."

"You must excuse me," said the Envoy, bewilderedly. "Why—"

"Because we—and I mean all the Conqueror races, and all the Submissive races—" said the Chief, strongly, "have no defenses in the emotional and philosophic areas. Look at what you told me about the Bahrin, and the Submissives the humans took over from the Bahrin. Having no strong emotional and philosophic persuasions of their own, they have become immediately infected by the human ones. They are like people unacquainted with a new disease who fall prey to an epidemic. The humans, being self-convinced of such things as justice and love, in spite of their own arbitrariness and violence, convince all of us who lack convictions having never needed them before. Do you remember how you said you felt when you saw the little Bahrin being patted on the head? *That's* how vulnerable we are!"

The Envoy shivered again, remembering.

"Now I see," he said.

"I thought you would," said the Chief, grimly. "The situation to my mind is serious, enough so to call for the greatest emergency measures possible. We mustn't make the mistake

of the creature under the bridge in the story. We were prepared to let the humans get by our community strength because we thought of them as embryo Conquerors, and we
hoped for better entertainment later. Now they come along
again, this time as something we can recognize as Conqueror-
plus. And this time we can't let them get by. I'm going to call
a meeting of our neighboring Conqueror executive Chiefs;
and get an agreement to hit the humans now with a coalition
big enough to wipe them out to the last one."

He reached for a button below a screen on his desk. But
before he could touch it, it came alight with the figure of his
own attaché.

"Sir—" began this officer; and then words failed him.

"Well?" barked the Chief.

"Sir—" the officer swallowed. "From the Shielded Worlds—
a message." The Chief stared long and hard.

"From the Shielded Worlds?" said the Chief. "How? From
the Shielded Worlds? When?"

"I know it's fantastic, sir. But one of our ships was passing
not too far from one of the Shielded Worlds and it found itself caught—"

"And you just now got the message?" The Chief cut him
short.

"Just this second, sir. I was just—"

"Let me have it. And keep your channel open," said the
Chief. "I've got some messages to send."

The officer made a movement on the screen and something
like a message cylinder popped out of a slot in the Chief's
desk. The Chief reached for it, and hesitated. Looking up,
he found the eyes of the Envoy upon him.

"Never—" said the Envoy, softly. "Never in known history
have they communicated with any of us. . . ."

"It's addressed to me," said the Chief, looking at the outside of the cylinder. "If they can read our minds, as we suspect, then they know what I've just discovered about the

humans and what I plan to do about it." He gave the cylinder a twist to open it. "Let's see what they have to say."

The cylinder opened up like a flower. A single white sheet unrolled within it to lie flat on the desk; and the message upon it in the common galactic code looked up at the Chief. The message consisted of just one word. The word was:—

NO.

I

It was raw, red war for all of them, from the moment the two ships intercepted each other, one degree off the plane of the ecliptic and three diameters out from the second planet of the star that was down on the charts as K94. K94 was a GO type star; and the yelping battle alarm of the trouble horn tumbled sixteen men to their stations. This was at thirteen hours, twenty-one minutes, four seconds of the ship's day.

Square in the scope of the laser screen, before the Survey Team Leader aboard the *Harrier*, appeared the gray, light-edged silhouette of a ship unknown to the ship's library. And the automatic reflexes of the computer aboard, that takes no account of men not yet into their vacuum suits, took over. The *Harrier* disappeared into no-time.

She came out again at less than a quarter-mile's distance from the stranger ship and released a five-pound weight at a velocity of five miles a second relative to the velocity of the alien ship. Then she had gone back into no-time again—but not before the alien, with computer-driven reflexes of its own, had rolled like the elongated cylinder it resembled, and laid out a soft green-colored beam of radiation which opened up the *Harrier* forward like a hot knife through butter left long on the table. Then it too was gone into no-time. The time aboard the *Harrier* was thirteen hours, twenty-two minutes and eighteen seconds; and on both ships there were dead.

"There are good people in the human race," Cal Hartlett had written only two months before, to his uncle on Earth, *"who feel that it is not right to attack other intelligent beings without warning—to drop five-pound weights at destructive relative velocities on a strange ship simply because you find it at large in space and do not know the race that built it.*

"What these gentle souls forget is that when two strangers encounter in space, nothing at all is known—and everything must be. The fates of both races may hinge on which one is first to kill the other and study the unknown carcass. Once contact is made, there is no backing out and no time for consideration. For we are not out here by chance, neither are they, and we do not meet by accident."

Cal Hartlett was Leader of the Mapping Section aboard the *Harrier,* and one of those who lived through that first brush with the enemy. He wrote what he wrote as clearly as if he had been Survey Leader and in command of the ship. At any moment up until the final second when it was too late, Joe Aspinall, the Survey Leader, could have taken the *Harrier* into no-time and saved them. He did not; as no commander of a Survey Ship ever has. In theory, they could have escaped.

In practice, they had no choice.

When the *Harrier* ducked back into no-time, aboard her they could hear the slamming of emergency bulkheads. The mapping room, the fore weight-discharge room and the sleeping quarters all crashed shut as the atmosphere of the ship whiffed out into space through the wound the enemy's beam had made. The men beyond the bulkheads and in the damaged sections would have needed to be in their vacuum suits to survive. There had not been time for that, so those men were dead.

The *Harrier* winked back into normal space.

Her computer had brought her out on the far side of the second planet, which they had not yet surveyed. It was larger than Earth, with somewhat less gravity but a deeper atmospheric envelope. The laser screen picked up the enemy reappearing almost where she had disappeared, near the edge of that atmosphere.

The *Harrier* winked back all but alongside the other and laid a second five-pound weight through the center of the cylindrical vessel. The other ship staggered, disappeared into no-time and appeared again far below, some five miles above planetary surface in what seemed a desperation attempt to gain breathing time. The *Harrier* winked after her—and came out within five hundred yards, square in the path of the green beam which it seemed was waiting for her. It opened up the drive and control rooms aft like a red-hot poker lays open a cardboard box.

A few miles below, the surface stretched up the peaks of titanic mountains from horizon to horizon.

"Ram!" yelled the voice of Survey Leader Aspinwall, in warning over the intercom.

The *Harrier* flung itself at the enemy. It hit like an elevator falling ten stories to a concrete basement. The cylindrical ship broke in half in midair and bodies erupted from it. Then its broken halves and the ruined *Harrier* were falling separately to the surface below and there was no more time for anyone to look. The clock stood at 13 hrs., 23 minutes and 4 seconds.

The power—except from emergency storage units—was all but gone. As Joe punched for a landing the ship fell angling past the side of a mountain that was a monster among giants, and jarred to a stop. Joe keyed the intercom of the control board before him.

"Report," he said.

In the Mapping Section Cal Hartlett waited for other voices to speak before him. None came. He thumbed his audio.

"The whole front part of the ship's dogged shut, Joe," he

said. "No use waiting for anyone up there. So—this is Number Six reporting. I'm all right."

"Number Seven," said another voice over the intercom. "Maury. O.K."

"Number Eight. Sam. O.K."

"Number Nine. John. O.K. . . ."

Reports went on. Numbers Six through Thirteen reported themselves as not even shaken up. From the rest there was no answer.

In the main Control Section, Joe Aspinwall stared bleakly at his dead control board. Half of his team was dead.

The time was 13 hours, 30 minutes, no seconds.

He shoved that thought from his mind and concentrated on the positive rather than the negative elements of the situation they were in. Cal Hartlett, he thought, was one. Since he could only have eight survivors of his Team, he felt a deep gratitude that Cal should be one of them. He would need Cal in the days to come. And the other survivors of the Team would need him, badly.

Whether they thought so at this moment or not.

"All right," said Joe, when the voices had ended. "We'll meet outside the main airlock, outside the ship. There's no power left to unseal those emergency bulkheads. Cal, Doug, Jeff—you'll probably have to cut your way out through the ship's side. Everybody into respirators and warmsuits. According to pre-survey—" he glanced at the instruments before him—"there's oxygen enough in the local atmosphere for the respirators to extract, so you won't need emergency bottles. But we're at twenty-seven thousand three hundred above local sea-level. So it'll probably be cold—even if the atmosphere's not as thin here as it would be at this altitude on Earth." He paused. "Everybody got that? Report!"

They reported. Joe unharnessed himself and got up from his seat. Turning around, he faced Maury Taller.

Maury, rising and turning from his own communications board on the other side of the Section, saw that the Survey

Leader's lean face was set in iron lines of shock and sorrow under his red hair. They were the two oldest members of the Team, whose average age had been in the mid-twenties. They looked at each other without words as they went down the narrow tunnel to the main airlock and, after putting on respirators and warmsuits, out into the alien daylight outside.

The eight of them gathered together outside the arrowhead shape of their *Harrier,* ripped open fore and aft and as still now as any other murdered thing.

Above them was a high, blue-black sky and the peaks of mountains larger than any Earth had ever known. A wind blew about them as they stood on the side of one of the mountains, on a half-mile wide shelf of tilted rock. It narrowed backward and upward like a dry streambed up the side of the mountain in one direction. In the other it broke off abruptly fifty yards away, in a cliff-edge that hung over eye-shuddering depths of a clefted valley, down in which they could just glimpse a touch of something like jungle greenness.

Beyond that narrow clefted depth lifted the great mountains, like carvings of alien devils too huge to be completely seen from one point alone. Several thousand feet above them on their mountain, the white spill of a glacier flung down a slope that was too steep for ice to have clung to in the heavier gravity of Earth. Above the glacier, which was shaped like a hook, red-gray peaks of the mountain rose like short towers stabbing the blue-dark sky. And from these, even as far down as the men were, they could hear the distant trumpeting and screaming of winds whistling in the peaks.

They took it all in in a glance. And that was all they had time to do. Because in the same moment that their eyes took in their surroundings, something no bigger than a man but tiger-striped and moving with a speed that was more than human, came around the near end of the dead *Harrier,* and went through the eight men like a predator through a huddle of goats.

Maury Taller and even Cal, who towered half a head over the rest of the men, all were brushed aside like cardboard cutouts of human figures. Sam Cloate, Cal's assistant in the mapping section, was ripped open by one sweep of a clawed limb as it charged past, and the creature tore out the throat of Mike DeWall with a sideways slash of its jaws. Then it was on Joe Aspinall.

The Survey Team Leader went down under it. Reflex that got metal cuffs on the gloves of his warmsuit up and crossed in front of his throat, his forearms and elbows guarding his belly, before he felt the ferocious weight grinding him into the rock and twisting about on top of him. A snarling, worrying, noise sounded in his ears. He felt teeth shear through the upper part of his thigh and grate on bone.

There was an explosion. He caught just a glimpse of Cal towering oddly above him, a signal pistol fuming in one big hand.

Then the worrying weight pitched itself full upon him and lay still. And unconsciousness claimed him.

II

When Joe came to, his respirator mask was no longer on his face. He was looking out, through the slight waviness of a magnetic bubble field, at ten mounds of small rocks and gravel in a row about twenty feet from the ship. Nine crosses and one six-pointed star. The Star of David would be for Mike DeWall. Joe looked up and saw the unmasked face of Maury Taller looming over him, with the dark outside skin of the ship beyond him.

"How're you feeling, Joe?" Maury asked.

"All right," he answered. Suddenly he lifted his head in fright. "My leg—I can't feel my leg!" Then he saw the silver anesthetic band that was clamped about his right leg, high on the thigh. He sank back with a sigh.

Maury said, "You'll be all right, Joe."

The words seemed to trip a trigger in his mind. Suddenly the implications of his damaged leg burst on him. He was the Leader!

"Help me!" he gritted, trying to sit up.

"You ought to lie still."

"Help me up, I said!" The leg was a dead weight. Maury's hands took hold and helped raise his body. He got the leg swung off the edge of the surface on which he had been lying, and got into sitting position. He looked around him.

The magnetic bubble had been set up to make a small, air-filled addition of breathable ship's atmosphere around the airlock entrance of the *Harrier*. It enclosed about as much space as a good-sized living room. Its floor was the mountain hillside's rock and gravel. A mattress from one of the ship's bunks had been set up on equipment boxes to make him a bed. At the other end of the bubble-enclosed space something as big as a man was lying zippered up in a gray cargo freeze-sack.

"What's that?" Joe demanded. "Where's everybody?"

"They're checking equipment in the damaged sections," answered Maury. "We shot you full of medical juices. You've been out about twenty hours. That's about three-quarters of a local day-and-night cycle locally, here." He grabbed the wounded man's shoulders suddenly with both hands. "Hold it! What're you trying to do?"

"Have a look in that freeze-sack there," grunted the Team Leader between his teeth. "Let go of me, Maury. I'm still in charge here!"

"Sit still," said Maury. "I'll bring it to you."

He went over to the bag, taking hold of one of the carrying handles he dragged it back. It came easily in the lesser gravity, only a little more than eight-tenths of Earth's. He hauled the thing to the bed and unzipped it.

Joe stared. What was inside was not what he had been expecting.

"Cute, isn't it?" said Maury.

They looked down at the hard-frozen gray body of a biped, with the back of its skull shattered and burnt by the flare of a signal pistol. It lay on its back. The legs were somewhat short for the body and thick, as the arms were thick. But elbow and knee joints were where they should be, and the hands had four stubby gray fingers, each with an opposed thumb. Like the limbs, the body was thick—almost waistless. There were deep creases, as if tucks had been taken in the skin, around the body under the armpits, around the waist and around the legs and arms.

The head, though, was the startling feature. It was heavy and round as a ball, sunk into thick folds of neck and all but featureless. Two long slits ran down each side into the neck and shoulder area. The slits were tight closed. Like the rest of the body, the head had no hair. The eyes were little pock-marks, like raisins sunk into a doughball, and there were no visible brow ridges. The nose was a snout-end set almost flush with the facial surface. The mouth was lipless, a line of skin folded together, through which now glinted barely a glimpse of close-set, large, tridentated teeth.

"What's this?" said Joe. "Where's the thing that attacked us?"

"This is it," said Maury. "One of the aliens from the other ship."

Joe stared at him. In the brighter, harsher light from the star K94 overhead, he noticed for the first time a sprinkling of gray hairs in the black shock above Maury's spade-shaped face. Maury was no older than Joe himself.

"What're you talking about?" said Joe. "I saw that thing that attacked me. And this isn't it!"

"Look," said Maury and turned to the foot of the bed. From one of the equipment boxes he brought up eight by ten inch density photographs. "Here," he said, handing them to the Survey Team Leader. "The first one is set for bone density."

Joe took them. It showed the skeleton of the being at his feet . . . and it bore only a relative kinship to the shape of the being itself.

Under the flesh and skin that seemed so abnormally thick, the skull was high-forebrained and well developed. Heavy brown ridges showed over deep wells for the eyes. The jaw and teeth were the prognathous equipment of a carnivorous animal.

But that was only the beginning of the oddities. Bony ridges of gill structures were buried under a long fold on either side of the head, neck and shoulders. The rib cage was enormous and the pelvis tiny, buried under eight or nine inches of the gray flesh. The limbs were literally double-jointed. There was a fantastic double structure of ball and socket that seemed wholly unnecessary. Maury saw the Survey Leader staring at one hip joint and leaned over to tap it with the blunt nail of his forefinger.

"Swivel and lock," said Maury. "If the joint's pulled out, it can turn in any direction. Then, if the muscles surrounding it contract, the two ball joints interlace those bony spurs there and lock together so that they operate as a single joint in the direction chosen. That hip joint can act like the hip joint on the hind leg of a quadruped, or the leg of a biped. It can even adapt for jumping and running with maximum efficiency. —Look at the toes and the fingers."

Joe looked. Hidden under flesh, the bones of feet and hands were not stubby and short, but long and powerful. And at the end of finger and toe bones were the curved, conical claws they had seen rip open Sam Cloate with one passing blow.

"Look at these other pictures now," said Maury, taking the first one off the stack Joe held. "These have been set for densities of muscle—that's this one here—and fat. Here. And this one is set for soft internal organs—here." He was down to the last. "And this one was set for the density of the skin. Look at that. See how thick it is, and how great folds of it are literally tucked away underneath in those creases.

"Now," said Maury, "look at this closeup of a muscle. See how it resembles an interlocking arrangement of innumerable tiny muscles? Those small muscles can literally shift to adapt to different skeletal positions. They can take away beef from one area and add it to an adjoining area. Each little muscle actually holds on to its neighbors, and they have little sphincter-sealed tube-systems to hook on to whatever blood-conduit is close. By increased hookup they can increase the blood supply to any particular muscle that's being overworked. There's parallel nerve connections."

Maury stopped and looked at the other man.

"You see?" said Maury. "This alien can literally be four or five different kinds of animal. Even a fish! And no telling how many varieties of each kind. We wondered a little at first why he wasn't wearing any kind of clothing, but we didn't wonder after we got these pictures. Why would he need clothing when he can adapt to any situation—Joe!" said Maury. "You see it, don't you? You see the natural advantage these things have over us all?"

Joe shook his head.

"There's no body hair," he said. "The creature that jumped me was striped like a tiger."

"Pigmentation. In response to emotion, maybe," said Maury. "For camouflage—or for terrifying the victims."

Joe sat staring at the pictures in his hand.

"All right," he said after a bit. "Then tell me how he happened to get here three or four minutes after we fell down here ourselves? And where did he come from? We rammed that other ship a good five miles up."

"There's only one way, the rest of us figured it out," said Maury. "He was one of the ones who were spilled out when we hit them. He must have grabbed our hull and ridden us down."

"That's impossible!"

"Not if he could flatten himself out and develop suckers like a starfish," said Maury. "The skin picture shows he could."

"All right," said Joe. "Then why did he try a suicidal trick like that attack—him alone against the eight of us?"

"Maybe it wasn't so suicidal," said Maury. "Maybe he

didn't see Cal's pistol and thought he could take the unarmed eight of us." Maury hesitated. "Maybe he could, too. Or maybe he was just doing his duty—to do as much damage to us as he could before we got him. There's no cover around here that'd have given him a chance to escape from us. He knew that we'd see him the first time he moved."

Joe nodded, looking down at the form in the freeze-sack. For the aliens of the other ship there would be one similarity with the humans—a duty either to get home themselves with the news of contact, at all costs; or failing that, to see their enemy did not get home.

For a moment he found himself thinking of the frozen body before him almost as if it had been human. From what strange home world might this individual now be missed forever? And what thoughts had taken place in that round, gray-skinned skull as it had fallen surfaceward clinging to the ship of its enemies, seeing the certainty of its own death approaching as surely as the rocky mountainside?

"Do we have record films of the battle?" Joe asked.

"I'll get them." Maury went off.

He brought the films. Joe, feeling the weakness of his condition stealing up on him, pushed it aside and set to examining the pictorial record of the battle. Seen in the film viewer, the battle had a remote quality. The alien ship was smaller than Joe had thought, half the size of the *Harrier*. The two dropped weights had made large holes in its midships. It was not surprising that it had broken apart when rammed.

One of the halves of the broken ship had gone up and melted in a sudden flare of green light like their weapons beam, as if some internal explosion had taken place. The other half had fallen parallel to the *Harrier* and almost as slowly—as if the fragment, like the dying *Harrier*, had had yet some powers of flight—and had been lost to sight at last on the opposite side of this mountain, still falling.

Four gray bodies had spilled from the alien ship as it broke apart. Three, at least, had fallen some five miles to their deaths. The record camera had followed their dwindling bodies. And Maury was right; these had been changing even as they fell, flattening and spreading out as if in an instinctive effort to slow their fall. But, slowed or not, a five-mile fall even in this lesser-than-Earth gravity was death.

Joe put the films aside and began to ask Maury questions.

The *Harrier*, Maury told him, would never lift again. Half her drive section was melted down to magnesium alloy slag. She lay here with food supplies adequate for the men who were left for four months. Water was no problem as long as everyone existed still within the ship's recycling system. Oxygen was available in the local atmosphere and respirators would extract it. Storage units gave them housekeeping power for ten years. There was no shortage of medical supplies, the tool shop could fashion ordinary implements, and there was a good stock of usual equipment.

But there was no way of getting off this mountain.

III

The others had come into the bubble while Maury had been speaking. They stood now around the bed. With the single exception of Cal, who showed nothing, they all had a new, taut, skinned-down look about their faces, like men who have been recently exhausted or driven beyond their abilities.

"Look around you," said Jeff Ramsey, taking over from Maury when Maury spoke of the mountain. "Without help we can't leave here."

"Tell him," said Doug Kellas. Like young Jeff, Doug had not shaved recently. But where Jeff's stubble of beard was blond, Doug's was brown-dark and now marked out the hollows under his youthful cheekbones. The two had been the youngest of the Team.

"Well, this is a hanging valley," said Jeff. Jeff was the surface man geologist and meterologist of the Team. "At one time a glacier used to come down this valley we're lying in, and over that edge there. Then the valley subsided, or the mountain rose or the climate changed. All the slopes below that cliff edge—any way down from here—brings you finally to a sheer cliff."

"How could the land raise that much?" murmured Maury, looking out and down at the green too far below to tell what it represented. Jeff shrugged.

"This is a bigger world than Earth—even if it's lighter," he said. "Possibly more liable to crustal distortion." He nodded at the peaks above them. "These are young mountains. Their height alone reflects the lesser gravity. That glacier up there couldn't have formed on that steep a slope on Earth."

"There's the Messenger," said Cal.

His deeper-toned voice brought them all around. He had been standing behind the rest, looking over their heads. He smiled a little dryly and sadly at the faint unanimous look of hostility on the faces of all but the Survey Leader's. He was unusual in the respect that he was so built as not to need their friendship. But he was a member of the Team as they were and he would have liked to have had that friendship—if it could have been had at any price short of changing his own naturally individualistic character.

"There's no hope of that," said Doug Kellas. "The Messenger was designed for launching from the ship in space. Even in spite of the lower gravity here, it'd never break loose of the planet."

The Messenger was an emergency device every ship carried. It was essentially a miniature ship in itself, with drive unit and controls for one shift through no-time and an attached propulsive unit to kick it well clear of any gravitic field that might inhibit the shift into no-time. It could be set with the location of a ship wishing to send a message back to Earth, and with the location of Earth at the moment of arrival—both figured in terms of angle and distance from the theoretical centerpoint of the galaxy, as determined by ship's observations. It would set off, translate itself through no-time in one jump back to a reception area just outside Earth's critical gravitic field, and there be picked up with the message it contained.

For the *Harrier* team, this message could tell of the aliens and call for rescue. All that was needed was the precise information concerning the *Harrier's* location in relation to Galactic Centerpoint and Earth's location.

In the present instance, this was no problem. The ship's computer log developed the known position and movement of Earth with regard to Centerpoint, with every shift and movement of the ship. And the position of the second planet of star K94 was known to the chartmakers of Earth recorded by last observation aboard the *Harrier*.

Travel in no-time made no difficulty of distance. In no-time all points coincided, and the ship was theoretically touching them all. Distance was not important, but location was. And a precise location was impossible—the very time taken to calculate it would be enough to render it impossibly inaccurate. What ships travelling by no-time operated on were calculations approximately as correct as possible—*and leave a safety factor,* read the rulebook.

Calculate not to the destination, but to a point safely short enough of it, so that the predictable error will not bring the ship out in the center of some solid body. Calculate safely short of the distance remaining . . . and so on by smaller and smaller jumps to a safe conclusion.

But that was with men aboard. With a mechanical unit like the Messenger, a one-jump risk could be taken.

The *Harrier* had the figures to risk it—but a no-time drive could not operate within the critical area of a gravitic field like this planet's. And, as Jeff had said, the propulsive unit of the Messenger was not powerful enough to take off from this mountainside and fight its way to escape from the planet.

"That was one of the first things I figured," said Jeff, now.

"We're more than four miles above this world's sea-level, but it isn't enough. There's too much atmosphere still above us."

"The Messenger's only two and a half feet long put together," said Maury. "It only weighs fifteen pounds earthside. Can't we send it up on a balloon or something? Did you think of that?"

"Yes," said Jeff. "We can't calculate exactly the time it would take for a balloon to drift to a firing altitude, and we have to know the time to set the destination controls. We can't improvise any sort of a booster propulsion unit for fear of jarring or affecting the destination controls. The Messenger is meant to be handled carefully and used in just the way it's designed to be used, and that's all." He looked around at them. "Remember, the first rule of a Survey Ship is that it never lands anywhere but Earth."

"Still," said Cal, who had been calmly waiting while they talked this out, "we can make the Messenger work."

"How?" challenged Doug, turning on him. "Just how?"

Cal turned and pointed to the wind-piping battlemented peaks of the mountain looming far above.

"I did some calculating myself," he said. "If we climb up there and send the Messenger off from the top, it'll break free and go."

None of the rest of them said anything for a moment. They had all turned and were looking up the steep slope of the mountain, at the cliffs, the glacier where no glacier should be able to hang, and the peaks.

"Any of you had any mountain-climbing experience?" asked Joe.

"There was a rock-climbing club at the University I went to," said Cal. "They used to practice on the rock walls of the bluffs on the St. Croix River—that's about sixty miles west of Minneapolis and St. Paul. I went out with them a few times."

No one else said anything. Now they were looking at Cal.

"And," said Joe, "as our nearest thing to an expert, you

think that—" he nodded to the mountain—"can be climbed carrying the Messenger along?"

Cal nodded.

"Yes," he said slowly. "I think it can. I'll carry the Messenger myself. We'll have to make ourselves some equipment in the tool shop, here at the ship. And I'll need help going up the mountain."

"How many?" said Joe.

"Three." Cal looked around at them as he called their names. "Maury, Jeff and Doug. All the able-bodied we've got."

Joe was growing paler with the effort of the conversation.

"What about John?" he asked looking past Doug at John Martin, Number Nine of the Survey Team. John was a short, rugged man with wiry hair—but right now his face was almost as pale as Joe's, and his warmsuit bulged over the chest.

"John got slashed up when he tried to pull the alien off you," said Cal calmly. "Just before I shot. He got it clear across the pectoral muscles at the top of his chest. He's no use to me."

"I'm all right," whispered John. It hurt him even to breathe and he winced in spite of himself at the effort of talking.

"Not all right to climb a mountain," said Cal. "I'll take Maury, Jeff and Doug."

"All right. Get at it then." Joe made a little, awkward gesture with his hand, and Maury stooped to help pull the pillows from behind him and help him lie down. "All of you—get on with it."

"Come with me," said Cal. "I'll show you what we're going to have to build ourselves in the tool shop."

"I'll be right with you," said Maury. The others went off. Maury stood looking down at Joe. They had been friends and teammates for some years.

"Shoot," whispered Joe weakly, staring up at him. "Get it off your chest, whatever it is, Maury." The effort of the last few minutes was beginning to tell on Joe. It seemed to him the

bed rocked with a seasick motion beneath him, and he longed
for sleep.

"You want Cal to be in charge?" said Maury, staring down
at him.

Joe lifted his head from the pillow. He blinked and made an
effort and the bed stopped moving for a moment under him.

"You don't think Cal should be?" he said.

Maury simply looked down at him without words. When
men work and sometimes die together as happens with tight
units like a Survey Team, there is generally a closeness
amongst them. This closeness, or the lack of it, is something
that is not easily talked about by the men concerned.

"All right," Joe said. "Here's my reasons for putting him in
charge of this. In the first place he's the only one who's done
any climbing. Secondly, I think the job is one he deserves." Joe
looked squarely back up at the man who was his best friend on
the Team. "Maury, you and the rest don't understand Cal. I
do. I know that country he was brought up in and I've had
access to his personal record. You all blame him for something he can't help."

"He's never made any attempt to fit in with the Team—"

"He's not built to fit himself into things. Maury—" Joe struggled up on one elbow. "He's built to make things fit him. Listen, Maury—he's bright enough, isn't he?"

"I'll give him that," said Maury, grudgingly.

"All right," said Joe. "Now listen. I'm going to violate Department rules and tell you a little bit about what made him
what he is. Did you know Cal never saw the inside of a formal
school until he was sixteen—and then the school was a university? The uncle and aunt who brought him up in the old
voyageur's-trail area of the Minnesota-Canadian border were
just brilliant enough and nutty enough to get Cal certified for
home education. The result was Cal grew up in the open
woods, in a tight little community that was the whole world,
as far as he was concerned. And that world was com-

pletely indestructible, reasonable and handlable by young Cal Hartlett."

"But—"

"Let me talk, Maury. I'm going to this much trouble," said Joe, with effort, "to convince you of something important. Add that background to Cal's natural intellect and you get a very unusual man. Do you happen to be able to guess what Cal's individual sense of security rates out at on the psych profile?"

"I suppose it's high," said Maury.

"It isn't simply high—it just isn't," Joe said. "He's off the scale. When he showed up at the University of Minnesota at sixteen and whizzed his way through a special ordering of entrance exams, the psychology department there wanted to put him in a cage with the rest of the experimental animals. He couldn't see it. He refused politely, took his bachelor's degree and went into Survey Studies. And here he is." Joe paused. "That's why he's going to be in charge. These aliens we've bumped into could be the one thing the human race can't match. We've got to get word home. And to get word home, we've got to get someone with the Messenger to the top of that mountain."

He stopped talking. Maury stood there.

"You understand me, Maury?" said Joe. "I'm Survey Leader. It's my responsibility. And in my opinion if there's one man who can get the Messenger to the top of the mountain, it's Cal."

The bed seemed to make a slow half-swing under him suddenly. He lost his balance. He toppled back off the support of his elbow, and the sky overhead beyond the bubble began to rotate slowly around him and things blurred.

Desperately he fought to hold on to consciousness. He had to convince Maury, he thought. If he could convince Maury, the others would fall in line. He knew what was wrong with them in their feelings toward Cal as a leader. It was the fact that the mountain was unclimbable. Anyone could see it was unclimbable. But Cal was going to climb it anyway, they all knew that, and in climbing it he would probably require the lives of the men who went with him.

They would not have minded that if he had been one of them. But he had always stood apart, and it was a cold way to give your life—for a man whom you had never understood, or been able to get close to.

"Maury," he choked. "Try to see it from Cal's—try to see it from his—"

The sky spun into a blur. The world blurred and tilted.

"Orders," Joe croaked at Maury. "Cal—command—"

"Yes," said Maury, pressing him back down on the bed as he tried blindly to sit up again. "All right. All right, Joe. Lie still. He'll have the command. He'll be in charge and we'll all follow him. I promise . . ."

IV

During the next two days, the Survey Leader was only intermittently conscious. His fever ran to dangerous levels, and several times he trembled and jerked as if on the verge of going into convulsions. John Martin also, although he was conscious and able to move around and even do simple tasks, was pale, high-fevered and occasionally thick-tongued for no apparent reason. It seemed possible there was an infective agent in the claw and teeth wounds made by the alien, with which the ship's medicines were having trouble coping.

With the morning of the third day when the climbers were about to set out both men showed improvement.

The Survey Leader came suddenly back to clear-headedness as Cal and the three others were standing, all equipped in the bubble, ready to leave. They had been discussing last-minute warnings and advices with a pale but alert John Martin when Joe's voice entered the conversation.

"What?" it said. "Who's alive? What was that?"

They turned and saw him propped up on one elbow on his makeshift bed. They had left him on it since the sleeping quarters section of the ship had been completely destroyed, and the sections left unharmed were too full of equipment to make practical places for the care of a wounded man. Now they saw his eyes taking in their respirator masks, packs, hammers, the homemade pitons and hammers, and other equipment including rope, slung about them.

"What did one of you say?" Joe demanded again. "What was it?"

"Nothing, Joe," said John Martin, coming toward him. "Lie down."

Joe waved him away, frowning. "Something about one being still alive. One what?"

Cal looked down at him. Joe's face had grown lean and fallen in even in these few days but the eyes in the face were sensible.

"He should know," Cal said. His calm, hard, oddly carrying baritone quieted them all. "He's still Survey Leader." He looked around at the rest but no one challenged his decision. He turned and went into the corridor of the ship, down to the main control room, took several photo prints from a drawer and brought them back. When he got back out, he found Joe now propped up on pillows but waiting.

"Here," said Cal, handing Joe the photos. "We sent survey rockets with cameras over the ridge up there for a look at the other side of the mountain. That top picture shows you what they saw."

Joe looked down at the top picture that showed a stony mountainside steeper than the one the *Harrier* lay on. On this rocky slope was what looked like the jagged, broken-off end of a blackened oil drum—with something white spilled out on the rock by the open end of the drum.

"That's what's left of the alien ship," said Cal. "Look at the closeup on the next picture."

Joe discarded the top photo and looked at the one beneath. Enlarged in the second picture he saw that the white something was the body of an alien, lying sprawled out and stiff.

"He's dead, all right," said Cal. "He's been dead a day or two anyway. But take a good look at the whole scene and tell me how it strikes you."

Joe stared at the photo with concentration. For a long moment he said nothing. Then he shook his head, slowly.

"Something's phony," he said at last, huskily.

"I think so too," said Cal. He sat down on the makeshift bed beside Joe and his weight tilted the wounded man a little toward him. He pointed to the dead alien. "Look at him. He's got nothing in the way of a piece of equipment he was trying to put outside the ship before he died. And that mountainside's as bare as ours. There was no place for him to go outside the ship that made any sense as a destination if he was that close to dying. And if you're dying on a strange world, do you crawl *out* of the one familiar place that's there with you?"

"Not if you're human," said Doug Kellas behind Cal's shoulder. There was the faintly hostile note in Doug's voice still. "There could be a dozen different reasons we don't know anything about. Maybe it's taboo with them to die inside a spaceship. Maybe he was having hallucinations at the end, that home was just beyond the open end of the ship. Anything."

Cal did not bother to turn around.

"It's possible you're right, Doug," he said. "They're about our size physically and their ship was less than half the size of the *Harrier*. Counting this one in the picture and the three that fell with the one that we killed here, accounts for five of them. But just suppose there were six. And the sixth one hauled the body of this one outside in case we came around for a look—just to give us a false sense of security thinking they were all gone."

Joe nodded slowly. He put the photos down on the bed and looked at Cal who stood up.

"You're carrying guns?" said Joe. "You're all armed in case?"

"We're starting out with sidearms," said Cal. "Down here the weight of them doesn't mean much. But up there . . ."

He nodded to the top reaches of the mountain and did not finish. "But you and John better move inside the ship nights and keep your eyes open in the day."

"We will." Joe reached up a hand and Cal shook it. Joe shook hands with the other three who were going. They put their masks on.

"The rest of you ready?" asked Cal, who by this time was already across the bubble enclosure, ready to step out. His voice came hollowly through his mask. The others broke away from Joe and went toward Cal, who stepped through the bubble.

"Wait!" said Joe suddenly from the bed. They turned to him. He lay propped up, and his lips moved for a second as if he was hunting for words. "—Good luck!" he said at last.

"Thanks," said Cal for all of them. "To you and John, too. We'll all need it."

He raised a hand in farewell. They turned and went.

They went away from the ship, up the steep slope of the old glacier stream bed that became more steep as they climbed. Cal was in the lead with Maury, then Jeff, then Doug bringing up the rear. The yellow bright rays of K94 struck back at them from the ice-scoured granite surface of the slope, gray with white veinings of quartz. The warmsuits were designed to cool as well as heat their wearers, but they had been designed for observer-wearers, not working wearers. At the bend-spots of arm and leg joints, the soft interior cloth of the warmsuits soon became damp with sweat as the four men toiled upward. And the cooling cycle inside the suits made these damp spots clammy-feeling when they touched the wearer. The respirator masks also became slippery with perspiration where the soft, elastic rims of their transparent faceplates pressed against brow and cheek and chin. And to the equipment-heavy men the *feel* of the angle of the steep rock slope seemed treacherously less than eyes trained to Earth gravity reported it. Like a subtly tilted floor in a fun house at an amusement park.

They climbed upward in silence as the star that was larger than the sun of Earth climbed in the sky at their backs. They moved almost mechanically, wrapped in their own thoughts. What the other three thought were personal, private thoughts having no bearing on the moment. But Cal in the lead, his strong-boned, rectangular face expressionless, was wrapped up in two calculations. Neither of these had anything to do with the angle of the slope or the distance to the top of the mountain.

He was calculating what strains the human material walking behind him would be able to take. He would need more than their grudging cooperation. And there was something else.

He was thinking about water.

Most of the load carried by each man was taken up with items constructed to be almost miraculously light and compact for the job they would do. One exception was the fifteen Earth pounds of components of the Messenger, which Cal himself carried in addition to his mountain-climbing equipment—the homemade crampons, pitons and ice axe-piton hammer—and his food and the sonic pistol at his belt. Three others were the two-gallon containers of water carried by each of the other three men. Compact rations of solid food they all carried, and in a pinch they could go hungry. But to get to the top of the mountain they would need water.

Above them were ice slopes, and the hook-shaped glacier that they had been able to see from the ship below.

That the ice could be melted to make drinking water was beyond question. Whether that water would be safe to drink was something else. There had been the case of another Survey ship on another world whose melted local ice water had turned out to contain as a deposited impurity a small wind-born organism that came to life in the inner warmth of men's bodies and attacked the walls of their digestive tracts. To play safe here, the glacier ice would have to be distilled.

Again, one of the pieces of compact equipment Cal himself

carried was a miniature still. But would he still have it by the time they reached the glacier? They were all ridiculously overloaded now.

Of that overload, only the Messenger itself and the climbing equipment, mask and warmsuit had to be held on to at all costs. The rest could and probably would go. They would probably have to take a chance on the melted glacier ice. If the chance went against them—how much water would be needed to go the rest of the way?

Two men at least would have to be supplied. Only two men helping each other could make it all the way to the top. A single climber would have no chance.

Cal calculated in his head and climbed. They all climbed.

From below, the descending valley stream bed of the former glacier had looked like not too much of a climb. Now that they were on it, they were beginning to appreciate the tricks the eye could have played upon it by sloping distances in a lesser gravity, where everything was constructed to a titanic scale. They were like ants inching up the final stories of the Empire State Building.

Every hour they stopped and rested for ten minutes. And it was nearly seven hours later, with K94 just approaching its noon above them, that they came at last to the narrowed end of the ice-smoothed rock, and saw, only a few hundred yards ahead, the splintered and niched vertical rock wall they would have to climb to the foot of the hook-shaped glacier.

v

They stopped to rest before tackling the distance between them and the foot of the rock wall. They sat in a line on the bare rock, facing downslope, their packloads leaned back against the higher rock. Cal heard the sound of the others breathing heavily in their masks, and the voice of Maury came somewhat hollowly through the diaphragm of his mask.

138 THE STAR ROAD

"Lots of loose rock between us and that cliff," said the older man. "What do you suppose put it there?"

"It's talus," answered Jeff Ramsey's mask-hollowed voice from the far end of the line. "Weathering—heat differences, or maybe even ice from snowstorms during the winter season getting in cracks of that rock face, expanding, and cracking off the sedimentary rock it's constructed of. All that weathering's made the wall full of wide cracks and pockmarks, see?"

Cal glanced over his shoulder.

"Make it easy to climb," he said. And heard the flat sound of his voice thrown back at him inside his mask. "Let's get going. Everybody up!"

They got creakily and protestingly to their feet. Turning, they fell into line and began to follow Cal into the rock debris, which thickened quickly until almost immediately they were walking upon loose rock flakes any size up to that of a garage door, that slipped or slid unexpectedly under their weight and the angle of this slope that would not have permitted such an accumulation under Earth's greater gravity.

"Watch it!" Cal threw back over his shoulder at the others. He had nearly gone down twice when loose rock under his weight threatened to start a miniature avalanche among the surrounding rock. He labored on up the talus slope, hearing the men behind swearing and sliding as they followed.

"Spread out!" he called back. "So you aren't one behind the other—and stay away from the bigger rocks."

These last were a temptation. Often as big as a small platform, they looked like rafts floating on top of the smaller shards of rock, the similarity heightened by the fact that the rock of the cliff-face was evidently planar in structure. Nearly all the rock fragments split off had flat faces. The larger rocks seemed to offer a temptingly clear surface on which to get away from the sliding depth of smaller pieces in which the boots of the men's warmsuits went mid-leg deep with each sliding step. But the big fragments, Cal had already discovered, were generally in precarious balance on the loose rock below them and the angled slope. The lightest step upon them was often enough to make them turn and slide.

He had hardly called the warning before there was a choked-off yell from behind him and the sound of more-than-ordinary roaring and sliding of rock.

He spun around. With the masked figures of Maury on his left and Doug on his right he went scrambling back toward Jeff Ramsey, who was lying on his back, half-buried in rock fragments and all but underneath a ten by six foot slab of rock that now projected reeflike from the smaller rock pieces around it.

Jeff did not stir as they came up to him, though he seemed conscious. Cal was first to reach him. He bent over the blond-topped young man and saw through the faceplate of the respirator mask how Jeff's lips were sucked in at the corners and the skin showed white in a circle around his tight mouth.

"My leg's caught." The words came tightly and hollowly through the diaphragm of Jeff's mask. "I think something's wrong with it."

Carefully, Cal and the others dug the smaller rock away. Jeff's right leg was pinned down under an edge of the big rock slab. By extracting the rock underneath it piece by piece, they got the leg loose. But it was bent in a way it should not have been.

"Can you move it?"

Jeff's face stiffened and beaded with sweat behind the mask faceplate.

"No."

"It's broken, all right," said Maury. "One down already," he added bitterly. He had already gone to work, making a splint from two tent poles out of Jeff's pack. He looked up at Cal as he worked, squatting beside Jeff. "What do we do now, Cal? We'll have to carry him back down?"

"No," said Cal. He rose to his feet. Shading his eyes against the sun overhead he looked down the hanging valley to the *Harrier,* tiny below them.

They had already used up nearly an hour floundering over the loose rock, where one step forward often literally had meant two steps sliding backward. His timetable, based on his water supplies, called for them to be at the foot of the ice slope leading to the hook glacier before camping for the night—and it was already noon of the long local day.

"Jeff," he said. "You're going to have to get back down to the *Harrier* by yourself." Maury started to protest, then shut up. Cal could see the other men looking at him.

Jeff nodded. "All right," he said. "I can make it. I can roll most of the way." He managed a grin.

"How's the leg feel?"

"Not bad, Cal." Jeff reached out a warmsuited hand and felt the leg gingerly. "More numb than anything right now."

"Take his load off," said Cal to Doug. "And give him your morphine pack as well as his own. We'll pad that leg and wrap it the best we can, Jeff, but it's going to be giving you a rough time before you get it back to the ship."

"I could go with him to the edge of the loose rock—" began Doug, harshly.

"No. I don't need you. Downhill's going to be easy," said Jeff.

"That's right," said Cal. "But even if he did need you, you couldn't go, Doug. *I* need you to get to the top of that mountain."

They finished wrapping and padding the broken leg with one of the pup tents and Jeff started off, half-sliding, half dragging himself downslope through the loose rock fragments.

They watched him for a second. Then, at Cal's order, they turned heavily back to covering the weary, strugglesome distance that still separated them from the foot of the rock face.

They reached it at last and passed into the shadow at its base. In the sunlight of the open slope the warmsuits had struggled to cool them. In the shadow, abruptly, the process went the other way. The cliff of the rock face was about two hundred feet in height, leading up to that same ridge over which the weather balloon had been sent to take pictures of the fragment of alien ship on the other side of the mountain. Between the steep rock walls at the end of the glacial valley, the rock face was perhaps fifty yards wide. It was torn and pocked and furrowed vertically by the splitting off of rock from it. It looked like a great chunk of plank standing on end, weathered along the lines of its vertical grain into a decayed roughness of surface.

The rock face actually leaned back a little from the vertical, but, looking up at it from its foot, it seemed not only to go straight up, but—if you looked long enough—to overhang, as if it might come down on the heads of the three men. In the shadowed depths of vertical cracks and holes, dark ice clung.

Cal turned to look back the way they had come. Angling down away behind them, the hanging valley looked like a giant's ski-jump. A small, wounded creature that was the shape of Jeff was dragging itself down the slope, and a child's toy, the shape of the *Harrier*, lay forgotten at the jump's foot.

Cal turned back to the cliff and said to the others, "Rope up."

He had already shown them how this was to be done, and they had practiced it back at the *Harrier*. They tied themselves together with the length of sounding line, the thinness of which Cal had previously padded and thickened so that a man could wrap it around himself to belay another climber without being cut in half. There was no worry about the strength of the sounding line.

"All right," said Cal, when they were tied together—himself in the lead, Maury next, Doug at the end. "Watch where I put my hands and feet as I climb. Put yours in exactly the same places."

"How'll I know when to move?" Doug asked hollowly through his mask.

"Maury'll wave you on, as I'll wave him on," said Cal. Already they were high enough up for the whistling winds up on the mountain peak to interfere with mask-impeded conversations conducted at a distance. "You'll find this cliff is easier than it looks. Remember what I told you about handling the rope. And don't look down."

"All right."

Cal had picked out a wide rock chimney rising twenty feet to a little ledge of rock. The inner wall of the chimney was studded with projections on which his hands and feet could find purchase. He began to climb.

When he reached the ledge he was pleasantly surprised to find that, in spite of his packload, the lesser gravity had allowed him to make the climb without becoming winded. Maury, he knew, would not be so fortunate. Doug, being the younger man and in better condition, should have less trouble, which was why he had put Doug at the end, so that they would have the weak man between them.

Now Cal stood up on the ledge, braced himself against the rock wall at his back and belayed the rope by passing it over his left shoulder, around his body and under his right arm.

He waved Maury to start climbing. The older man moved to the wall and began to pull himself up as Cal took in the slack of the rope between them.

Maury climbed slowly but well, testing each hand and foothold before he trusted his weight to it. In a little while he was beside Cal on the ledge, and the ascent of Doug began. Doug climbed more swiftly, also without incident. Shortly they were all on the ledge.

Cal had mapped out his climb on this rock face before they had left, studying the cliff with powerful glasses from the *Harrier* below. Accordingly, he now made a traverse, moving horizontally across the rock face to another of the deep, vertical clefts in the rock known as chimneys to climbers. Here he belayed the rope around a projection and, by gesture and shout, coached Maury along the route.

Maury, and then Doug, crossed without trouble.

Cal then led the way up the second chimney, wider than the first and deeper. This took them up another forty-odd feet to a ledge on which all three men could stand or sit together.

Cal was still not winded. But looking at the other two, he saw that Maury was damp-faced behind the faceplate of his mask. The older man's breath was whistling in the respirator. It was time, thought Cal, to lighten loads. He had never expected to get far with some of their equipment in any case, but he had wanted the psychological advantage of starting the others out with everything needful.

"Maury," he said, "I think we'll leave your sidearm here, and some of the other stuff you're carrying."

"I can carry it," said Maury. "I don't need special favors."

"No," said Cal. "You'll leave it. I'm the judge of what's ahead of us, and in my opinion the time to leave it's now." He helped Maury off with most of what he carried, with the exception of a pup tent, his climbing tools and the water container and field rations. Then as soon as Maury was rested, they tackled the first of the two really difficult stretches of the cliff.

This was a ten-foot traverse that any experienced climber would not have found worrisome. To amateurs like themselves it was spine-chilling.

The route to be taken was to the left and up to a large, flat piece of rock wedged in a wide crack running diagonally up the rock face almost to its top. There were plenty of available footrests and handholds along the way. What would bother them was the fact that the path they had to take was around a boss, or protuberance of rock. To get around the boss it was necessary to move out over the empty atmosphere of a clear drop to the talus slope below.

Cal went first.

He made his way slowly but carefully around the outcurve of the rock, driving in one of his homemade pitons and attaching an equally homemade snap-ring to it, at the outermost point in the traverse. Passing the line that connected him to Maury through this, he had a means of holding the other men to the cliff if their holds should slip and they have to depend on the rope on their way around. The snap-ring and piton were also a psychological assurance.

Arrived at the rock slab in the far crack, out of sight of the other two, Cal belayed the rope and gave two tugs. A second later a tug came back. Maury had started crossing the traverse.

He was slow, very slow, about it. After agonizing minutes Cal saw Maury's hand come around the edge of the boss. Slowly he passed the projecting rock to the rock slab. His face was pale and rigid when he got to where Cal stood. His breath came in short, quick pants.

Cal signaled on the rope again. In considerably less time than Maury had taken Doug came around the boss. There was a curious look on his face.

"What is it?" asked Cal.

Doug glanced back the way he had come. "Nothing, I guess," he said. "I just thought I saw something moving back there. Just before I went around the corner. Something I couldn't make out."

Cal stepped to the edge of the rock slab and looked as far back around the boss as he could. But the ledge they had come from was out of sight. He stepped back to the ledge.

"Well," he said to the others, "the next stretch is easier."

VI

It was. The crack up which they climbed now slanted to the right at an almost comfortable angle.

They went up it using hands and feet like climbing a ladder. But if it was easy, it was also long, covering better than a hundred feet of vertical rock face. At the top, where the crack pinched out, there was the second tricky traverse across the rock face, of some eight feet. Then a short climb up a cleft and they stood together on top of the ridge.

Down below, they had been hidden by the mountain walls from the high winds above. Now for the first time, as they emerged onto the ridge they faced and felt them.

The warmsuits cut out the chill of the atmosphere whistling down on them from the mountain peak, but they could feel the pressure of it molding the suits to their bodies. They stood now once more in sunlight. Behind them they could see the hanging valley and the *Harrier*. Ahead was a cwm, a hollow in the steep mountainside that they would have to cross to get to a further ridge leading up to the mountain peak. Beyond and below the further ridge, they could see the far, sloping side of the mountain and, black against it, the tiny, oil-drum-end fragment of alien ship with a dot of white just outside it.

"We'll stay roped," said Cal. He pointed across the steep-sloping hollow they would need to cross to reach the further rocky ridge. The hollow seemed merely a tilted area with occasional large rock chunks perched on it at angles that to Earth eyes seemed to defy gravity. But there was a high shine where the sun's rays struck.

"Is that ice?" said Maury, shading his eyes.

"Patches of it. A thin coating over the rocks," said Cal. "It's time to put on the crampons."

They sat down and attached the metal frameworks to their boots that provided them with spiked footing. They drank sparingly of the water they carried and ate some of their rations. Cal glanced at the descending sun, and the blue-black sky above them. They would have several hours yet to cross the cwm, in daylight. He gave the order to go, and led off.

He moved carefully out across the hollow, cutting or kicking footholds in patches of ice he could not avoid. The slope was like a steep roof. As they approached the deeper center of the cwm, the wind from above seemed to be funnelled at them so that it was like a hand threatening to push them into a fall.

Some of the rock chunks they passed were as large as small houses. It was possible to shelter from the wind in their lees. At the same time, they often hid the other two from Cal's sight, and this bothered him. He would have preferred to be able to watch them in their crossings of the ice patches, so that if one of them started to slide he would be prepared to belay the rope. As it was, in the constant moan and howl of the wind, his first warning would be the sudden strain on the rope itself. And if one of them fell and pulled the other off the mountainside, their double weight could drag Cal loose.

Not for the first time, Cal wished that the respirator masks they wore had been equipped with radio intercom. But these were not and there had been no equipment aboard the *Harrier* to convert them.

They were a little more than halfway across when Cal felt a tugging on the line.

He looked back. Maury was waving him up into a shelter of one of the big rocks. He waved back and turned off from the direct path, crawling up into the ice-free overhang. Behind him, as he turned, he saw Maury coming toward him, and behind Maury, Doug.

"Doug wants to tell you something!" Maury shouted against the wind noise, putting his mask up close to Cal's.

"What is it?" Cal shouted.

"—Saw it again!" came Doug's answer.

"Something moving?" Doug nodded. "Behind us?" Doug's mask rose and fell again in agreement. "Was it one of the aliens?"

"I think so!" shouted Doug. "It could be some sort of animal. It was moving awfully fast—I just got a glimpse of it!"

"Was it—" Doug shoved his masked face closer, and Cal raised his voice—"was it wearing any kind of clothing that you could see?"

"No!" Doug's head shook back and forth.

"What kind of life could climb around up here without freezing to death—unless it had some protection?" shouted Maury to them both.

"We don't know!" Cal answered. "Let's not take chances. If it is an alien, he's got all the natural advantages. Don't take chances. You've got your gun, Doug. Shoot anything you see moving!"

Doug grinned and looked harshly at Cal from inside his mask.

"Don't worry about me!" he shouted back. "Maury's the one without a gun."

"We'll both keep an eye on Maury! Let's get going now. There's only about another hour or so before the sun goes behind those other mountains—and we want to be in camp underneath the far ridge before dark!"

He led off again and the other two followed.

As they approached the far ridge, the wind seemed to lessen somewhat. This was what Cal had been hoping for—that the far ridge would give them some protection from the assault of the atmosphere they had been enduring in the open. The dark wall of the ridge, some twenty or thirty feet in sudden height at the edge of the cwm, was now only a hundred yards or so away. It was already in shadow from the descending sun, as were the downslope sides of the big rock chunks. Long shadows stretched toward a far precipice edge where the cwm ended, several thousand feet below. But the open icy spaces were now ruddy and brilliant with the late sunlight. Cal though wearily of the pup tents and his sleeping bag.

Without warning a frantic tugging on the rope roused him. He jerked around, and saw Maury, less than fifteen feet behind him, gesturing back the way they had come. Behind Maury, the rope to Doug led out of sight around the base of one of the rock chunks.

Then suddenly Doug slid into view.

Automatically Cal's leg muscles spasmed tight, to take the sudden jerk of the rope when Doug's falling body should draw it taut. But the jerk never came.

Sliding, falling, gaining speed as he descended the rooftop-steep slope of the cwm, Doug's body no longer had the rope attached to it. The rope still lay limp on the ground behind Maury. And then Cal saw something he had not seen before. The dark shape of Doug was not falling like a man who finds himself sliding down two thousand feet to eternity. It was making no attempt to stop its slide at all. It fell limply, loosely, like a dead man—and indeed, just at that moment, it slid far upon a small, round boulder in his path which tossed it into the air like a stuffed dummy, arms and legs asprawl, and it came down indifferently upon the slope beyond and continued, gaining speed as it went.

Cal and Maury stood watching. There was nothing else they could do. They saw the dark shape speeding on and on, until finally it was lost for good among the darker shapes of the boulders farther on down the cwm. They were left without knowing whether it came eventually to rest against some rock, or continued on at last to fall from the distant edge of the precipice to the green, unknown depth that was far below them.

After a little while Maury stopped looking. He turned and climbed on until he had caught up with Cal. His eyes were accusing as he pulled in the loose rope to which Doug had been attached. They looked at it together.

The rope's end had been cut as cleanly as any knife could have cut it.

The sun was just touching the further mountains. They turned without speaking and climbed on to the foot of the ridge wall.

Here the rocks were free of ice. They set up a single pup tent and crawled into it with their sleeping bags together, as the sun went down and darkness flooded their barren and howling perch on the mountainside.

VII

They took turns sitting up in their sleeping bags, in the darkness of their tiny tent, with Cal's gun ready in hand.

Lying there in the darkness, staring at the invisible tent roof nine inches above his nose, Cal recognized that in theory the aliens could simply be better than humans—and that was that. But, Cal, being the unique sort of man he was, found that he could not believe such theory.

And so, being the unique sort of man he was, he discarded it. He made a mental note to go on trying to puzzle out the alien's vulnerability tomorrow . . . and closing his eyes, fell into a light doze that was the best to be managed in the way of sleep.

When dawn began to lighten the walls of their tent they managed, with soup powder, a little of their precious water and a chemical thermal unit, to make some hot soup and get it into them. It was amazing what a difference this made, after the long, watchful and practically sleepless night. They put some of their concentrated dry rations into their stomachs on top of the soup and Cal unpacked and set up the small portable still.

He took the gun and his ice-hammer and crawled outside the tent. In the dawnlight and the tearing wind he sought ice which they could melt and then distill to replenish their containers of drinking water. But the only ice to be seen within any reasonable distance of their tent was the thin ice-glaze— *verglas,* mountaineers back on Earth called it—over which they had struggled in crossing the cwm the day before. And Cal dared not take their only gun too far from Maury, in case the alien made a sudden attack on the tent.

There was more than comradeship involved. Alone, Cal knew, there would indeed be no hope of his getting the Messenger to the mountaintop. Not even the alien could do that job alone—and so the alien's strategy must be to frustrate the human party's attempt to send a message.

It could not be doubted that the alien realized what their reason was for trying to climb the mountain. A race whose spaceships made use of the principle of no-time in their drives, who was equipped for war, and who responded to attack with the similarities shown so far, would not have a hard time figuring out why the human party was carrying the equipment on Cal's pack up the side of a mountain.

More, the alien, had he had a companion, would probably have been trying to get message equipment of his own up into favorable dispatching position. Lacking a companion his plan must be to frustrate the human effort. That put the humans at an additional disadvantage. They were the defenders, and could only wait for the attacker to choose the time and place of his attempt against them.

And it would not have to be too successful an attempt, at that. It would not be necessary to kill either Cal or Maury, now that Doug was gone. To cripple one of them enough so that he could not climb and help his companion climb, would be enough. In fact, if one of them were crippled Cal doubted even that they could make it back to the *Harrier*. The alien then could pick them off at leisure.

Engrossed in his thoughts, half-deafened by the ceaseless wind, Cal woke suddenly to the vibration of something thundering down on him.

He jerked his head to stare upslope—and scrambled for his life. It was like a dream, with everything in slow motion —and one large chunk of rock with its small host of lesser rocks roaring down upon him.

Then—somehow—he was clear. The miniature avalanche went crashing by him, growing to a steady roar as it grew in size sweeping down alongside the ridge. Cal found himself at the tent, from which Maury was half-emerged, on hands and knees, staring down at the avalanche.

Cal swore at himself. It was something he had been told, and had forgotten. Such places as they had camped in last night were natural funnels for avalanches of loose rock. So, he remembered now, were wide cracks like the sloping one in the cliff face they had climbed up yesterday—as, indeed, the cwm itself was on a large scale. And they had crossed the cwm in late afternoon, when the heat of the day would have been most likely to loosen the frost that held precariously balanced rocks in place.

Only fool luck had gotten them this far!

"Load up!" he shouted to Maury. "We've got to get out of here."

Maury had already seen that for himself. They left the pup-tent standing. The tent in Cal's load would do. With that the Messenger, their climbing equipment, their sleeping bags and their food and water, they began to climb the steeply sloping wall of the ridge below which they had camped. Before they were halfway up it, another large rock with its attendant avalanche of lesser rocks came by below them.

Whether the avalanches were alien-started, or the result of natural causes, made no difference now. They had learned their lesson the hard way. From now on, Cal vowed silently, they would stick to the bare and open ridges unless there was absolutely no alternative to entering avalanche territory. And only after every precaution.

In the beginning Cal had kept a fairly regular check on how Maury was doing behind him. But as the sun rose in the bluish-black of the high altitude sky overhead the weariness of his body seemed to creep into his mind and dull it. He still turned his head at regular intervals to see how Maury was doing. But sometimes he found himself sitting and staring at his companion without any real comprehension of why he should be watching over him.

The blazing furnace of K94 overhead, climbing toward its noontime zenith, contributed to this dullness of the mind. So did the ceaseless roaring of the wind which had long since deafened them beyond any attempt at speech. As the star overhead got higher in the sky this and the wind noise combined to produce something close to hallucinations . . . so that once he looked back and for a moment seemed to see the alien following them, not astraddle the ridge and hunching themselves forward as they were, but walking along the knive-edge of rock like a monkey along a branch, foot over foot, and grasping the rock with toes like fingers, oblivious of the wind and the sun.

Cal blinked and, the illusion—if that was what it was—was gone. But its image lingered in his brain with the glare of the sun and the roar of the wind.

His eyes had fallen into the habit of focusing on the rock only a dozen feet ahead of him. At last he lifted them and saw the ridge broaden, a black shadow lying sharply across it. They had come to the rock walls below the hanging glacier they had named the Hook.

They stopped to rest in the relative wind-break shelter of the first wall, then went on.

Considering the easiness of the climb they made remarkably slow progress. Cal slowly puzzled over this until, like the slow brightening of a candle, the idea grew in him to check the absolute altimeter at his belt.

They were now nearly seven thousand feet higher up than they had been at the wreck of the *Harrier*. The mask respirators had been set to extract oxygen for them from the local atmosphere in accordance with the *Harrier* altitude. Pausing on a ledge, Cal adjusted his mask controls.

For a minute there seemed to be no difference at all. And then he began to come awake. His head cleared. He became sharply conscious, suddenly of where he stood—on a ledge of rock, surrounded by rock walls with, high overhead, the blue-black sky and brilliant sunlight on the higher walls. They were nearly at the foot of the third, and upper, battlement of the rock walls.

He looked over the edge at Maury, intending to signal the man to adjust his mask controls. Maury was not even looking up, a squat, lumpish figure in the warmsuit totally covered, with the black snout of the mask over his face. Cal tugged at the rope and the figure raised its face. Cal with his gloved hands made adjusting motions at the side of his mask. But the other's face below, hidden in the shadow of the faceplate, stared up without apparent comprehension. Cal started to yell down to him—here the wind noise was lessened to the point where a voice might have carried—and then thought better of it.

Instead he tugged on the rope in the signal they had repeated an endless number of times; and the figure below, foreshortened to smallness stood dully for a moment and then began to climb. His eyes sharpened by the fresh increase in the oxygen flow provided by his mask Cal watched that slow climb almost with amazement carefully taking in the rope and belaying it as the other approached.

There was a heaviness, an awkwardness, about the warmsuited limbs, as slowly—but strongly enough—they pulled the climber up toward Cal. There was something abnormal about their movement. As the other drew closer, Cal stared more and more closely until at last the gloves of the climber fastened over the edge of the ledge.

Cal bent to help him. But, head down not looking, the other hoisted himself up alongside Cal and a little turned away.

Then in that last instant the combined flood of instinct and a lifetime of knowledge cried certainty. And Cal knew.

The warmsuited figure beside him was Maury no longer.

VIII

Reflexes have been the saving of many a man's life. In this case, Cal had been all set to turn and climb again, the moment Maury stood beside him on the edge. Now recognizing that somewhere among these rocks, in the past fumbling hours of oxygen starvation, Maury had ceased to live and his place had been taken by the pursuing alien, Cal's reflexes took over.

If the alien had attacked the moment he stood upright on the ledge, different reflexes would have locked Cal in physical combat with the enemy. When the alien did not attack, Cal turned instinctively to the second prepared response of his body and began automatically to climb to the next ledge.

There was no doubt that any other action by Cal, any hesitation, any curiosity about his companion would have forced the alien into an immediate attack. For then there would have been no reason not to attack. As he climbed, Cal felt his human brain beginning to work again after the hours of dullness. He had time to think.

His first thought was to cut the line that bound them together, leaving the alien below. But this would precipitate the attack Cal had already instinctively avoided. Any place Cal could climb at all, the alien could undoubtedly climb with ease. Cal's mind chose and discarded possibilities. Suddenly he remembered the gun that hung innocently at his hip.

With that recollection, the situation began to clear and settle in his mind. The gun evened things. The knowledge that it was the alien on the other end of the rope, along with the gun, more than evened things. Armed and prepared, he could afford to risk the present situation for a while. He could play a game of pretense as well as the alien could, he thought.

That amazing emotional center of gravity, Cal's personal sense of security and adequacy that had so startled the psychology department at the university was once more in command of the situation. Cal felt the impact of the question—why was the alien pretending to be Maury? Why had he adapted himself to man-shape, put on man's clothes and fastened himself to the other end of Cal's climbing rope?

Perhaps the alien desired to study the last human that opposed him before he tried to destroy it. Perhaps he had some hope of rescue by his own people, and wanted all the knowledge for them he could get. If so it was a wish that cut two ways. Cal would not be sorry of the chance to study a living alien in action.

And when the showdown came—there was the gun at Cal's belt to offset the alien's awesome physical natural advantage.

They continued to climb. Cal watched the other figure below him. What he saw was not reassuring.

With each wall climbed, the illusion of humanity grew stronger. The clumsiness Cal had noticed at first—the appearance of heaviness—began to disappear. It began to take on a smoothness and a strength that Maury had never shown in the climbing. It began in fact, to look almost familiar. Now Cal could see manlike hunching and bulgings of the shoulder muscles under the warmsuit's shapelessness, as the alien climbed and a certain trick of throwing the head from right to left to keep a constant watch for a better route up the face of the rock wall.

It was what he did himself, Cal realized suddenly. The alien was watching Cal climb ahead of him and imitating even the smallest mannerisms of the human.

They were almost to the top of the battlements, climbing more and more in sunlight. K94 was already far down the slope of afternoon. Cal began to hear an increase in the wind noise as they drew close to the open area above. Up there was the tumbled rock-strewn ground of a terminal moraine and then the snow slope to the hook glacier.

Cal had planned to camp for the night above the moraine at the edge of the snow slope. Darkness was now only about an hour away and with darkness the showdown must come between himself and the alien. With the gun, Cal felt a fair amount of confidence. With the showdown, he would probably discover the reason for the alien's impersonation of Maury.

Now Cal pulled himself up the last few feet. At the top of the final wall of the battlements the windblast was strong. Cal found himself wondering if the alien recognized the gun as a killing tool. The alien which had attacked them outside the *Harrier* had owned neither weapons nor clothing. Neither had the ones filmed as they fell from the enemy ship, or the one lying dead outside the fragment of that ship on the other side of the mountain. It might be that they were so used to their natural strength and adaptability they did not understand the use of portable weapons. Cal let his hand actually brush against the butt of the sidearm as the alien climbed on to the top of the wall and stood erect, faceplate turned a little from Cal.

But the alien did not attack.

Cal stared at the other for a long second, before turning and starting to lead the way through the terminal moraine, the rope still binding them together. The alien moved a little behind him, but enough to his left so that he was within Cal's range of vision, and Cal was wholly within his. Threading his way among the rock rubble of the moraine, Cal cast a glance at the yellow orb of K94, now just hovering above the sharp peaks of neighboring mountains around them.

Night was close. The thought of spending the hours of darkness with the other roped to him cooled the back of Cal's neck. Was it darkness the alien was waiting for?

Above them, as they crossed the moraine the setting sun struck blazing brilliance from the glacier and the snow slope. In a few more minutes Cal would have to stop to set up the pup-tent, if he hoped to have enough light to do so. For a moment the wild crazy hope of a notion crossed Cal's mind that the alien had belatedly chosen life over duty. That at this late hour, he had changed his mind and was trying to make friends.

Cold logic washed the fantasy from Cal's mind. This being trudging almost shoulder to shoulder with him was the same creature than had sent Doug's limp and helpless body skidding and falling down the long ice-slope to the edge of an abyss. This companion alongside was the creature that had stalked Maury somewhere among the rocks of the mountainside and disposed of him, and stripped his clothing off and taken his place.

Moreover, this other was of the same race and kind as the alien who had clung to the hull of the falling *Harrier* and, instead of trying to save himself and get away on landing, had made a suicidal attack on the eight human survivors. The last thing that alien had done, when there was nothing else to be done was to try to take as many humans as possible into death with him.

This member of the same race walking side by side with Cal would certainly do no less.

But why was he waiting so long to do it? Cal frowned hard inside his mask. That question had to be answered. Abruptly he stopped. They were through the big rubble of the moraine, onto a stretch of gravel and small rock. The sun was already partly out of sight behind the mountain peaks. Cal untied the rope and began to unload the pup tent.

Out of the corner of his eyes, he could see the alien imitating his actions. Together they got the tent set up and their sleeping bags inside. Cal crawled in the tiny tent and took off his boots. He felt the skin between his shoulder blades crawl as a second later the masked head of his companion poked itself through the tent opening and the other crept on hands and knees to the other sleeping bag. In the dimness of the tent with the last rays of K94 showing thinly through its walls, the shadow on the far tent wall was a monstrous parody of a man taking off his boots.

The sunlight failed and darkness filled the tent. The wind moaned loudly outside. Cal lay tense, his left hand gripping the gun he had withdrawn from its holster. But there was no movement.

The other had gotten into Maury's sleeping bag and lay with his back to Cal. Facing that back, Cal slowly brought the gun to bear. The only safe thing to do was to shoot the alien now, before sleep put Cal completely at the other's mercy.

Then the muzzle of the gun in Cal's hand sank until it pointed to the fabric of the tent floor. To shoot was the only safe thing—and it was also the only impossible thing.

Ahead of them was the snow-field and the glacier, with its undoubted crevasses and traps hidden under untrustworthy caps of snow. Ahead of them was the final rock climb to the summit. From the beginning, Cal had known no one man could make this final stretch alone. Only two climbers roped together could hope to make it safely to the top.

Sudden understanding burst on Cal's mind. He quietly reholstered the gun. Then, muttering to himself, he sat up suddenly without any attempt to hide the action, drew a storage cell lamp from his pack and lit it. In the sudden illumination that burst on the tent he found his boots and stowed them up alongside his bag.

He shut the light off and lay down again, feeling cool and clear-headed. He had had only a glimpse in turning, but the glimpse was enough. The alien had shoved Maury's pack up into a far corner of the tent as far away from Cal as possible. But the main pockets of that pack now bulked and swelled as they had not since Cal had made Maury lighten his load on the first rock climb.

Cal lay still in the darkness with a grim feeling of humor inside him. Silently, in his own mind he took his hat off to his enemy. From the beginning he had assumed that the only possible aim one of the other race could have would be to frustrate the human attempt to get word back to the human base—so that neither race would know of the two ships' encounter.

Cal had underestimated the other. And he should not have, for technologically they were so similar and equal. The aliens had used a no-time drive. Clearly, they had also had a no-time rescue signalling device like the Messenger, which needed to be operated from the mountaintop.

The alien had planned from the beginning to join the human effort to get up into Messenger-firing position, so as to get his own device up there.

He too, had realized—in spite of his awesome natural advantage over the humans—that no single individual could make the last stage of the climb alone. Two, roped together, would have a chance. He needed Cal as much as Cal needed him.

In the darkness, Cal almost laughed out loud with the irony of it. He need not be afraid of sleeping. The showdown would come only at the top of the mountain.

Cal patted the butt of the gun at his side and smiling, he fell asleep.

But he did not smile, the next morning when, on waking, he found the holster empty.

IX

When he awoke to sunlight through the tent walls the form beside him seemed not to have stirred, but the gun was gone.

As they broke camp, Cal looked carefully for it. But there was no sign of it either in the tent, or in the immediate vicinity of the camp. He ate some of the concentrated rations he carried and drank some of the water he still carried. He made a point not to look to see if the alien was imitating him. There was a chance, he thought, that the alien was still not sure whether Cal had discovered the replacement.

Cal wondered coldly where on the naked mountainside Maury's body might lie—and whether the other man had recognized the attacker who had killed him, or whether death had taken him unawares.

Almost at once they were on the glacier proper. The glare of ice was nearly blinding. Cal stopped and uncoiled the rope from around him. He tied himself on, and the alien in Maury's warmsuit, without waiting for a signal, tied himself on also.

Cal went first across the ice surface, thrusting downward with the forearm-length handle of his homemade ice axe. When the handle penetrated only the few inches of top snow and jarred against solidity, he chipped footholds like a series of steps up the steep pitch of the slope. Slowly they worked their way forward.

Beyond the main length of the hook rose a sort of tower of rock that was the main peak. The tower appeared to have a cup-shaped area or depression in its center—an ideal launching spot for the Messenger, Cal had decided, looking at it through a powerful telescopic viewer from the wreck of the *Harrier*. A rare launching spot in this landscape of steeply tilted surfaces.

Without warning a shadow fell across Cal's vision. He started and turned to see the alien towering over him. But, before he could move, the other had begun chipping at the ice higher up. He cut a step and moved up ahead of Cal. He went on, breaking trail, cutting steps for Cal to follow.

A perverse anger began to grow in Cal. He was aware of the superior strength of the other, but there was something contemptuous about the alien's refusal to stop and offer Cal his turn. Cal moved up close behind the other and abruptly began chipping steps in a slightly different direction. As he chipped, he moved up them, and gradually the two of them climbed apart.

When the rope went taut between them they both paused and turned in each other's direction—and without warning the world fell out from underneath Cal.

He felt himself plunging. The cruel and sudden jerk of the rope around his body brought him up short and he dangled, swaying between ice-blue walls.

He craned his head backward and looked up. Fifteen feet above him were two lips of snow, and behind these the blue-black sky. He looked down and saw the narrowing rift below him plunge down into darkness beyond vision.

For a moment his breath caught in his chest.

Then there was a jerk on the rope around him, and he saw the wall he was facing drop perhaps eighteen inches. He had been lifted. The jerk came again, and again. Steadily it progressed. A strength greater than that of any human was drawing him up.

Slowly, jerk by jerk, Cal mounted to the edge of the crevasse—to the point where he could reach up and get his gloved hands on the lip of ice and snow, to the point where he could get his forearms out on the slope and help lift his weight from the crevasse.

With the aid of the rope he crawled out at last on the downslope side of the crevasse. Just below him, he saw the alien in Maury's clothing, buried almost to his knees in loose snow, half kneeling, half-crouching on the slope with the rope in his grasp. The alien did not straighten up at once. It was as if even his great strength had been taxed to the utmost.

Cal trembling stared at the other's crouched immobility. It made sense. No physical creature was possessed of inexhaustible energy—and the alien had also been climbing a mountain. But, the thought came to chill Cal's sudden hope, if the alien had been weakened, Cal had been weakened also. They stood in the same relationship to each other physically that they had to begin with.

After a couple of minutes, Cal straightened up. The alien straightened up also, and began to move. He stepped out and took the lead off to his left, circling around the crevasse revealed by Cal's fall. He circled wide, testing the surface before him.

They were nearing the bend of the hook—the point at which they could leave the glacier for the short slope of bare rock leading up to the tower of the main peak and the cup-shaped spot from which Cal had planned to send off the Messenger. The hook curved to their left. Its outer bulge reached to the edge of a ridge on their right running up to the main peak, so that there was no avoiding a crossing of this final curve of the glacier. They had been moving closer to the ice-edge of the right-hand ridge, and now they were close enough to see how it dropped sheer, a frightening distance to rocky slopes far below.

The alien, leading the way, had found and circled a number of suspicious spots in the glacier ice. He was now a slack thirty feet of line in front of Cal, and some fifty feet from the ice-edge of the rim.

Suddenly, with almost no noise—as if it had been a sort of monster conjuring feat—the whole edge of the ice disappeared.

The alien and Cal both froze in position.

Cal, ice axe automatically dug in to anchor the other, was still on what seemed to be solid ice-covered rock. But the alien was revealed to be on an ice-bridge, all that was left of what must have been a shelf of glacier overhanging the edge of the rocky ridge. The rock was visible now—inside the alien's position. The ice-bridge stretched across a circular gap in the edge of the glacier, to ice-covered rock at the edge of the gap ahead and behind. It was only a few feet thick and the sun glinted on it.

Slowly, carefully, the masked and hidden face of the alien turned to look back at Cal, and the darkness behind his face-plate looked square into Cal's eyes.

For the first time there was direct communication between them. The situation was their translator and there was no doubt between them about the meanings of their conversation. The alien's ice-bridge might give way at any second. The jerk of the alien's fall on the rope would be more than the insecure anchor of Cal's ice-hammer could resist. If the alien fell while Cal was still roped to him, they would both go.

On the other hand, Cal could cut himself loose. Then, if the ice-bridge gave way, Cal would have lost any real chance of making the peak. But he would still be alive.

The alien made no gesture asking for help. He merely looked.

Well, which is it to be? the darkness behind his faceplate asked. If Cal should cut loose, there was only one thing for the alien to do, and that was to try to crawl on across the ice-bridge on his own—an attempt almost certain to be disastrous.

Cal felt a cramping in his jaw muscles. Only then did he realize he was smiling—a tight-lipped, sardonic smile. Careful not to tauten the rope between them, he turned and picked up the ice axe, then drove it into the ice beyond and to his left. Working step by step, from anchor point to anchor point, he made his way carefully around the gap, swinging well inside it, to a point above the upper end of the ice-bridge. Here he hammered and cut deeply into the ice until he stood braced in a two-foot hole with his feet flat against a vertical wall, lying directly back against the pull of the rope leading to the alien.

The alien had followed Cal's movements with his gaze. Now, as he saw Cal bracing himself, the alien moved forward and Cal took up the slack in the rope between them. Slowly, carefully, on hands and knees like a cat stalking in slow motion a resting butterfly, the alien began to move forward across the ice-bridge.

One foot—two feet—and the alien froze suddenly as a section of the bridge broke out behind him.

Now there was no way to go but forward. Squinting over the lower edge of his faceplate and sweating in his warmsuit, Cal saw the other move forward again. There were less than ten feet to go to solid surface. Slowly, the alien crept forward. He had only five feet to go, only four, only three—

The ice-bridge went out from under him.

X

The shock threatened to wrench Cal's arms from their shoulder-sockets—but skittering, clawing forward like a cat in high gear, the alien was snatching at the edge of the solid ice. Cal suddenly gathered in the little slack in the line and threw his weight into the effort of drawing the alien forward.

Suddenly the other was safe, on solid surface. Quickly, without waiting, Cal began to climb.

He did not dare glance down to see what the alien was do-ing; but from occasional tautenings of the rope around his shoulders and chest, he knew that the other was still tied to him. This was important, for it meant that the moment of their showdown was not yet. Cal was gambling that the other, perhaps secure in the knowledge of his strength and his ability to adapt, had not studied the face of this tower as Cal had studied it through the telescopic viewer from the *Harrier*.

From that study, Cal had realized that it was a face that he himself might be able to climb unaided. And that meant a face that the alien certainly could climb unaided. If the alien should realize this, a simple jerk on the rope that was tied around Cal would settle the problem of the alien as far as human competition went. Cal would be plucked from his meager hand and footholds like a kitten from the back of a chair, and the slope below would dispose of him. He sweated now, climbing, trying to remember the path up the towerside as he had planned it out, from handhold to handhold, gazing through the long-distance viewer.

He drew closer to the top. For some seconds and minutes now, the rope below him had been completely slack. He dared not look down to see what that might mean. Then finally he saw the edge of the cup-shaped depression above him, bulg-ing out a little from the wall.

A second more and his fingers closed on it. Now at last he

had a firm handhold. Quickly he pulled himself up and over
the edge. For a second perspiration blurred his vision. Then
he saw the little, saucer sloping amphitheater not more than
eighteen feet wide, and the further walls of the tower enclos-
ing it on three sides.

Into the little depression the light of K94 blazed from the
nearly black sky. Unsteadily Cal got to his feet and turned
around. He looked down the wall he had just climbed.

The alien still stood at the foot of the wall. He had braced
himself there, evidently to belay Cal against a fall that would
send him skidding down the rock slope below. Though what
use to belay a dead man, Cal could not understand, since the
more than thirty feet of fall would undoubtedly have killed
him. Now, seeing Cal upright and in solid position, the alien
put his hands out toward the tower wall as if he would start
to climb.

Cal immediately hauled taut on the line, drew a knife
from his belt and, reaching as far down as possible, cut the
line.

The rope end fell in coils at the alien's feet. The alien was
still staring upward as Cal turned and went as quickly as he
could to the center of the cup-shaped depression.

The wind had all but died. In the semi-enclosed rock depression the reflected radiation of the star overhead made it
hot. Cal unsnapped his pack and let it drop. He stripped off
the gloves of his warmsuit and, kneeling, began to open up
the pack. His ears were alert. He heard nothing from outside
the tower, but he knew that he had minutes at most.

He laid out the three sections of the silver-plated Messenger, and began to screw them together. The metal was warm
to his touch after being in the sun-warmed backpack, and his
fingers, stiff and cramped from gripping at handholds, fumbled. He forced himself to move slowly, methodically, to con-
centrate on the work at hand and forget the alien now

climbing the tower wall with a swiftness no human could have
matched.

Cal screwed the computer-message-beacon section of the
nose tight to the drive section of the middle. He reached for
the propulsive unit that was the third section. It rolled out of
his hand. He grabbed it up and began screwing it on to the
two connected sections.

The three support legs were still in the pack. He got the
first one out and screwed it on. The next stuck for a moment,
but he got it connected. His ear seemed to catch a scratching
noise from the outside of the tower where the alien would be
climbing. He dug in the bag, came out with the third leg and
screwed it in. Sweat ran into his eyes inside the mask faceplate, and he blinked to clear his vision.

He set the Messenger upright on its three legs. He bent over
on his knees, facemask almost scraping the ground to check
the level indicator.

Now he was sure he heard a sound outside on the wall of
the tower. The leftmost leg was too long. He shortened it.
Now the middle leg was off. He lengthened that. He shortened
the leftmost leg again . . . slowly . . . there, the Messenger
was leveled.

He glanced at the chronometer on his wrist. He had set it
with the ship's chronometer before leaving. Sixty-six ship's
hours thirteen minutes, and . . . the sweep second hand was
moving. He fumbled with two fingers in the breast pocket of
his warmsuit, felt the small booklet he had made up before
leaving and pulled it out. He flipped through the pages of
settings, a row of them for each second of time. Here they
were . . . sixty-three hours, thirteen minutes—

A gust of wind flipped the tiny booklet from his stiffened
fingers. It fluttered across the floor of the cup and into a crack
in the rock wall to his right. On hands and knees he scrambled after it, coming up against the rock wall with a bang.

The crack reached all the way through the further wall,

narrowing until it was barely wide enough for daylight to enter—or a booklet to exit. The booklet was caught crossways against the unevenness of the rock sides. He reached in at arm's length. His fingers touched it. They shoved it a fraction of an inch further away. Sweat rolled down his face.

He ground the thickness of his upper arm against the aperture of the crack. Gently, gently, he maneuvered two fingers into position over the near edge of the booklet. The fingers closed. He felt it. He pulled back gently. The booklet came.

He pulled it out.

He was back at the Messenger in a moment, finding his place in the pages again. Sixteen hours—fourteen minutes—the computer would take four minutes to warm and fire the propulsive unit.

A loud scratching noise just below the lip of the depression distracted him for a second.

He checked his chronometer. Sixty-three hours, sixteen minutes plus . . . moving on toward thirty seconds. Make it sixty-three hours sixteen minutes even. Setting for sixty-three hours, sixteen minutes plus four minutes—sixty-three hours, twenty minutes.

His fingers made the settings on the computer section as the second hand of his chronometer crawled toward the even minute . . .

There.

His finger activated the computer. The Messenger began to hum faintly, with a soft internal vibration.

The sound of scraping against rock was right at the lip of the depression, but out of sight.

He stood up. Four minutes the Messenger must remain undisturbed. Rapidly, but forcing himself to calmness, he unwound the rest of the rope from about him and unclipped it. He was facing the lip of the depression over which the alien would come, but as yet there was no sign. Cal could not risk the time to step to the depression's edge and make sure.

The alien would not be like a human being, to be dislodged

by a push as he crawled over the edge of the lip. He would come adapted and prepared. As quickly as he could without fumbling, Cal fashioned a slipknot in one end of the rope that hung from his waist.

A gray, wide, flat parody of a hand slapped itself over the lip of rock and began to change form even as Cal looked. Cal made a running loop in his rope and looked upward. There was a projection of rock in the ascending walls on the far side of the depression that would do. He tossed his loop up fifteen feet toward the projection. It slipped off—as another hand joined the first on the lip of rock. The knuckles were becoming pale under the pressure of the alien's great weight.

Cal tossed the loop again. It caught. He drew it taut.

He backed off across the depression, out of line with the Messenger, and climbed a few feet up the opposite wall. He pulled the rope taut and clung to it with desperate determination.

And a snarling tiger's mask heaved itself into sight over the edge of rock, a tiger body following. Cal gathered his legs under him and pushed off. He swung out and downward, flashing toward the emerging alien, and they slammed together, body against fantastic body.

For a fraction of a second they hung together, toppling over space while the alien's lower extremities snatched and clung to the edge of rock.

Then the alien's hold loosened. And wrapped together, still struggling, they fell out and down toward the rock below accompanied by a cascade of rocks.

XI

"Waking in a hospital," Cal said later, "when you don't expect to wake at all, has certain humbling effects."

It was quite an admission for someone like himself, who had by his very nature omitted much speculation on either humbleness or arrogance before. He went deeper into the subject with Joe Aspinall when the Survey Team Leader visited him in that same hospital back on Earth. Joe by this time, with a cane, was quite ambulatory.

"You see," Cal said, as Joe sat by the hospital bed in which Cal lay, with the friendly and familiar sun of Earth making the white room light about them, "I got to the point of admiring that alien—almost of liking him. After all, he saved my life, and I saved his. That made us close, in a way. Somehow, now that I've been opened up to include creatures like him, I seem to feel closer to the rest of my own human race. You understand me?"

"I don't think so," said Joe.

"I mean, I needed that alien. The fact brings me to think that I may need the rest of you, after all. I never really believed I did before. It made things lonely."

"I can understand that part of it," said Joe.

"That's why," said Cal, thoughtfully, "I hated to kill him, even if I thought I was killing myself at the same time."

"Who? The alien?" said Joe. "Didn't they tell you? You didn't kill him."

Cal turned his head and stared at his visitor.

"No, you didn't kill him!" said Joe. "When the rescue ship came they found you on top of him and both of you halfway down that rock slope. Evidently landing on top of him saved you. Just his own natural toughness saved him—that and being able to spread himself out like a rug and slow his fall. He got half a dozen broken bones—but he's alive right now."

Cal smiled. "I'll have to go say hello to him when I get out of here."

"I don't think they'll let you do that," said Joe. "They've got him guarded ten deep someplace. Remember, his people still represent a danger to the human race greater than anything we've ever run into."

"Danger?" said Cal. "They're no danger to us."

It was Joe who stared at this. "They've got a definite weakness," said Cal. "I figured they must have. They seemed too good to be true from the start. It was only in trying to beat him out to the top of the mountain and get the Messenger off that I figured out what it had to be, though."

"What weakness? People'll want to hear about this!" said Joe.

"Why, just what you might expect," said Cal. "You don't get something without giving something away. What his race had gotten was the power to adapt to any situation. Their weakness is that same power to adapt."

"What're you talking about?"

"I'm talking about my alien friend on the mountain," said Cal, a little sadly. "How do you suppose I got the Messenger off? He and I both knew we were headed for a showdown when we reached the top of the mountain. And he had the natural advantage of being able to adapt. I was no match for him physically. I had to find some advantage to outweigh that advantage of his. I found an instinctive one."

"Instinctive . . ." said Joe, looking at the big, bandaged man under the covers and wondering whether he ought not to ring for the nurse.

"Of course, instinctive," said Cal thoughtfully, staring at the bed sheet. "His instincts and mine were diametrically opposed. He adapted to fit the situation. I belonged to a people who adapted situations to fit *them*. I couldn't fight a tiger with my bare hands, but I could fight something half-tiger, half something else."

"I think I'll just ring for the nurse," said Joe, leaning forward to the button on the bedside table.

"Leave that alone," said Cal calmly. "It's simple enough. What I had to do was force him into a situation where he would be between adaptations. Remember, he was as exhausted as I was, in his own way; and not prepared to quickly understand the unexpected."

"What unexpected?" Joe gaped at him. "You talk as if you

thought you were in control of the situation all the way."

"Most of the way," said Cal. "I knew we were due to have a showdown. I was afraid we'd have it at the foot of the tower —but he was waiting until we were solidly at the top. So I made sure to get up to that flat spot in the tower first, and cut the rope. He had to come up the tower by himself."

"Which he was very able to do."

"Certainly—in one form. He was in one form coming up," said Cal. "He changed to his fighting form as he came over the edge—and those changes took energy. Physical and nervous, if not emotional energy, when he was pretty exhausted already. Then I swung at him like Tarzan as he was balanced, coming over the edge of the depression in the rock."

"And had the luck to knock him off," said Joe. "Don't tell me with someone as powerful as that it was anything but luck. I was there when Mike and Sam got killed at the *Harrier,* remember."

"Not luck at all," said Cal, quietly. "A foregone conclusion. As I say, I'd figured out the balance sheet for the power of adaptation. It had to be instinctive. That meant that if he was threatened, his adaptation to meet the threat would take place whether consciously he wanted it to or not. He was barely into tiger-shape, barely over the edge of the cliff, when I hit him and threatened to knock him off into thin air. He couldn't help himself. He adapted."

"Adapted!" said Joe, staring.

"Tried to adapt—to a form that would enable him to cling to his perch. That took the strength out of his tiger-fighting form, and I was able to get us both off the cliff together instead of being torn apart the minute I hit him. The minute we started to fall, he instinctively spread out and stopped fighting me altogether."

Joe sat back in his chair. After a moment, he swore.

"And you're just now telling me this?" he said.

Cal smiled a little wryly.

"I'm surprised you're surprised," he said. "I'd thought people back here would have figured all this out by now. This
character and his people can't ever pose any real threat to us.
For all their strength and slipperiness, their reaction to life is
passive. They adapt to it. Ours is active—we adapt it to us.
On the instinctive level, we can always choose the battlefield
and the weapons, and win every time in a contest."

He stopped speaking and gazed at Joe, who shook his head
slowly.

"Cal," said Joe at last, "you don't think like the rest of us."

Cal frowned. A cloud passing beyond the window dimmed
the light that had shone upon him.

"I'm afraid you're right," he said quietly. "For just a while,
I had hopes it wasn't so."

THE CATCH

"Sure, Mike. Gee!" said the young Tolfian excitedly, and went dashing off from the spaceship in the direction of the temporary camp his local people had set up at a distance of some three hundred yards across the grassy turf of the little valley. Watching him go, Mike Wellsbauer had to admit that in motion he made a pretty sight, scooting along on his hind legs, his sleek black-haired otterlike body leaning into the wind of his passage, and his wide, rather paddle-shaped tail extended behind him to balance the weight of his erected body. All the same . . .

"I don't like it," Mike murmured. "I don't like it one bit."

"First signs of insanity," said a female and very human voice behind him. He turned about.

"All right, Penny," he said. "You can laugh. But this could turn out to be the most unfunny thing that ever happened to the human race. Where is the rest of the crew?"

Peony Matsu sobered, the small gamin grin fading from her pert face, as she gazed up at him.

"Red and Tommy are still trying to make communication contact with home base," she said. "Alvin's out checking the flora—he can't be far." She stared at him curiously. "What's up now?"

"I want to know what they're building."

"Something for us, I'll bet."

"That's what I'm afraid of. I've just sent for the local squire." Mike peered at the alien camp. Workers were still zipping around it in that typical Tolfian fashion that seemed to dictate that nobody went anywhere except at a run. "This time he's going to give me a straight answer."

"I thought," said Penny, "he had."

"Answers," said Mike, shortly. "Not necessarily straight ones." He heaved a sudden sigh, half of exhaustion, half of exasperation. "That young squirt was talking to me right now in English. In *English!* What can you do?"

Penny bubbled with laughter in spite of herself.

"All right, now hold it!" snapped Mike, glaring at her. "I tell you that whatever this situation is, it's serious. And letting ourselves be conned into making a picnic out of it may be just what they want."

"All right," said Penny, patting him on the arm. "I'm serious. But I don't see that their learning English is any worse than the other parts of it—"

"It's the whole picture," growled Mike, not waiting for her to finish. He stumped about to stand half-turned away from her, facing the Tolfian camp, and she gazed at his short, blocky, red-haired figure with tolerance and a scarce-hidden affection. "The first intelligent race we ever met. They've got science we can't hope to touch for nobody knows how long, they belong to some Interstellar Confederation or other with races as advanced as themselves—and they fall all over themselves learning English and doing every little thing we ask for. *'Sure, Mike!'*—that's what he said to me just now . . . *'Sure, Mike!'* I tell you, Penny—"

"Here they come now," she said.

A small procession was emerging from the camp. It approached the spaceship at a run, single file, the tallest Tolfian figure in the lead, and the others grading down in size behind until the last was a half-grown alien that was pretty sure to be the one Mike had sent on the errand.

"If we could just get through to home base back on Altair A—" muttered Mike; and then he could mutter no more, because the approaching file was already dashing into hearing distance. The lead Tolfian raced to the very feet of Mike and sat down on his tail. His muzzle was gray with age and authority and the years its color represented had made him almost as tall as Mike.

"Mike!" he said, happily.

The other Tolfians had dispersed themselves in a semicircle and were also sitting on their tails and looking rather like a group of racetrack fans on shooting sticks.

"Hello, Moral," said Mike, in a pleasantly casual tone. "What're you building over there now?"

"A terminal—a transport terminal, I suppose you'd call it in English, Mike," said Moral. "It'll be finished in a few hours. Then you can all go to Barzalac."

"Oh, we can, can we?" said Mike. "And where is Barzalac?"

"I don't know if you know the sun, Mike," said Moral, seriously. "We call it Aimna. It's about a hundred and thirty light-years from ours. Barzalac is the Confederation center— on its sixth planet."

"A hundred and thirty light-years?" said Mike, staring at the Tolfian.

"Isn't that right?" said Moral, confusedly. "Maybe I've got your terms wrong. I haven't been speaking your language since yesterday—"

"You speak it just fine. Just fine," said Mike. "Nice of you all to go to the trouble to learn it."

"Oh, it wasn't any trouble," said Moral. "And for you humans—well," he smiled, "nothing's too good, you know."

He said the last words rather shyly, and ducked his head for a second as if to avoid Mike's eyes.

"That's very nice," said Mike. "Now, would you mind if I asked you again *why* nothing's too good?"

"Oh, didn't I make myself clear before?" said Moral, in distressed tones. "I'm sorry—the thing is, we've met others of your people before."

"I got that, all right," said Mike. "Another race of humans, some thousands or dozens of thousands of years ago. And they aren't around any more?"

"I am very sorry," said Moral, with tears in his eyes. "Very, very sorry—"

"They died off?"

"Our loss—the loss of all the Confederation—was deeply felt. It was like losing our own, and more than our own."

"Yes," said Mike. He locked his hands behind his back and took a step up and down on the springy turf before turning back to the Tolfian squire. "Well, now, Moral, we wouldn't want that to happen to us."

"Oh, no!" cried Moral. "It mustn't happen. Somehow—we must insure its not happening."

"My attitude, exactly," said Mike, a little grimly. "Now, to get back to the matter at hand—why did you people decide to build your transportation center right here by our ship?"

"Oh, it's no trouble, no trouble at all to run one up," said Moral. "We thought you'd want one convenient here."

"Then you have others?"

"Of course," said Moral. "We go back and forth among the Confederation a lot." He hesitated. "I've arranged for them to expect you tomorrow—if it's all right with you."

"Tomorrow? On Barzalac?" cried Mike.

"If it's all right with you."

"Look, how fast is this . . . transportation, or whatever you call it?"

Moral stared at him.

"Why, I don't know, exactly," he said. "I'm just a sort of a rural person, you know. A few millionths of a second, I believe you'd say, in your terms?"

Mike stared. There was a moment's rather uncomfortable silence. Mike drew a deep breath.

"I see," he said.

"I have the honor of being invited to escort you," said Moral, eagerly. "If you want me, that is. I . . . I rather

look forward to showing you around the museum in Barzalac.
And after all, it was *my* property you landed on."

"Here we go again," said Mike under his breath. Only
Penny heard him. "What museum?"

"What museum?" echoed Moral, and looked blank. "Oh,
the museum erected in honor of those other humans. It has
everything," he went on eagerly, "artifacts, pictures—the
whole history of these other people, together with the Confederation. Of course"—he hesitated with shyness again—
"there'll be experts around to give you the real details. As I
say, I'm only a sort of rural person—"

"All right," said Mike, harshly. "I'll quit beating around
the bush. Just why do you want us to go to Barzalac?"

"But the heads of the Confederation," protested Moral.
"They'll be expecting you."

"Expecting us?" demanded Mike. "For what?"

"Why to take over the Confederation, of course," said
Moral, staring at him as if he thought the human had taken
leave of his senses. "You are going to, aren't you?"

Half an hour later, Mike had a council of war going in the
lounge of Exploration Ship 29XJ. He paced up and down
while Penny, Red Sommers, Tommy Anotu, and Alvin Long-
hand sat about in their gimballed armchairs, listening.

". . . The point's this," Mike was saying, "we can't get
through to base at all because of the distance. Right, Red?"

"The equipment just wasn't designed to carry more than a
couple of light-years, Mike," answered Red. "You know that.
To get a signal from here to Altair we'd need a power plant
nearly big enough to put this ship in its pocket."

"All right," said Mike. "Point one—we're on our own. That
leaves it up to me. And my duty as captain of this vessel is to
discover anything possible about an intelligent life form like
this—particularly since the human race's never bumped into
anything much brighter than a horse up until now."

"You're going to go?" asked Penny.

"That's the question. It all depends on what's behind the way these Tolfians are acting. That transporter of theirs could just happen to be a fine little incinerating unit, for all we know. Not that I'm not expendable—we all are. But the deal boils down to whether I'd be playing into alien hands by going along with them, or not."

"You don't think they're telling the truth?" asked Alvin, his lean face pale against the metal bulkhead behind him.

"I don't know!" said Mike, pounding one fist into the palm of his other hand and continuing to pace. "I just don't know. Of all the fantastic stories—that there are, or have been, other ethnic groups of humans abroad in the galaxy! And that these humans were so good, so wonderful that their memory is revered and this Confederation can't wait to put our own group up on the pedestal the other bunch vacated!"

"What happened to the other humans, Mike?" asked Tommy.

"Moral doesn't know, exactly. He knows they died off, but he's hazy on the why and how. He thinks a small group of them may have just pulled up stakes and moved on—but he thinks maybe that's just a legend. And that's *it*." He pounded his fist into his palm again.

"What's it?" asked Penny.

"The way he talked about it—the way these Tolfians are," said Mike. "They're as bright as we are. Their science—and they know it as well as we do—is miles ahead of us. Look at that transporter, if it's true, that can whisk you light-years in millisecond intervals. Does it make any sense at all that a race that advanced—let alone a bunch of races that advanced—would want to bow down and say 'Master' to *us?*"

Nobody said anything.

"All right," said Mike, more calmly, "you know as well as I do it doesn't. That leaves us right on the spike. Are they telling the truth, or aren't they? If they aren't, then they are obviously setting us up for something. If they are—then there's a catch in it somewhere, because the whole story is just too good to be true. They need us like an idiot uncle, but they claim that now that we've stumbled on to them, they can't think of existing without us. They want us to take over. *Us!*"

Mike threw himself into his own chair and threw his arms wide.

"All right, everybody," he said. "Let's have some opinions."

There was a silence in which everybody looked at everybody else.

"We could pack up and head for home real sudden-like," offered Tommy.

"No," Mike gnawed at his thumb. "If they're this good, they could tell which way we went and maybe track us. Also, we'd be popping off for insufficient reason. So far we've encountered nothing obviously inimical."

"This planet's Earth-like as they come," offered Alvin—and corrected himself, hastily. "I don't mean that perhaps the way it sounded. I mean it's as close to Earth conditions as any of the worlds we've colonized extensively up until now."

"I know," muttered Mike. "Moral says the Confederation worlds are all that close—and *that* I can believe. Now that we know that nearly all suns have planets, and if these people can really hop dozens of light-years in a wink, there'll be no great trouble in finding a good number of Earth-like worlds in this part of the galaxy."

"Maybe that's it. Maybe it's just a natural thing for life forms on worlds so similar to hang together," offered Red.

"Sure," said Mike. "Suppose that was true, and suppose we were their old human-style buddies come back. Then there'd be a reason for a real welcome. But we aren't."

"Maybe they think we're just pretending not to be their old friends," said Red.

"No," Mike shook his head. "They can take one look at our ship here and see what we've got. Their old buddies wouldn't come back in anything as old-fashioned as a spaceship; and they'd hardly be wanted if they did. Besides, welcoming an old friend and inviting him to take over your home and business are two different things."

"Maybe—" said Red, hesitantly, "it's all true, but they've got it in for their old buddies for some reason, and all this is just setting us up for the ax."

Mike slowly lifted his head and exchanged a long glance with his Communications officer.

"That does it," he said. "Now you say it. That, my friends, was the exact conclusion I'd come to myself. Well, that ties it."

"What do you mean, Mike?" cried Penny.

"I mean that's it," said Mike. "If that's the case, I've got to see it through and find out about it. In other words, tomorrow I go to Barzalac. The rest of you stay here; and if I'm not back in two days, blast off for home."

"Mike," said Penny, as the others stared at him, "I'm going with you."

"No," said Mike.

"Yes, I am," said Penny, "I'm not needed here, and—"

"Sorry," said Mike. "But I'm captain. And you stay, Penny."

"Sorry, captain," retorted Penny. "But I'm the biologist. And if we're going to be running into a number of other alien life forms—" She let the sentence hang.

Mike threw up his hands in helplessness.

The trip through the transporter was, so far as Mike and Penny had any way of telling, instantaneous and painless. They stepped through a door-shaped opaqueness and found themselves in a city.

The city was even almost familiar. They had come out on a sort of plaza or court laid out on a little rise, and they were able to look down and around them at a number of low buildings. These glowed in all manners of colors and were remarkable mainly for the fact that they had no roofs as such, but were merely obscured from overhead view by an opaqueness similar to that in the transporter. The streets on which they were set stretched in all directions, and streets and buildings were clear to the horizon.

"The museum," said Moral, diffidently, and the two humans turned about to find themselves facing a low building fronting on the court that stretched wide to the left and right and far before them. Its interior seemed split up into corridors.

They followed Moral in through the arch of an entrance that stood without respect to any walls on either side and down a corridor. They emerged into a central interior area dominated by a single large statue in the area's center. Penny caught her breath, and Mike stared. The statue was, indubitably, that of a human—a man.

The stone figure was dressed only in a sort of kilt. He stood with one hand resting on a low pedestal beside him; gazing downward in such a way that his eyes seemed to meet those of whoever looked up at him from below. The eyes were gentle, and the lean, middle-aged face was a little tired and careworn, with its high brow and the sharp lines drawn around the corners of the thin mouth. Altogether, it most nearly resembled the face of a man who is impatient with the time it is taking to pose for his sculptor.

"Moral! Moral!" cried a voice; and they all turned to see a being with white and woolly fur that gave him a rather polar-bear look, trotting across the polished floor toward them. He approached in upright fashion and was as four-limbed as Moral—and the humans themselves, for that matter.

"You *are* Moral, aren't you?" demanded the newcomer, as he came up to them. His English was impeccable. He bowed to the humans—or at least he inclined the top half of his body toward them. Mike, a little uncertainly, nodded back. "I'm Arrjhanik."

"Oh, yes . . . yes," said Moral. "The Greeter. These are the humans, Mike Wellsbauer and Peony Matsu. May I . . .

how do you put it . . . present Arrjhanik a Bin. He is a
Siniloid, one of the Confederation's older races."

"So honored," said Arrjhanik.

"We're both very pleased to meet you," said Mike, feeling
on firmer ground. There were rules for *this* kind of alien contact.

"Would you . . . could you come right now?" Arrjhanik
appealed to the humans. "I'm sorry to prevent you from seeing the rest of the museum at this time"—Mike frowned; and
his eyes narrowed a little—"but a rather unhappy situation
has come up. One of our Confederate heads—the leader of
one of the races that make up our Confederation—is dying.
And he would like to see you before . . . you understand."

"Of course," said Mike.

"If we had known in advance— But it comes rather suddenly on the Adrii—" Arrjhanik led them off toward the
entrance of the building and they stepped out into sunlight
again. He led them back to the transporter from which they
had just emerged.

"Wait a minute," said Mike, stopping. "We aren't going
back to Tolfi, are we?"

"Oh, no. No," put in Moral from close behind him. "We're
going to the Chamber of Deputies." He gave Mike a gentle
push; and a moment later they had stepped through into a
small and pleasant room half-filled with a dozen or so beings
each so different one from the other that Mike had no chance
to sort them out and recognize individual characteristics.

Arrjhanik led them directly to the one piece of furniture in
the room which appeared to be a sort of small table incredibly
supported by a single wire-thin leg at one of the four corners.
On the surface of this lay a creature or being not much bigger
than a seven-year-old human child and vaguely catlike in
form. It lay on its side, its head supported a little above the
table's surface by a cube of something transparent but ap-

parently not particularly soft, and large colorless eyes in its head focused on Mike and Penny as they approached.

Mike looked down at the small body. It showed no signs of age, unless the yellowish-white of the thin hair covering its body was a revealing shade. Certainly the hair itself seemed brittle and sparse.

The Adri—or whatever the proper singular was—stirred its head upon its transparent pillow and its pale eyes focused on Mike and Penny. A faint, drawn out rattle of noise came from it.

"He says," said Arrjhanik, at Mike's elbow, "'You cannot refuse. It is not in you.'"

"Refuse what?" demanded Mike, sharply. But the head of the Adri lolled back suddenly on its pillow and the eyes filmed and glazed. There was a little murmur that could have been something reverential from all the beings standing about; and without further explanation the body of the being that had just died thinned suddenly to a ghostly image of itself, and was gone.

"It was the Confederation," said Arrjhanik, "that he knew you could not refuse."

"Now wait a minute," said Mike. He swung about so that he faced them all, his stocky legs truculently apart. "Now, listen—you people are acting under a misapprehension. *I* can't accept or refuse anything. I haven't the authority. I'm just an explorer, nothing more."

"No, no," said Arrjhanik, "there's no need for you to say that you accept or not, and speak for your whole race. That is a formality. Besides, we know you will not refuse, you humans. How could you?"

"You might be surprised," said Mike. Penny hastily jogged his elbow.

"Temper!" she whispered. Mike swallowed, and when he spoke again, his voice sounded more reasonable.

"You'll have to bear with me," he said. "As I say, I'm an

explorer, not a diplomat. Now, what did you all want to see me about?"

"We wanted to see you only for our own pleasure," said Arrjhanik. "Was that wrong of us? Oh, and yes—to tell you that if there is anything you want, anything the Confederation can supply you, of course you need only give the necessary orders—"

"It is so good to have you here," said one of the other beings.

A chorus of voices broke out in English all at once, and the aliens crowded around. One large, rather walruslike alien offered to shake hands with Mike, and actually did so in a clumsy manner.

"Now, wait. Wait!" roared Mike. The room fell silent. The assembled aliens waited, looking at him in an inquiring manner.

"Now, listen to me!" snapped Mike. "And answer one simple question. What is all this you're trying to give to us humans?"

"Why, everything," said Arrjhanik. "Our worlds, our people, are yours. Merely ask for what you want. In fact—please ask. It would make us feel so good to serve you, few though you are at the moment here."

"Yes," said the voice of Moral, from the background. "If you'll forgive me speaking up in this assemblage—they asked for nothing back on Tolfi, and I was forced to exercise my wits for things to supply them with. I'm afraid I may have botched the job."

"I sincerely hope not," said Arrjhanik, turning to look at the Tolfian. Moral ducked his head, embarrassedly.

"Mike," said Arrjhanik, turning back to the human, "something about all this seems to bother you. If you would just tell us what it is—"

"All right," said Mike. "I will." He looked around at all of them. "You people are all being very generous. In fact, you're being so generous it's hard to believe. Now, I accept the fact that you may have had contact with other groups of humans before us. There's been speculation back on our home world that our race might have originated elsewhere in the galaxy, and that would mean there might well be other human groups in existence we don't even know of. But even assuming that you may have reached all possible limits of love and admiration for the humans you once knew, it still doesn't make sense that you would be willing to just make us a gift of all you possess, to bow down to a people who—we're not blind, you know —possess only a science that is childlike compared with your own."

To Mike's surprise, the reaction to this little speech was a murmur of admiration from the group.

"So analytical. So very human!" said the walruslike alien warmly in tones clearly pitched to carry to Mike's ear.

"Indeed," said Arrjhanik, "we understand your doubts. You are concerned about what, in our offer, is . . . you have a term for it—"

"The catch," said Mike grimly and bluntly. "What's the catch?"

"The catch. Yes," said Arrjhanik. "You have to excuse me. I've only been speaking this language of yours for—"

"Just the last day or so, I know," said Mike, sourly.

"Well, no. Just for the last few hours, actually. But—" went on Arrjhanik, "while there's no actual way of putting your doubts to rest, it really doesn't matter. More of your people are bound to come. They will find our Confederation open and free to all of them. In time they will come to believe. It would be presumptuous of us to try to convince you by argument."

"Well, just suppose you try it anyway," said Mike, unaware that his jaw was jutting out in a manner which could not be otherwise than belligerent.

"But we'd be only too happy to!" cried Arrjhanik, enthusiastically. "You see"—he placed a hand or paw, depending on how you looked at it, gently on Mike's arm—"all that we have nowadays, we owe to our former humans. This science you make such a point of—they developed it in a few short thousand years. The Confederation was organized by them. Since they've been gone—"

"Oh, yes," interrupted Mike. "Just how did they go? Mind telling me that?"

"The strain—the effort of invention and all, was too much for them," said Arrjhanik, sadly. He shook his head. "Ah," he said, "they were a great people—you *are* a great people, you humans. Always striving, always pushing, never giving up. We others are but pale shadows of your kind. I am afraid, Mike, that your cousins worked themselves to death, and for our sake. So you see, when you think we are giving you something that is ours, we are really just returning what belongs to you, after all."

"Very pretty," said Mike. "I don't believe it. No race could survive who just gave everything away for nothing. And somewhere behind all this is the catch I spoke of. That's what you're not telling me—what all of you will be getting out of it, by turning your Confederation over to us."

"But . . . now I understand!" cried Arrjhanik. "You *didn't* understand. *We* are the ones who will be getting. You humans will be doing all the giving. Surely you should know that! It's your very nature that ensures that, as our friend who just died, said. You humans can't help yourselves, you can't keep from it!"

"Keep from what?" yelled Mike, throwing up his hands in exasperation."

"Why," said Arrjhanik, "I was sure you understood. Why from assuming all authority and responsibility, from taking over the hard and dirty job of running our Confederation and making it a happy, healthy place for us all to live, safe and protected from any enemies. *That* is what all the rest of us have been saddled with these thousands of years since that

other group of your people died; and I can't tell you"—
Arrjhanik, his eyes shining, repeated his last words strongly
and emphatically—"I can't tell you how badly things have
gone to pot, and how very, very glad we are to turn it all over
to you humans, once again!"

JACKAL'S MEAL

If there should follow a thousand swords to carry my bones away—
Belike the price of a jackal's meal were more than a thief could
  pay . . .
"The Ballad of East and West," by Rudyard Kipling

In the third hour after the docking of the great, personal
spaceship of the Morah Jhan—on the planetoid outpost of
the 469th Corps which was then stationed just outside the
Jhan's spatial frontier—a naked figure in a ragged gray cloak
burst from a crate of supplies being unloaded off the huge
alien ship. The figure ran around uttering strange cries for a
little while, eluding the Morah who had been doing the un-
loading, until it was captured at last by the human Military
Police guarding the smaller, courier vessel, alongside, which
had brought Ambassador Alan Dormu here from Earth to
talk with the Jhan.

The Jhan himself, and Dormu—along with Marshal Sayers
Whin and most of the other ranking officers, Morah and
human alike—had already gone inside, to the Headquarters
area of the outpost, where an athletic show was being put on
for the Jhan's entertainment. But the young captain in charge
of the Military Police, on his own initiative, refused the strong
demands of the Morah that the fugitive be returned to them.
For it, or he, showed signs of being—or of once having been—a
man, under his rags and dirt and some surgicallike changes
that had been made in him.

One thing was certain. He was deathly afraid of his Morah pursuers; and it was not until he was shut in a room out of sight of them that he quieted down. However, nothing could bring him to say anything humanly understandable. He merely stared at the faces of all those who came close to him, and felt their clothing as someone might fondle the most precious fabric made—and whimpered a little when the questions became too insistent, trying to hide his face in his arms but not succeeding because of the surgery that had been done to him.

The Morah went back to their own ship to contact their chain of command, leading ultimately up to the Jhan; and the young Military Police captain lost no time in getting the fugitive to his Headquarters' Section and the problem, into the hands of his own commanders. From whom, by way of natural military process, it rose through the ranks until it came to the attention of Marshal Sayers Whin.

"Hell's Bells—" exploded Whin, on hearing it. But then he checked himself and lowered his voice. He had been drawn aside by Harold Belman, the one-star general of the Corps who was his aide; and only a thin door separated him from the box where Dormu and the Jhan sat, still watching the athletic show. "Where is the . . . Where is he?"

"Down in my office, sir."

"This has got to be quite a mess!" said Whin. He thought rapidly. He was a tall, lean man from the Alaskan back country and his temper was usually short-lived. "Look, the show in there'll be over in a minute. Go in. My apologies to the Jhan. I've gone ahead to see everything's properly fixed for the meeting at lunch. Got that?"

"Yes, Marshal."

"Stick with the Jhan. Fill in for me."

"What if Dormu—"

"Tell him nothing. Even if he asks, play dumb. I've got to have time to sort this thing out, Harry! You understand?"

"Yes, sir," said his aide.

Whin went out a side door of the small anteroom, catching himself just in time from slamming it behind him. But once out in the corridor, he strode along at a pace that was almost a run.

He had to take a lift tube down eighteen levels to his aide's office. When he stepped in there, he found the fugitive surrounded by the officer of the day and some officers of the Military Police, including General Mack Stigh, Military Police Unit Commandant. Stigh was the ranking officer in the room; and it was to him Whin turned.

"What about it, Mack?"

"Sir, apparently he escaped from the Jhan's ship—"

"Not that. I know that. Did you find out who he is? What he is?" Whin glanced at the fugitive who was chewing hungrily on something grayish-brown that Whin recognized as a Morah product. One of the eatables supplied for the lunch meeting with the Jhan that would be starting any moment now. Whin grimaced.

"We tried him on our own food," said Stigh. "He wouldn't eat it. They may have played games with his digestive system, too. No, sir, we haven't found out anything. There've been a few undercover people sent into Morah territory in the past twenty years. He could be one of them. We've got a records search going on. Of course, chances are his record wouldn't be in our files, anyway."

"Stinking Morah," muttered a voice from among the officers standing around. Whin looked up quickly, and a new silence fell.

"Records search. All right," Whin said, turning back to Stigh, "that's good. What did the Morah say when what's-his-name—that officer on duty down at the docks—wouldn't give him up?"

"Captain—?" Stigh turned and picked out a young officer with his eyes. The young officer stepped forward.

"Captain Gene McKussic, Marshal," he introduced himself.

"You were the one on the docks?" Whin asked.

"Yes, sir."

"What did the Morah say?"

"Just—that he wasn't human, sir," said McKussic. "That he was one of their own experimental pets, made out of one of their own people—just to look human."

"What else?"

"That's all, Marshal."

"And you didn't believe them?"

"Look at him, sir—" McKussic pointed at the fugitive, who by this time had finished his food and was watching them with bright but timid eyes. "He hasn't got a hair on him, except where a man'd have it. Look at his face. And the shape of his head's human. Look at his fingernails, even—"

"Yes—" said Whin slowly, gazing at the fugitive. Then he raised his eyes and looked around at the other officers. "But none of you thought to get a doctor in here to check?"

"Sir," said Stigh, "we thought we should contact you, first—"

"All right. But get a doctor *now!* Get two of them!" said Whin. One of the other officers turned to a desk nearby and spoke into an intercom. "You know what we're up against, don't you—all of you?" Whin's eyes stabbed around the room. "This is just the thing to blow Ambassador Dormu's talk with the Morah Jhan sky high. Now, all of you, except General Stigh, get out of here. Go back to your quarters and stay on tap until you're given other orders. And keep your mouths shut."

"Marshal," it was the young Military Police captain, McKussic, "we aren't going to give him back to the Morah, no matter what, are we, sir . . ."

He trailed off. Whin merely looked at him.

"Get to your quarters, Captain!" said Stigh, roughly.

The room cleared. When they were left alone with the fugitive, Stigh's gaze went slowly to Whin.

"So," said Whin, "you're wondering that too, are you, Mack?"

"No, sir," said Stigh. "But word of this is probably spreading through the men like wildfire, by this time. There'll be no stopping it. And if it comes to the point of our turning back to the Morah a man who's been treated the way this man has—"

"They're soldiers!" said Whin, harshly. "They'll obey orders." He pointed at the fugitive. "That's a soldier."

"Not necessarily, Marshal," said Stigh. "He could have been one of the civilian agents—"

"For my purposes, he's a soldier!" snarled Whin. He took a couple of angry paces up and down the room in each direction, but always wheeling back to confront the fugitive. "Where are those doctors? I've got to get back to the Jhan and Dormu!"

"About Ambassador Dormu," Stigh said. "If he hears something about this and asks us—"

"Tell him nothing!" said Whin. "It's my responsibility! I'm not sure he's got the guts—never mind. The longer it is before the little squirt knows—"

The sound of the office door opening brought both men around.

"The little squirt already knows," said a dry voice from the doorway. Ambassador Alan Dormu came into the room. He was a slight, bent man, of less than average height. His fading blond hair was combed carefully forward over a balding forehead; and his face had deep, narrow lines that testified to even more years than hair and forehead.

"Who told you?" Whin gave him a mechanical grin.

"We diplomats always respect the privacy of our sources," said Dormu. "What difference does it make—as long as I found out? Because you're wrong, you know, Marshal. I'm the one who's responsible. I'm the one who'll have to answer the Jhan when he asks about this at lunch."

"Mack," said Whin, continuing to grin and with his eyes still fixed on Dormu, "see you later."

"Yes, Marshal."

Stigh went toward the door of the office. But before he

reached it, it opened and two officers came in; a major and a lieutenant colonel, both wearing the caduceus. Stigh stopped and turned back.

"Here're the doctors, sir."

"Fine. Come here, come here, gentlemen," said Whin. "Take a look at this."

The two medical officers came up to the fugitive, sitting in the chair. They maintained poker faces. One reached for a wrist of the fugitive and felt for a pulse. The other went around back and ran his fingers lightly over the upper back with its misshapen and misplaced shoulder sockets.

"Well?" demanded Whin, after a restless minute. "What about it? Is he a man, all right?"

The two medical officers looked up. Oddly, it was the junior in rank, the major, who answered.

"We'll have to make tests—a good number of tests, sir," he said.

"You've no idea—now?" Whin demanded.

"Now," spoke up the lieutenant colonel, "he could be either Morah or human. The Morah are very, very, good at this sort of thing. The way those arms—We'll need samples of his blood, skin, bone marrow—"

"All right. All right," said Whin. "Take the time you need. But not one second more. We're all on the spot here, gentlemen. Mack—" he turned to Stigh, "I've changed my mind. You stick with the doctors and stand by to keep me informed."

He turned back to Dormu.

"We'd better be getting back upstairs, Mr. Ambassador," he said.

"Yes," answered Dormu, quietly.

They went out, paced down the corridor and entered the lift tube in silence.

"You know, of course, how this complicates things, Marshal," said Dormu, finally, as they began to rise up the tube together. Whin started like a man woken out of deep thought.

"What? You don't have to ask me that," he said. His voice took on an edge. "I suppose you'd expect my men to just stand around and watch, when something like that came running out of a Morah ship?"

"*I* might have," said Dormu. "In their shoes."

"Don't doubt it." Whin gave a single, small grunt of a laugh, without humor.

"I don't think you follow me," said Dormu. "I didn't bring up the subject to assign blame. I was just leading into the fact the damage done is going to have to be repaired, at any cost; and I'm counting on your immediate—note the word, Marshal —*immediate* cooperation, if and when I call for it."

The lift had carried them to the upper floor that was their destination. They got off together. Whin gave another humorless little grunt of laughter.

"You're thinking of handing him back, then?" Whin said.

"Wouldn't you?" asked Dormu.

"Not if he's human. No," said Whin. They walked on down a corridor and into a small room with another door. From beyond that other door came the faint smell of something like incense—it was, in fact, a neutral odor, tolerable to human and Morah alike and designed to hide the differing odors of one race from another. Also, from beyond the door, came the sound of three musical notes, steadily repeated; two notes exactly the same, and then a third, a half-note higher.

Tonk, tonk, TINK! . . .

"It's establishing a solid position for confrontation with the Jhan that's important right now," said Dormu, as they approached the other door. "He's got us over a barrel on the subject of this talk anyway, even without that business downstairs coming up. So it's the confrontation that counts. Nothing else."

They opened the door and went in.

Within was a rectangular, windowless room. Two tables had been set up. One for Dormu and Whin; and one for the

Jhan, placed at right angles to the other table but not quite touching it. Both tables had been furnished and served with food; and the Jhan was already seated at his. To his right and left, each at about five feet of distance from him, flamed two purely symbolic torches in floor standards. Behind him stood three ordinary Morah—two servers, and a musician whose surgically-created, enormous forefinger tapped steadily at the bars of something like a small metal xylophone, hanging vertically on his chest.

The forefinger tapped in time to the three notes Whin and Dormu had heard in the room outside but without really touching the xylophone bars. The three notes actually sounded from a speaker overhead, broadcast throughout the station wherever the Jhan might be, along with the neutral perfume. They were a courtesy of the human hosts.

"Good to see you again, gentlemen," said the Jhan, through the mechanical interpreter at his throat. "I was about to start without you."

He sat, like the other Morah in the room, unclothed to the waist, below which he wore, though hidden now by the table, a simple kilt, or skirt, of dark red, feltlike cloth. The visible skin of his body, arms and face was a reddish brown in color, but there was only a limited amount of it to be seen. His upper chest, back, arms, neck and head—excluding his face—was covered by a mat of closely-trimmed, thick, gray hair, so noticeable in contrast to his hairless areas, that it looked more like a garment—a cowled half-jacket—than any natural growth upon him.

The face that looked out of the cowl-part was humanoid, but with wide jawbones, rounded chin and eyes set far apart over a flat nose. So that, although no one feature suggested it, his face as a whole had a faintly feline look.

"Our apologies," said Dormu, leading the way forward. "The marshal just received an urgent message for me from Earth, in a new code. And only I had the key to it."

"No need to apologize," said the Jhan. "We've had our musician here to entertain us while we waited."

Dormu and Whin sat down at the opposite ends of their table, facing each other and at right angles to the Jhan. The Jhan had already begun to eat. Whin stared deliberately at the foods on the Jhan's table, to make it plain that he was not avoiding looking at them, and then turned back to his own plate. He picked up a roll and buttered it.

"Your young men are remarkable in their agility," the Jhan said to Dormu. "We hope you will convey them our praise—"

They talked of the athletic show; and the meal progressed. As it was drawing to a close, the Jhan came around to the topic that had brought him to this meeting with Dormu.

". . . It's unfortunate we have to meet under such necessities," he said.

"My own thought," replied Dormu. "You must come to Earth some time on a simple vacation."

"We would like to come to Earth—in peace," said the Jhan.

"We would hope not to welcome you any other way," said Dormu.

"No doubt," said the Jhan. "That is why it puzzles me, that when you humans can have peace for the asking—by simply refraining from creating problems—you continue to cause incidents, to trouble us and threaten our sovereignty over our own territory of space."

Dormu frowned.

"Incidents?" he echoed. "I don't recall any incidents. Perhaps the Jhan has been misinformed?"

"We are not misinformed," said the Jhan. "I refer to your human settlements on the fourth and fifth worlds of the star you refer to as 27J93; but which we call by a name of our own. Rightfully so because it is in our territory."

Tonk, tonk, TINK . . . went the three notes of the Morah music.

"It seems to me—if my memory is correct," murmured Dormu, "that the Treaty Survey made by our two races jointly, twelve years ago, left Sun 27J93 in unclaimed territory outside both our spatial areas."

"Quite right," said the Jhan. "But the Survey was later amended to include this and several other solar systems in our territory."

"Not by us, I'm afraid," said Dormu. "I'm sorry, but my people can't consider themselves automatically bound by whatever unilateral action you choose to take without consulting us."

"The action was not unilateral," said the Jhan, calmly. "We have since consulted with our brother Emperors—the Morah Selig, the Morah Ben, the Morah Yarra and the Morah Ness. All have concurred in recognizing the solar systems in question as being in our territory."

"But surely the Morah Jhan understands," said Dormu, "that an agreement only between the various political segments of one race can't be considered binding upon a people of another race entirely?"

"We of the Morah," said the Jhan, "reject your attitude that race is the basis for division between Empires. Territory is the only basis upon which Empires may be differentiated. Distinction between the races refers only to differences in shape or color; and as you know we do not regard any particular shape or color as sacredly, among ourselves, as you do; since we make many individuals over into what shape it pleases us, for our own use, or amusement."

He tilted his head toward the musician with the enormous, steadily jerking, forefinger.

"Nonetheless," said Dormu, "the Morah Jhan will not deny his kinship with the Morah of the other Morah Empires."

"Of course not. But what of it?" said the Jhan calmly. "In our eyes, your empire and those of our brothers, are in all ways similar. In essence you are only another group possessing a territory that is not ours. We make no difference between you and the empires of the other Morah."

"But if it came to an armed dispute between you and us," said Dormu, "would your brother Emperors remain neutral?"

"We hardly expect so," said the Morah Jhan, idly, pushing aside the last container of food that remained on the table before him. A server took it away. "But that would only be because, since right would be on our side, naturally they would rally to assist us."

"I see," said Dormu.

Tonk, tonk, TINK . . . went the sound of the Morah music.

"But why must we talk about such large and problematical issues?" said the Jhan. "Why not listen, instead, to the very simple and generous disposition we suggest for this matter of your settlements under 27J93? You will probably find our solution so agreeable that no more need be said on the subject."

"I'd be happy to hear it," said Dormu.

The Jhan leaned back in his seat at the table.

"In spite of the fact that our territory has been intruded upon," he said, "we ask only that you remove your people from their settlements and promise to avoid that area in future, recognizing these and the other solar systems I mentioned earlier as being in our territory. We will not even ask for ordinary reparations beyond the purely technical matter of your agreement to recognize what we Morah have already recognized, that the division of peoples is by territory, and not by race."

He paused. Dormu opened his mouth to speak.

"Of course," added the Jhan, "there is one additional, trivial concession we insist on. A token reparation—so that no precedent of not asking for reparations be set. That token concession is that you allow us corridors of transit across your spatial territory, through which our ships may pass without inspection between our empire and the empires of our brother Morah."

Dormu's mouth closed. The Jhan sat waiting. After a moment, Dormu spoke.

"I can only say," said Dormu, "that I am stunned and overwhelmed at these demands of the Morah Jhan. I was sent to this meeting only to explain to him that our settlements under Sun number 27J93 were entirely peaceful ones, constituting no human threat to his empire. I have no authority to treat with the conditions and terms just mentioned. I will have to contact my superiors back on Earth for instructions—and that will take several hours."

"Indeed?" said the Morah Jhan. "I'm surprised to hear you were sent all the way here to meet me with no more instructions than that. That represents such a limited authority that I almost begin to doubt the good will of you and your people in agreeing to this meeting."

"On our good will, of course," said Dormu, "the Morah Jhan can always depend."

"Can I?" The wide-spaced eyes narrowed suddenly in the catlike face. "Things seem to conspire to make me doubt it. Just before you gentlemen joined me I was informed of a most curious fact by my officers. It seems some of your Military Police have kidnapped one of my Morah and are holding him prisoner."

"Oh?" said Dormu. His face registered polite astonishment. "I don't see how anything like that could have happened." He turned to Whin. "Marshal, did you hear about anything like that taking place?"

Whin grinned his mechanical grin at the Morah Jhan.

"I heard somebody had been picked up down at the docks," he said. "But I understood he was human. One of our people who'd been missing for some time—a deserter, maybe. A purely routine matter. It's being checked out, now."

"I would suggest that the marshal look more closely into the matter," said the Jhan. His eyes were still slitted. "I promise him he will find the individual is a Morah; and of course, I expect the prisoner's immediate return."

"The Morah Jhan can rest assured," said Whin, "any Morah held by my troops will be returned to him, immediately."

"I will expect that return then," said the Jhan, "by the time

Ambassador Dormu has received his instructions from Earth and we meet to talk again."

He rose, abruptly; and without any further word, turned and left the room. The servers and the musician followed him.

Dormu got as abruptly to his own feet and led the way back out of the room in the direction from which he and Whin had come.

"Where are you going?" demanded Whin. "We go left for the lifts to the Message Center."

"We're going back to look at our kidnapped prisoner," said Dormu. "I don't need the Message Center."

Whin looked sideways at him.

"So . . . you *were* sent out here with authority to talk on those terms of his, after all, then?" Whin asked.

"We expected them," said Dormu briefly.

"What are you going to do about them?"

"Give in," said Dormu. "On all but the business of giving them corridors through our space. That's a first step to breaking us up into territorial segments."

"Just like that—" said Whin. "You'll give in?"

Dormu looked at him, briefly.

"You'd fight, I suppose?"

"If necessary," said Whin. They got into the lift tube and slipped downward together.

"And you'd lose," said Dormu.

"Against the Morah Jhan?" demanded Whin. "I know within ten ships what his strength is."

"No. Against all the Morah," answered Dormu. "This situation's been carefully set up. Do you think the Jhan would ordinarily be that much concerned about a couple of small settlements of our people, away off beyond his natural frontiers? The Morah—all the Morah—have started to worry about our getting too big for them to handle. They've set up a coalition of all their so-called Empires to contain us before that happens. If we fight the Jhan, we'll find ourselves fighting them all."

The skin of Whin's face grew tight.

"Giving in to a race like the Morah won't help," he said.

"It may gain us time," said Dormu. "We're a single, integrated society. They aren't. In five years, ten years, we can double our fighting strength. Meanwhile their coalition members may even start fighting among themselves. That's why I was sent here to do what I'm doing—give up enough ground so that they'll have no excuse for starting trouble at this time; but not enough ground so that they'll feel safe in trying to push further."

"Why won't they—if they know they can win?"

"Jhan has to count the cost to him personally, if he starts the war," said Dormu, briefly. They got off the lift tube. "Which way's the Medical Section?"

"There"—Whin pointed. They started walking. "What makes you so sure he won't think the cost is worth it?"

"Because," said Dormu, "he has to stop and figure what would happen if, being the one to start the war, he ended up more weakened by it than his brother-emperors were. The others would turn on him like wolves, given the chance; just like he'd turn on any of them. And he knows it."

Whin grunted his little, humorless laugh.

They found the fugitive lying on his back on an examination table in one of the diagnostic rooms of the Medical Section. He was plainly unconscious.

"Well?" Whin demanded bluntly of the medical lieutenant colonel. "Man, or Morah?"

The lieutenant colonel was washing his hands. He hesitated, then rinsed his fingers and took up a towel.

"Out with it!" snapped Whin. "Marshal," the lieutenant colonel hesitated again, "to be truthful . . . we may never know."

"Never know?" demanded Dormu. General Stigh came into

the room, his mouth open as if about to say something to Whin. He checked at the sight of Dormu and the sound of the ambassador's voice.

"There's human RNA involved," said the lieutenant colonel. "But we know that the Morah have access to human bodies from time to time, soon enough after the moment of death so that the RNA might be preserved. But bone and flesh samples indicate Morah, rather than human origin. He could be human and his RNA be the one thing about him the Morah didn't monkey with. Or he could be Morah, treated with human RNA to back up the surgical changes that make him resemble a human. I don't think we can tell, with the facilities we've got here; and in any case—"

"In any case," said Dormu, slowly, "it may not really matter to the Jhan."

Whin raised his eyebrows questioningly; but just then he caught sight of Stigh.

"Mack?" he said. "What is it?"

Stigh produced a folder.

"I think we've found out who he is," the Military Police general said. "Look here—a civilian agent of the Intelligence Service was sent secretly into the spatial territory of the Morah Jhan eight years ago. Name—Paul Edmonds. Description— superficially the same size and build as this man here." He nodded at the still figure on the examining table. "We can check the retinal patterns and fingerprints."

"It won't do you any good," said the lieutenant colonel. "Both fingers and retinas conform to the Morah pattern."

"May I see that?" asked Dormu. Stigh passed over the folder. The little ambassador took it. "Eight years ago, I was the State Dpartment's Liaison Officer with the Intelligence Service."

He ran his eyes over the information on the sheets in the folder.

"There's something I didn't finish telling you," said the lieutenant colonel, appealing to Whin, now that Dormu's attention was occupied. "I started to say I didn't think we could tell whether he's man or Morah; but in any case—the question's probably academic. He's dying."

"Dying?" said Dormu sharply, looking up from the folder. "What do you mean?"

Without looking, he passed the folder back to Stigh.

"I mean . . . he's dying," said the lieutenant colonel, a little stubbornly. "It's amazing that any organism, human or Morah, was able to survive, in the first place, after being cut up and altered that much. His running around down on the docks was evidently just too much for him. He's bleeding to death internally from a hundred different pinpoint lesions."

"Hm-m-m," said Whin. He looked sharply at Dormu. "Do you think the Jhan would be just as satisfied if he got a body back, instead of a live man?"

"Would you?" retorted Dormu.

"Hm-m-m . . . no. I guess I wouldn't," said Whin. He turned to look grimly at the unconscious figure on the table; and spoke almost to himself. "If he *is* Paul Edmonds—"

"Sir," said Stigh, appealingly.

Whin looked at the general. Stigh hesitated.

"If I could speak to the marshal privately for a moment—" he said.

"Never mind," said Whin. The line of his mouth was tight and straight. "I think I know what you've got to tell me. Let the ambassador hear it, too."

"Yes, sir." But Stigh still looked uncomfortable. He glanced at Dormu, glanced away again, fixed his gaze on Whin. "Sir, word about this man has gotten out all over the Outpost. There's a lot of feeling among the officers and men alike—a lot of feeling against handing him back . . ."

He trailed off.

"You mean to say," said Dormu sharply, "that they won't obey if ordered to return this individual?"

"They'll obey," said Whin, softly. Without turning his head, he spoke to the lieutenant colonel. "Wait outside for us, will you, Doctor?"

The lieutenant colonel went out, and the door closed behind him. Whin turned and looked down at the fugitive on the table. In unconsciousness the face was relaxed, neither human nor Morah, but just a face, out of many possible faces. Whin looked up again and saw Dormu's eyes still on him.

"You don't understand, Mr. Ambassador," Whin said, in the same soft voice. "These men are veterans. You heard the doctor talking about the fact that the Morah have had access to human RNA. This outpost has had little, unreported, border clashes with them every so often. The personnel here have seen the bodies of the men we've recovered. They know what it means to fall into Morah hands. To deliberately deliver anyone back into those hands is something pretty hard for them to take. But they're soldiers. They won't refuse an order."

He stopped talking. For a moment there was silence in the room.

"I see," said Dormu. He went across to the door and opened it. The medical lieutenant colonel was outside, and he turned to face Dormu in the opened door. "Doctor, you said this individual was dying."

"Yes," answered the lieutenant colonel.

"How long?"

"A couple of hours—" the lieutenant colonel shrugged helplessly. "A couple of minutes. I've no way of telling, nothing to go on, by way of comparable experience."

"All right." Dormu turned back to Whin. "Marshal, I'd like to get back to the Jhan as soon as the minimum amount of time's past that could account for a message to Earth and back."

An hour and a half later, Whin and Dormu once more entered the room where they had lunched with the Jhan. The tables were removed now; and the servers were gone. The musician was still there; and, joining him now, were two grotesqueries of altered Morah, with tiny, spidery bodies and great, grinning heads. These scuttled and climbed on the heavy, thronelike chair in which the Jhan sat, grinning around it and their Emperor, at the two humans.

"You're prompt," said the Jhan to Dormu. "That's promising."

"I believe you'll find it so," said Dormu. "I've been authorized to agree completely to your conditions—with the minor exceptions of the matter of recognizing that the division of peoples is by territory and not by race, and the matter of spatial corridors for you through our territory. The first would require a referendum of the total voting population of our people, which would take several years; and the second is beyond the present authority of my superiors to grant. But both matters will be studied."

"This is not satisfactory."

"I'm sorry," said Dormu. "Everything in your proposal that it's possible for us to agree to at this time has been agreed to. The Morah Jhan must give us credit for doing the best we can on short notice to accommodate him."

"Give you credit?" The Jhan's voice thinned; and the two bigheaded monsters playing about his feet froze like startled animals, staring at him. "Where is my kidnapped Morah?"

"I'm sorry," said Dormu, carefully, "that matter has been investigated. As we suspected, the individual you mention turns out not to be a Morah, but a human. We've located his records. A Paul Edmonds."

"What sort of lie is this?" said the Jhan. "He is a Morah. No human. You may let yourself be deluded by the fact he looks like yourselves, but don't try to think you can delude us with looks. As I told you, it's our privilege to play with the shapes of individuals, casting them into the mold we want, to amuse ourselves; and the mold we played with in this case, was like your own. So be more careful in your answers. I would not want to decide you deliberately kidnapped this Morah, as an affront to provoke me."

"The Morah Jhan," said Dormu, colorlessly, "must know how unlikely such an action on our part would be—as unlikely as the possibility that the Morah might have arranged to turn this individual loose, in order to embarrass us in the midst of these talks."

The Jhan's eyes slitted down until their openings showed hardly wider than two heavy pencil lines.

"*You* do not accuse *me*, human!" said the Jhan. "*I* accuse *you!* Affront my dignity; and less than an hour after I lift ship from this planetoid of yours, I can have a fleet here that will reduce it to one large cinder!"

He paused. Dormu said nothing. After a long moment, the slitted eyes relaxed, opening a little.

"But I will be kind," said the Jhan. "Perhaps there is some excuse for your behavior. You have been misled, perhaps—by this business of records, the testimony of those amateur butchers you humans call physicians and surgeons. Let me set your mind at rest. I, the Morah Jhan, assure you that this prisoner of yours is a Morah, one of my own Morah; and no human. Naturally, you will return him now, immediately, in as good shape as when he was taken from us."

"That, in any case, is not possible," said Dormu.

"How?" said the Jhan.

"The man," said Dormu, "is dying."

The Jhan sat without motion or sound for as long as a man might comfortably hold his breath. Then, he spoke.

"The *Morah*," he said. "I will not warn you again."

"My apologies to the Morah Jhan," said Dormu, tonelessly. "I respect his assurances, but I am required to believe our own records and experienced men. The *man*, I say, is dying."

The Jhan rose suddenly to his feet. The two small Morah scuttled away behind him toward the door.

"I will go to the quarters you've provided me, now," said the Jhan, "and make my retinue ready to leave. In one of your hours, I will reboard my ship. You have until that moment to return my Morah to me."

He turned, went around his chair and out of the room. The door shut behind him.

Dormu turned and headed out the door at their side of the room. Whin followed him. As they opened the door, they saw Stigh, waiting there. Whin opened his mouth to speak, but Dormu beat him to it.

"Dead?" Dormu asked.

"He died just a few minutes ago—almost as soon as you'd both gone in to talk to the Jhan," said Stigh.

Whin slowly closed his mouth. Stigh stood without saying anything further. They both waited, watching Dormu, who did not seem to be aware of their gaze. At Stigh's answer, his face had become tight, his eyes abstract.

"Well," said Whin, after a long moment and Dormu still stood abstracted, "it's a body now."

His eyes were sharp on Dormu. The little man jerked his head up suddenly and turned to face the marshal.

"Yes," said Dormu, a little strangely. "He'll have to be buried, won't he? You won't object to a burial with full military honors?"

"Hell, no!" said Whin. "He earned it. When?"

"Right away." Dormu puffed out a little sigh like a weary man whose long day is yet far from over. "Before the Jhan leaves. And not quietly. Broadcast it through the Outpost."

Whin swore gently under his breath, with a sort of grim happiness.

"See to it!" he said to Stigh. After Stigh had gone, he added softly to Dormu. "Forgive me. You're a good man once the chips are down, Mr. Ambassador."

"You think so?" said Dormu, wryly. He turned abruptly toward the lift tubes. "We'd better get down to the docking area. The Jhan said an hour—but he may not wait that long."

The Jhan did not wait. He cut his hour short, like someone eager to accomplish his leaving before events should dissuade him. He was at the docking area twenty minutes later; and only the fact that it was Morah protocol that his entourage must board before him, caused him to be still on the dock when the first notes of the Attention Call sounded through the Outpost.

The Jhan stopped, with one foot on the gangway to his vessel. He turned about and saw the dockside Military Police all now at attention, facing the nearest command screen three meters wide by two high, which had just come to life on the side of the main docking warehouse. The Jhan's own eyes went to the image on the screen—to the open grave, the armed soldiers, the chaplain and the bugler.

The chaplain was already reading the last paragraph of the burial service. The religious content of the human words could have no meaning to the Jhan; but his eyes went comprehendingly, directly to Dormu, standing with Whin on the other side of the gangway. The Jhan took a step that brought him within a couple of feet of the little man.

"I see," the Jhan said. "He is dead."

"He died while we were last speaking," answered Dormu, without inflection. "We are giving him an honorable funeral."

"I see—" began the Jhan, again. He was interrupted by the sound of fired volleys as the burial service ended and the blank-faced coffin began to be let down into the pulverized rock of the Outpost. A command sounded from the screen. The soldiers who had just fired went to present arms—along with every soldier in sight in the docking area—as the bugler raised his instrument and taps began to sound.

"Yes." The Jhan looked around at the saluting Military Police, then back at Dormu. "You are a fool," he said, softly. "I had no conception that a human like yourself could be so much a fool. You handled my demands well—but what value is a dead body, to anyone? If you had returned it, I would have taken no action—this time, at least, after your concessions on the settlements. But you not only threw away all you'd gained, you flaunted defiance in my face, by burying the body before I could leave this Outpost. I've no choice now—after an affront like that. I must act."

"No," said Dormu.

"No?" The Jhan stared at him.

"You have no affront to react against," said Dormu. "You erred only through a misunderstanding."

"Misunderstanding?" said the Jhan. "*I* misunderstood? I not only did not misunderstand, I made the greatest effort to see that you did not misunderstand. I cannot let you take a Morah from me, just because he looks like a human. And he *was* a Morah. You did not need your records, or your physicians, to tell you that. My word was enough. But you let your emotions, the counsel of these lesser people, sway you—to your disaster, now. Do you think I didn't know how all these soldiers of yours were feeling? But *I* am the Morah Jhan. Did you think I would lie over anything so insignificant as one stray pet?"

"No," said Dormu.

"Now—" said the Jhan. "Now, you face the fact. But it is too late. You have affronted me. I told you it is our privilege and pleasure to play with the shapes of beings, making them into what we desire. I told you the shape did not mean he was human. I told you he was Morah. You kept him and buried him anyway, thinking he was human—thinking he was that lost spy of yours." He stared down at Dormu. "I told you he was a Morah."

"I believed you," said Dormu.

The Jhan's eyes stared. They widened, flickered, then narrowed down until they were nothing but slits, once more.

"You believed me? You *knew* he was a Morah?"

"I knew," said Dormu. "I was Liaison Officer with the Intelligence Service at the time Edmonds was sent out—and later when his body was recovered. We have no missing agent here."

His voice did not change tone. His face did not change expression. He looked steadily up into the face of the Jhan.

"I explained to the Morah Jhan, just now," said Dormu, almost pedantically, "that through misapprehension, he had erred. We are a reasonable people, who love peace. To soothe the feelings of the Morah Jhan we will abandon our settlements, and make as many other adjustments to his demands as are reasonably possible. But the Jhan must not confuse one thing with another."

"What thing?" demanded the Jhan. "With what thing?"

"Some things we do not permit," said Dormu. Suddenly, astonishingly, to the watching Whin, the little man seemed to grow. His back straightened, his head lifted, his eyes looked almost on a level up into the slit-eyes of the Jhan. His voice sounded hard, suddenly, and loud. "The Morah belong to the Morah Jhan; and you told us it's your privilege to play with their shapes. Play with them then—in all but a single way. Use any shape but one. You played with that shape, and forfeited your right to what we just buried. Remember it, Morah Jhan! *the shape of Man belongs to Men, alone!*"

He stood, facing directly into the slitted gaze of Jhan, as the bugle sounded the last notes of taps and the screen went blank. About the docks, the Military Police lowered their weapons from the present-arms position.

For a long second, the Jhan stared back. Then he spoke.

"I'll be back!" he said; and, turning, the red kilt whipping about his legs, he strode up the gangplank into his ship.

"But he won't," muttered Dormu, with grim satisfaction, gazing at the gangplank, beginning to be sucked up into the ship now, preparatory to departure.

"Won't?" almost stammered Whin, beside him. "What do you mean . . . *won't?*"

Dormu turned to the marshal.

"If he were really coming back with all weapons hot, there was no need to tell me." Dormu smiled a little, but still grimly. "He left with a threat because it was the only way he could save face."

"But you . . ." Whin was close to stammering again; only this time with anger. "You knew that . . . that creation . . . wasn't Edmonds from the start! If the men on this Outpost had known it was a stinking Morah, they'd have been ready to hand him back in a minute. You let us all put our lives on the line here—for something that only *looked* like a man!"

Dormu looked at him.

"Marshal," he said. "I told you it was the confrontation with the Jhan that counted. We've got that. Two hours ago, the Jhan and all the other Morah leaders thought they knew us. Now they—a people who think shape isn't important—suddenly find themselves facing a race who consider their shape sacred. This is a concept they are inherently unable to understand. If that's true of us, what else may not be true? Suddenly, they don't understand us at all. The Morah aren't fools. They'll go back and rethink their plans, now—all their plans."

Whin blinked at him, opened his mouth angrily to speak—closed it again, then opened it once more.

"But you risked . . ." he ran out of words and ended shaking his head, in angry bewilderment. "And you let me bury it—with honors!"

"Marshal," said Dormu, suddenly weary, "it's your job to win wars, after they're started. It's my job to win them before they start. Like you, I do my job in any way I can."

There was nothing to do. There was no place to go. He swam up to consciousness on the sleepy languor of that thought. Nothing to do, no place to go, tomorrow is forever. Could sleep, but body wants to wake up. His body was a cork floating up from deep water, up, up to the surface.

He opened his eyes. Sunlight and blue sky; sky so blue that if you looked at it long enough you could begin to imagine yourself falling into it. No clouds; just blue, blue sky.

He felt as if he had slept the clock of eternity around and back again until the hands of time were in the same position they had held when he went to sleep. When had that been? It was a long time ago, too far back to remember. He stopped worrying about it.

He lay supine, his arms flung wide, his legs asprawl. He became conscious of short blades of grass tickling the backs of his hands. There was a tiny breeze from somewhere that now and again brushed his face with its cool wing. And an edge of white cloud was creeping into the patch of blue that gradually filled his field of vision.

Slowly, physical awareness crept back to him. He felt smooth, loose clothing lying lightly against his skin, the expansion and contraction of his chest, the hard ground pressure against the long length of his back. And suddenly he was complete. The thousand disconnected sensations flowed together and became one. He was aware of himself as a single united entity, alive and alone, lying stretched out, exposed and vulnerable in an unknown place.

Brain pulsed, nerves tensed, muscles leaped.

He sat up.

"Where am I?"

He sat on a carpet of green turf that dipped gradually away ahead and on either side of him to a ridiculously close horizon. He twisted his head and looked over his shoulder. Behind him was a gravel walk leading to a small building that looked very airy and light. The front, beneath a thick ivory roof that soared flat out, apparently unsupported for several yards beyond the front itself, was one large window. He could see, like looking into the cool dimness of a cave, big, comfortable chairs, low tables, and what might possibly be a viseo.

Hesitantly, he rose to his feet and approached the building.

At the entrance he paused. There was no door, only a variable force-curtain to keep the breezes out; and he pushed his hand through it carefully, as if to test the atmosphere inside. But there was only the elastic stretch and sudden yield that was like pushing your fist through the wall of a huge soap bubble, and then a pleasant coolness beyond, so he withdrew his hand and, somewhat timidly, entered.

The room illuminated itself. He looked around. The chairs, the tables, everything was just as he had seen it from outside, through the window. And the thing that looked like a viseo *was* a viseo.

He walked over to it and examined it curiously. It was one of the large models, receiver and record-player, with its own built-in library of tapes. He left it and went on through an interior doorway into the back of the house.

Here were two more rooms, a bedroom and a kitchen. The bed was another force-field—expensive and luxurious. The kitchen had a table and storage lockers through whose transparent windows he could see enough eatables and drinkables stored there to last one man a hundred years.

At the thought of one man living in this lap of luxury for a hundred years, the earlier realization that he was alone came back to him. This was not his place. It did not belong to him. The owner could not be far off.

He went hurriedly back through the living room and out into the sunlight. The green turf stretched away on every side of him, empty, unrelieved by any other living figure.

"Hello!" he called.

His voice went out and died, without echoes, without answer. He called again, his voice going a trifle shrill.

"Hello? Anybody here? Hello! *Hello!*"

There was no answer. He looked down the gravel path to his right, to the short horizon. He looked down the path to his left and his breath caught in his throat.

He began to run in a senseless, brain-numbing, chest-constricting panic.

The grass streamed silently by on both sides of him, and his feet pounded on the gravel of the path. He ran until his lungs heaved with exhaustion and the pounding of his heart seemed to shake his thin body, when at last fatigue forced him to a halt. He stood and looked around him.

The building was out of sight now, and he found himself on the edge of a forest of tall flowers. Ten feet high or more, they lay like a belt across his way, and the path led through them. Green-stemmed, with long oval leaves gracefully reaching out, with flat, broad-petaled blue blossoms spread to the bright sky, they looked like the graceful creations of a lost dream. There was no odor, but his head seemed to whirl when he looked at them.

Somehow they frightened him; their height and their multitude seemed to look down on him as an intruder. He hesitated at that point where the path began to wind among them, no longer straight and direct as it had been through the grass. He felt irrational fear at the thought of pushing by them—but the loneliness behind him was worse.

He went on.

Once among the flowers, he lost all sense of time and distance. There was nothing but the gravel beneath his feet, a patch of blue sky overhead and the flowers, only the flowers. For a while he walked; and then, panic taking him again at the apparent endlessness of the green stems, he burst into a fear-stricken run which ended only when exhaustion once more forced him to a walk. After that, he plodded hopelessly, his desire to escape fighting a dull battle with increasing weariness.

He came out of it suddenly. One moment the flowers were all around him; then the path took an abrupt twist to the right and he was standing on the edge of a new patch of turf through which the path ran straight as ever.

He stopped, half disbelieving what he saw. With a little inarticulate grunt of relief, he stepped free of the flower-shadowed pathway and went forward between new fields of grass.

He did not have much farther to go. In a few minutes he topped a small rise and his walk came to an end.

There, in front of him, was the building.

The very same building he had run away from earlier.

He approached it slowly, trying to cling to the hope that it was not the same building, that he had somehow gone somewhere else, rather than that he had traveled in a circle. But the identity was too complete. There was the large window, the chairs, the viseo. There was the door to the bedroom and the one to the kitchen.

Moving like a man in a dream, he walked forward and into the house.

He knew where he was going now. He remembered what he had seen before—a bottle of light, amber-colored liquid among the stores in the kitchen. He found it among a thickly crowded bank of others of its kind and took off the cap humbly. He put the bottle to his lips.

The liquor burned his throat. Tears sprang to his eyes at the fire of it and he was glad, for the sensation gave him a feeling of reality that he had not yet had among the dreamlike emptiness of his surroundings.

Taking the bottle, he went outside to the grass in front of the building.

"This is good," he thought, taking another drink, and sitting down on the grass. "This is here and now, a departure point from which to figure out the situation. *I drink, therefore I am.* The beginning of a philosophy."

He drank again.

"But where do I go from there? Where is this? Who am I?"

He frowned suddenly. Well, who was he? The question went groping back and lost itself in a maze of shadows where his memory should have been. Almost, but not quite, he knew. He shook his head impatiently.

"Never mind that now. Plenty of time to figure that out later. The thing is to discover where I am, first."

Where was he, then? The drink was beginning to push soft fingers of numbness into his mind. The grass was Earth grass and the building was a human-type structure. But the flowers weren't like anything on Earth. Were they like anything on any other planet he'd ever been on?

He wrinkled his forehead in a frown, trying to remember. If only he could recall where he had been before he woke up! He thought he had been on Earth, but he wasn't sure. The things he wanted to remember seemed to skitter away from his recollection just before he touched them.

He lay back on the grass.

Where was he? He was in a place where one walked in circles. He was in a place where things were too perfect to be natural. The grass looked like a lawn and there were acres of it. There were acres of flowers, too. But the grass was real grass; and from what he'd seen of the flowers, they were real and natural as well.

Yet there was something wrong. He felt it. There was a strange air of artificiality about it all.

He lay back on the grass, staring at the sky and taking occasional drinks from the bottle. Without realizing it, he was getting very drunk.

His mind cast about like the nose of a hunting dog. Something about the place in which he found himself was wrong, but the something continued to elude him. Maybe it had to do with the fact that he couldn't seem to remember things. Whatever it was, it was something that told him clearly and unarguably that he wasn't on Earth or any of the planets he'd ever known or heard of.

He looked to the right and he looked to the left. He looked down and he looked up, and realization came smashing through the drunken fog in his mind.

There was no Sun in the sky.

He rose to his feet, the bottle in his hand, for a horrible suspicion was forming in his mind. He turned away from the house, looked at the chronometer on his wrist and began to walk.

When he got back to the house, the bottle in his hand was empty. But all the alcohol inside him could not shut out the truth from his mind. He was alone, on a tiny world that was half green grass and half great blue flowers. A pretty world, a silent, dreaming world beneath a bright, eternal sky. An empty world, and he was on it—

Alone.

He went away from the world, as far as drink would take him. And for many days—or was it weeks?—reality became a hazy thing, until the poor, starved body could take no more and so collapsed. Then there was no remembrance, but when he came back to himself at last, he found a little miracle had happened during that blank period.

Memory of a part of his life had come back to him.

Born and raised on Earth, in Greater Los Angeles, he had
been pitched neck and crop off his native planet at the age of
twenty-one, along with some other twenty million youngsters
for which overcrowded Earth had no room. Overpopulation
was a problem. Those without jobs were deported when they
reached the age of maturity. And what chance had a poor
young man to get an Earthside job when rich colonials wanted
them? For Earth was the center of government and trade.

He was spared the indignity of deportation. His family
scraped up the money for passage to Rigel IV and arranged
a job in a typographers' office for him there. They would continue to pull strings, they said, and he was to work hard and
save as much as he could in the hope of being able eventually
to buy his way back—although this was a forlorn hope; the
necessary bribes for citizenship would run to several million
credits. They saw him off with a minimum of tears; Father,
Mother, and a younger sister, who herself would be leaving
in a couple of years.

He went on to Rigel IV, filled with the determination of
youth to conquer all obstacles; to make his fortune in the ap-
proved fashion and return, trailing clouds of glory, to his
astounded and delighted parents.

But Rigel IV proved strangely indifferent to his enthusiasm.
The earlier colonists had seen his kind before. They resented
his Earth-pride, they laughed at his squeamishness where the
local aliens were concerned, and they played upon his exag-
gerated fears of the *Devils,* as the yet-unknown alien races
beyond the spatial frontier were called. They had only con-
tempt for his job in the typographers' office and no one liked
him well enough to offer him any other occupation.

So he sat at his desk, turning out an occasional map copy
on his desk duplicator for the stray customers that wandered
in. He stared out the window at the red dust in the streets and
in the air, calculating over and over again how many hundreds of years of hoarding his salary would be required to

save up the bribe money for citizenship, and dreaming of the lost beauty of the cool white moonlight of Earth.

Above all else, he remembered and yearned for moonlight. It became to him the symbol of all that he wished for and could not have. And he began to seek it—more and more often—in the contents of a bottle.

And so the breakup came. Though there was little to do at his job, a time came when he could not even do that, but sprawled on his bed in the hotel, dreaming of moonlight, while the days merged one into the other endlessly.

Termination came in the form of a note from his office and two months' salary.

Further than that, his recovered memory would not go. He lay for the equivalent of some days, recuperating; and when he was able to move around again, he discovered to his relief that he was now able to leave the remaining bottles in the liquor section alone.

Shortly after, he discovered that the house walls were honeycombed with equipment and control panels, behind sliding doors. He gazed at these with wonder, but for some reason could not bring himself to touch them.

One in particular drew him and repelled him even more than the rest. It was by far the simplest of the lot, having only four plain switches on it. The largest one, a knife switch with a red handle, exerted the strongest influence over him. The urge to pull it was so strong that he could not bear to stand staring at it for more than a few minutes, without reaching out his hand toward it. But no sooner did his fingertips approach the red handle than a reaction set in. A paralysis rooted him to the spot, his heart pounded violently, and sweat oozed coldly from his pores. He would be forced then to close the panel and not go back to it for several hours. Finally, he compromised with his compulsion. There were three smaller switches: and finally, gingerly, he reached out his hand to the first of these, one time when he had been staring at it, and pulled it.

The light went out.

He screamed in blind animal fear and slapped wildly at the panel. The switch moved again beneath his hand and the light came back on. Sobbing, he leaned against the panel, gazing in overwhelming relief out through the big front window at the good green grass and the brightness of the sky beyond.

It was some time before he could bring himself to touch that switch again. Finally he summoned up the nerve to pull it once more and stood a long while in the darkness, with thudding heart, letting his eyes grow accustomed to it.

Eventually he found he could see again, but faintly. He groped his way through the gloom of the front room and lifted his face to the sky outside, from which the faint glow came.

And this time he did not cry out.

The night sky was all around him and filled with stars. It was the bright shine of them that illuminated his little world with a sort of ghostly brilliance. Stars, stars, in every quarter of the heavens, stars. But it was not just their presence alone that struck him rigid with horror.

Like all of his generation, he knew how the stars looked from every planet owned by man. What schoolchild did not? He could glance at the stars from a position in any quarter of the human sector of space and tell roughly from the arrangement overhead where that position was. Consequently, his sight of the stars told him where he was now; and it was this knowledge that gripped him with mind-freezing terror.

He was adrift, alone on a little, self-contained world, ten miles in diameter, a pitiful little bubble of matter, in the territory of the *Devils,* in the unknown regions *beyond the farthest frontier.*

He could not remember what happened immediately after that. Somehow, he must have gotten back inside and closed the light switch, for when he woke again to sanity, the light had hidden the stars once more. But fear had come to live with him. He knew now that malice or chance had cut him irrevocably off from his own kind and thrust him forth to be the prey or sport of whatever beings held this unknown space.

But from that moment, memory of his adult life began to return. Bit by bit, from the further past, and working closer in time, it came. And at first he welcomed almost sardonically the life-story it told. Now that he knew where he was, whatever his history turned out to be, it could make no difference.

As time went on, though, interest in the man he had been obsessed him, and he seized on each individual recollection as it emerged from the mist, grasping at it almost frantically. The viseo that he kept running, purely for the sake of human-seeming companionship, played unheeded while he hunted desperately through the hazy corridor of his mind.

He remembered his name now. It was Helmut Perran.

Helmut Perran had gone from despondency to hopelessness after his dismissal from the job at the typographers. He was a confirmed alcoholic now, and with labor shortage common on an expanding planet, he had no trouble finding enough occasional work to keep himself in liquor. He nearly succeeded in killing himself off, but his youth and health saved him.

They dragged him back to existence in the snake ward of the local hospital, and psyched a temporary cure on him. Helmut had gone downhill socially until he reached rock bottom, until there was no further for him to go. He began to come back up again, but by a different route.

He came up in the shadowy no-man's-land just across the border of the law. He was passer, pimp and come-on man. He fronted for a gambling outfit. He made some money and went into business for himself as a promoter of crooked money-making schemes, and he ended as advance agent for a professional smuggling outfit.

Oddly enough, the business was only technically illegal. With the mushroom growth of the worlds, dirty politics and graft had mushroomed as well. Tariffs were passed often for the sole purpose of putting money in the pockets of customs officials. Unnecessary red tape served the same purpose. The upshot was that graft became an integral part of interstellar business. The big firms had their own agents to cut through these difficulties with the golden knife of credits. The smaller firms, or those who could less afford the direct graft, did business with smuggling outfits.

These did not actually smuggle; they merely saw to it that the proper men and machines were blind when a shipment that had been arranged for came through regular channels. They dealt with the little men—the spaceport guard, the berthing agent, the customs agent who checked the invoice—where the big firms made direct deals with the customs house head, or the political appointee in charge of that governmental section. It was more risky than the way of the big firms, but also much less expensive.

Helmut Perran, as advance agent, made the initial contacts. It was his job to determine who were the men who would have to be fixed, to take the risk of approaching them cold, and either to bribe them into cooperation or make sure that another man who could be bribed took their place at the proper time.

It was a job that paid well. But by this time, Helmut was ambitious. He was sick of illegality and he thought he saw a way back to Earth and the moonlight. He shot for a job as fixer with one of the big firms that dealt directly with the head men in Customs—and got it.

It was as simple as that. He was now respectable, wealthy, and his chance would come.

He worked for the big firm faithfully for five years before it did. Then there came along a transfer of goods so large and involved that he was authorized to arrange for bribes of more than three million credits. He made the arrangement, took the credits, and skipped to Earth, where, with more than enough money to cover it, he at last bought his coveted Earth citizenship.

After that, they came and got him, as he knew they would. They got him a penal sentence of ten years, but they couldn't manage revocation of the citizenship. Through the hell of the little question room and the long trial, he carried a miniature picture in his mind of the broad white streets of Los Angeles in the moonlight and the years ahead.

But there the memory ended. He had a vague recollection of days in some penal institution, and then the mists were thick again. He beat hard knuckles against his head in a furious rage to remember.

What had happened?

They couldn't have touched him while he was serving his sentence. And once he had put in his ten years, he would be a free man with the full rights of his Earth citizenship. Then let them try anything. They were a firm of colossal power, but Earth was filled with such colossi; and the Earth laws bore impartially on all. What, then, had gone wrong?

He groaned, rocking himself in his chair like a child, in his misery. But he was close to the answer, so close. Give him just a bit more time—

But he was not allowed the time. Before he could bring the answer to the front of his mind, the *Devils* came.

Their coming was heralded by the high-pitched screaming of a siren, which cut off abruptly as the spaceship came through the bright opaqueness of the sky, like the Sun through a cloud, and dropped gently toward the ground, its bright metal sides gleaming as if they had been freshly buffed. It landed not fifty feet from him. The weight of it sank its rounded bottom deep beneath the surface of the sod, so that it looked like a huge metal bowl turned face-down on the grass.

A port opened in its side and two bipedal, upright creatures stepped out of it and came toward him.

As they approached him, time seemed to slip a cog and
move very slowly. He had a chance to notice small individual
differences between them. They were both shorter than he by
at least a head, although the one on Helmut's left was slightly
taller. They were covered with what seemed to be white fur,
all but two little black buttons of eyes apiece. And they
seemed to have more than the ordinary number of joints in
their legs and arms, for these limbs bent like rubber hose when
they walked or gesticulated. They were carrying a square box
between them.

Helmut stood still, waiting for them. The only thought in
his mind was that now he would never get to know how he
had happened to be here, and he was sorry, for he had grown
fond of the man he had once been, not the one he later turned
out to be, as you might be fond of a distant relative. Meanwhile, he could feel his breath coming with great difficulty and
his heart thumping inside him as it had thumped that time he
had first tried the switch that turned off the light.

He watched them come up to a few feet from him and set
the box down.

As soon as it was resting on the grass, it began to vibrate
and a hum came from it that was pitched at about middle C.
It went up in volume until it was about as loud as a man saying "aaaah" when a doctor holds down his tongue with a
depressor to look at his throat. When it had reached this
point, it broke suddenly from a steady sound into a series of
short, intermittent hums that gradually resolved themselves
into syllables. He realized that the box was talking to him, one
syllable at a time.

"Do not be afraid," it said. "We wish to talk to you."

Helmut said nothing. He wanted to hear what the box had
to say, but, at the same time, a compulsion was mounting
within him. It screamed that these others were horrible and

unnatural and dangerous, that nothing they said was true, that he must turn and run to safety before it was too late.

They had been watching him for a long time, the box went on to tell him. They had listened from a safe distance to the viseo tapes he had run on the machine and finally translated his language. They had done their best to understand him from a distance and had failed, for he seemed to be unhappy and to dislike being where he was and what he was doing. And if this was so, why was he doing it? They did not understand. Where had he come from and who was he? Why was he here?

Helmut looked at the four little black eyes that gazed at him like the puzzled, half-friendly eyes of a bear he had seen in a zoo while he was a boy back on Earth. There was no possible way for white-furred faces to have shown expression, but he thought he read kindness in them, and the long loneliness of his stay on the sphere rose up and almost choked him with a desire to answer them. But that savagely irrational corner of his mind surged forward to combat the impulse toward friendliness.

He opened his mouth. Only a garbled croak came out.

He turned and ran.

He raced to the building and burst through the entrance. He threw himself at the panel that hid the switches, pulling it open and sliding aside the door that covered them. He reached for the red-handled switch, hesitated, and looked over his shoulder at the two creatures. They stood as he had left them. For the last time, he wavered under the urge to go back to them, to tell them his story, at least to listen to their side once—first.

But they were Devils!

The fear and anger inside him surged up, beating down everything else. He grasped the red switch firmly and threw it home.

What followed after that was nightmare.

He had been sitting for a long time in the cold hall and nobody had paid any attention to him. Occasionally, men in
Space Guard uniforms or the white coats of laboratory
workers would go past him into the Warden's office, and come
out again a little later. But all of these went past him as if he
did not exist.

He shifted uncomfortably in the chair they had given him.
They had outfitted him in fresh civilian clothes, which felt
clinging and uncomfortable after the long months of running
around on the sphere half-naked. The clothes, like the stiff
waiting-room chair, the hall, and the parade of passing men
all chafed on him and shrieked at him that he did not belong.
He hated them.

The parade in and out of the office went on.

Finally, the door to the office opened and a young Guardsman stuck his head out.

"You can come in now," he said.

Helmut got to his feet. He did it awkwardly, the unaccus-
tomed clothing seeming to stick to him, his legs half-asleep
from the long wait in the chair.

He walked through the door and the young Guard shut it
behind him. The Warden, a spare man of Helmut's age, with
a military stiffness in his bearing and noncommittal mouth
and eyes, looked up from his desk.

"You can go, Price," he said to the Guard; and, to Helmut,
"Sit down, Perran."

Helmut lowered himself clumsily into the armchair across
the desk from the Warden as the young Guardsman went out
the door. The Warden stared at him for a moment.

"Well, Perran," he said, "you deserve to congratulate yourself. You're one of our lucky ones."

Helmut stared back at him, numbly, for a long time. Then,
abruptly, it was like being sick. Without warning, a sob came
choking up in his throat and he laid his head on the desk in
front of him and began to cry.

The Warden lit a cigarette and smoked it for a while, staring out the window. The sound of Helmut's sobs was strained in the silence of the office. When they had dwindled somewhat, the Warden spoke again to Helmut.

"You'll get over it," he said. "That's just the conditioning wearing off. If you didn't break down and cry, you'd have been in serious psychological trouble. You'll be all right now."

Helmut lifted his head from the desk.

"What happened to me?" he asked, his throat hoarse. "What happened?"

The Warden puffed on his cigarette. "You were assigned to one of our Mousetraps," he answered. "It's a particularly hazardous duty for which criminals can volunteer. Normally, we only get men under death sentence or those with life terms. You're an exception."

"But I *didn't* volunteer!"

"In your case," said the Warden, "there may have been some dirty work along the line. We are investigating. Of course, if that turns out to be the case, you'll be entitled to reparation. I don't suppose you remember how you came to be on the Mousetrap, do you?"

Helmut shook his head.

"It's not surprising," said the Warden. "Few do, although, theoretically, the conditioning is supposed to disappear after you capture a specimen. Briefly, you were given psychological treatment in order to fit you for existence alone in the Mousetrap. It's necessary, because usually our Baits live their life out on the sphere without attracting any alien life. You were one of the lucky ones, Perran."

"But what it it?" asked Helmut. "What is it for?"

"The Mousetrap system?" the Warden answered. "It's our first step in the investigation of alien races with a view to integrating them into human economy. We take a sphere like the one you were on, put a conditioned criminal on it, and shove it off into unexplored territory where we have reason to suspect the presence of new races. With luck, the alien investigates the sphere and our conditioned Bait snaps the trap shut on him. Lacking luck, the Mousetrap is either not investigated or the aliens aren't properly trapped. Our conditioned man, in that case, blows it up—and himself along with it.

"As I say, you were lucky. You're back here safe on Kronbar, and we've got a fine couple of hitherto undiscovered specimens for our laboratory to investigate. What if those creatures had beaten you to the switch?"

Helmut shuddered and covered his eyes, as if, by doing so, he could shut the memory from his mind.

"The Guard Ship was so long coming," he muttered. "So long! Days. And I had to watch them all that time caught in a force-field like flies in a spider web. I couldn't go away without stepping out of the building and being caught myself. And they kept talking to me with that little box of theirs. They couldn't understand why I did it. They kept asking me over and over again why I did it. But they got weaker and weaker and finally they died. Then they just hung there because the force-field wouldn't let them fall over."

His voice dwindled away.

The Warden cleared his throat with a short rasp. "A trying time, I'm sure," he said. "But you have the consolation of knowing that you have performed a very useful duty for the human race." He stood up. "And now, unless you have some more questions—"

"When can I go home?" asked Helmut. "Back to Earth."

The Warden looked a trifle embarrassed. "Your capture of the aliens entitles you to a pardon; and of course you have Earth Citizenship—but I'm afraid we won't be able to let you leave Kronbar."

Helmut stared at him from a face that seemed to have gone entirely wooden. His lips moved stiffly.

"Why not?" he croaked.

"Well, you see," said the Warden, leading the way to a different door than the one through which Helmut had entered, "these specimens you brought back seem to be harmless, and inside of a month or two we'll probably have a task force out there to put them completely under our thumb. But we've had a little trouble before, when we'd release a Bait and it would turn out later that the aliens had in some way *infected* him. So there happens to be a blanket rule that successful Baits have to live out the rest of their life on Kronbar." He opened the door invitingly. "You can go out this way, if you want. Private entrance. It leads directly to the street."

Slowly, Helmut rose to his feet and shambled over to the door. For one last time a vision of moonlight on the bay at Santa Monica mocked him. A wild scheme flashed through his head in which he overpowered the Warden, stole his uniform and bluffed his way to a Guard Patrol ship, where he forced the crew to take him either to Earth, or, failing that, out beyond the Frontier to warn the white-furred kin of the two alien beings he had killed.

Then the scheme faded from his mind. It was no use. The odds were too great. There were too many like the Warden. There were always too many of them for Helmut and those like him. He turned away from the Warden, ignoring the Warden's outstretched hand.

He went out the door and down the steps into the brilliant daylight of Kronbar.

Kronbar, the Bright Planet, so-called because, since it winds an eccentric orbit around the twin stars of a binary system, there is neither dark nor moonlight, and the Sun is always shining.